Thanks to Aerin Lua for designing the cover!

Content Warnings on final page

Nonymous

Nonymous

*To the child who first accused me of being a selkie,
I hope the world is kind to you.*

Chapter 1

There was nowhere in any realm more boring to be than at one of *Interthrifter*'s many, many locations.

This was, strictly speaking, a far from true sentiment, but since they'd only originally been conned into working there due to a series of far from true sentiments, Nico had decided that it was one that they were more than entitled to hold.

Interthrifter was a 'marvel of magic'. Each location had to be meticulously planned out for years before its official opening date due to the sheer amount of spellwork required to make the concept even work. As the only store that stocked clothing for every single species, each location had to simultaneously cater to every possible customer's size, abilities, weaknesses, and preferences. The front door had to be enchanted to stretch or squish to match the size-class of each potential shopper that graced its welcome mat. The roof was built at a steep incline so that any species who fell on the 'Big' range of the Universal Size Scale could shop in relative comfort while smaller species could continue on further right until they found their wares housed beneath a ceiling a little less overwhelmingly distant. Giant-ish sized clothing and up resided in an entirely separate pocket dimension accessible only through an external slide that always smelt slightly of peppermint, for some reason.

In more recent years, they'd even started installing tanks (though luckily, Nico's location hadn't seen that particular renovation yet) for strictly-mer species to swim up into after a few protests about how *Interthrifer*'s 'every species welcome' mission statement wasn't technically true erupted in a couple of bigger cities. As far as Nico had heard though, the introduction of said tanks had led to exactly zero new customers. It appeared that few mer-aligned peoples were jumping (metaphorically, obviously. Nico was fairly certain that most of them couldn't jump) at the opportunity to spend hours swimming up a series of poorly maintained tubes just for the privilege of pointing at mostly non-water safe clothing from behind a pane of glass.

Regardless of whether or not all of *Interthrifer*'s unique design elements were entirely useful though, they at least should have been exciting. When the first location officially opened its doors a few years before Nico was born, it apparently had been. People would come from far and wide to experience its ingenuity. Back then, it had been equal parts tourist attraction and store.

That was what Nico had been sold on when they first arrived in Bayside at sixteen, looking to make their mark somewhere slightly bigger than the village that they'd grown up in. Brochures about all the exciting bits of innovative spellwork that they'd be surrounded by daily. Promises of meeting every type of creature from every walk of life. *Interthrifter* was far from just an entry level job, it was an experience. An experience that paid a copper more an hour than every other store in the market district. Which had definitely been appealing to an out of place teenage runaway living alone for the first time in their life.

Nico still would have applied without that extra incentive though. As someone who'd only grown-up hearing about *Interthrifter*, it had seemed like the perfect job opportunity for them. A place for all of the outsides and in-betweens of society that couldn't effectively do their shopping at a store catering exclusively to one size class. One of the few places built specifically for outcasts instead of against them.

Nico was (as far as they knew) entirely human and therefore perfectly capable of doing all their shopping at Middle-targeted establishments, but a place like *Interthrifter* had still felt like exactly where they were supposed to be. They were a margins person, after all. Despite their rather boring lineage. Neither girl nor boy nor able-bodied nor fully reliant on their cane. Neither shy nor loud nor smart nor dumb, just something a bit more oxymoronic. By sixteen, they'd already transformed their past into an ever-stretching trail of battered and mutilated boxes that they'd had to force their way out of. If there was anywhere in any realm that they could have belonged, it should have been *Interthrifter*.

They'd been tricked, though. They'd gotten less than a week into their initial four-month contract before realizing it and back then, they still skewed a bit too close to quiet to quit. Now that they could, they'd already dumped too much time into the store for it to feel worthwhile.

Because *Interthrifter* might have started out as a thrift store catering to outsiders, but then it had started multiplying. Franchising. Nico's birth-village had somehow miraculously remained untouched by any chain clothing stores, so they hadn't been able to recognize the kind of unfathomable evils that those always inevitably summoned until they were already locked in for the long-haul. The greatest foe of all retail workers. A darkness capable of shaking even the bravest of employees to their very cores:

bored teenagers with too much time on their hands.

"If you're naked right now, that's technically illegal."

The (alleged) old gnomish woman who'd just tried to skirt around the glamour-checkpoint at the store's entrance froze. Her eyes widened, just a bit too far to convincingly pass as natural, if you were paying enough attention. Nico had gotten used to paying enough attention. The (potential) woman clutched her purse to her chest. "My word!"

"So... are you?" Nico got up from the desk to confront her. They leaned against the doorframe once they reached it, partially for support, but mostly to keep the (potential) woman from barging through without getting scanned first. Not that that would have done much, if she was a hidden fae. A slightly-shorter-than average teenage human would be easy for any magic user to get past, if they were planning on throwing all decorum and decency out the window. Even if that teenage human came with a cool cane. And a ridiculously sick purple mullet. "Because I'd rather save you the fine and me the paperwork if we could just like, skip past that part here. With the weekend coming up and all."

"Why, I never..." the (alleged) gnome fluttered her eyelids in (supposed) shock. "You cannot just ask a customer something like that!"

Nico sighed. They risked glancing towards the clock then instantly regretted it. As far as Todd claimed, there was no time-manipulation laced into *Interthrifter*'s architecture, but after three years on the job, they'd still never gotten used to how impossible slowly the world seemed to move from within its walls. "Not a customer yet, actually." Nico reminded her. People never seemed to like it when they did that, but pissing off the guests that pissed them off without technically saying anything rude enough to go against company policy was one of Nico's few comforts during shifts. "Customers tend to buy things and if you are naked right now, I'm guessing you're not planning on doing that."

"I'm not—" The (possible) gnome flushed orange. She stomped her wooden-clogged foot in what might have passed as general gnomish frustration, but Nico had deal with enough would-be fae shoplifters to know how they reacted to getting caught in a lie. "I refuse to even entertain such a ridiculous—"

"It's our location policy," Nico jerked a thumb towards the poster in the window. It was enchanted to match the font-requirements of whichever species was currently reading it, but they weren't quite sure what effect glamours had on spellwork like that. They read it aloud, just in case. "If potential customers opt out of walking through the glamour checkpoint, then—"

"I've heard those cause—"

"Yes," Nico waved her off. "I'm sure a million different incredibly serious debilitating side effects never once backed up by anyone ever. Which is why we have to let you opt out, but if you do, policy says 'employees are welcome and encouraged to inquire as to said potential customer's level of nakedness before performing manual glamour checks. On account of potential customers not informing them of said level of nakedness ahead of time being illegal and also just downright nasty." They had personally been responsible for that part of the phrasing, back when they'd been seventeen. Todd was a mostly absentee location owner, but at least he was the kind of absent boss who trusted his employees to make any reasonable policy changes that they deemed necessary. "Or you could just, you know, say the sentence 'I'm super not naked right now' so I can be sure you're definitely not a secret fae doing an incredibly bad job at lying and we can both continue on with our days. But if you let me do a manual check and you were planning on sneaking in with nothing on just so you'd have an easier time concealing anything you smuggle out with you, we'd have to make physical contact. So not letting me know you're naked ahead of time would be you know, wildly inappropriate and definitely fine worthy?"

The (almost certainly not) gnome's eyebrows drew together. "Manual glamour checks are... physical?"

Nico stopped themself just before rolling their eyes in front of the (almost certainly not) customer. It was clearly this person's first time in a non-fae store. "Extremely so, yes." They pulled a pair of plastic gloves out of their pocket to accentuate the point. The creature in the doorway had glamoured sleeves all the way down to her wrists so like in most cases, Nico would have only had to try and pinch the fabric above her arm to check and see if they were being deceived, but over the years they'd learn that the gloves were an incredibly useful tool in speeding up these kinds of interactions.

The (definitely not) old woman sighed and then—with a loud pop and a flash of light that Nico had gotten so good at anticipating that they didn't even blink anymore—her head was replaced with a pimply faery teenager's.

"You could've just let me in," he grumbled. Even grumbling though, his voice was higher than the old woman's had been. Whiney.

8

"*You* could've put half a second of research into how glamour checkpoints worked before trying to shoplift," Nico rebutted.

The teen rolled his eyes and turned to go, but Nico caught his (real) sleeve.

"You owe me five copper," they informed him.

He frowned. "I didn't buy anything. You didn't even let me through the door."

"Right, and you almost ruined my day," they held out a hand. "Copper, please."

He glared. "That's extortion."

"And now that I know what your actual face looks like, if I went and described you to someone, this would be public nudity."

The faery sighed, dug through his pocket, and forked over the coin.

And then he left. And that was that. And in about an hour, Nico would forget about the entire confrontation.

Interthrifter was not boring. Not technically. A couple of years ago, they would have turned that encounter into an entire epic to tell back at The House. But by this point, Nico had seen every kind of customer and scenario imaginable. There'd been a recent influx in fae teens glamouring themselves as other species to try and get through loss prevention procedures, but even that was barely noteworthy anymore. It happened every time the schools let out for a holiday and with summer quickly approaching, they already knew that it definitely wouldn't be the last ill-informed would-be shoplifter that they'd be seeing that month. Even the most magical of encounters no longer piqued Nico's interest because they'd been through ever possible scenario dozens of time already. It was all routine. All just more mess to slog through.

They pressed against the head of their armlet (when they'd bought it years ago the owner had said the golden snake chasing its own tail had had some kind of important precautionary meaning, but Nico never learned what that meaning had actually been. They'd been too distracted by the armlet being magical and golden and snakey and badass.) and waited for their cane to expand and unwind. They clomped back over to their desk.

And then, they got through another Friday shift. They carried sunshades for vampires and banshees. Swept away pixie dust from change rooms and shook it off of clothing to keep the werewolves from getting agitated. Answered, "to the left" and "we don't technically carry anything, this is a thrift store" and "yes humans can sometimes have purple hair actually, it was a fairly inexpensive potion" and "no I'm not (insert any number of decidedly non-humanish species here)" and "we don't have that in another size, actually. Because this is a thrift store" and "nope, no curses here, I'm afraid" and every other question that was thrown at them with ease because they'd encountered all of them dozens of times before. They had scripts for everything, even when a witch came in, noticed their cane, and then scampered over with promises of fame, fortune, and full mobility. If they'd only sign their soul away on the dotted line and join their downline, of course. And then they'd only have to recruit six more witches of their own to get it back!

"I'm already in a coven, actually," they'd say (they weren't). "The cane's just to attract potential recruits."

Witches were full of sleezy recruitment tactics, so like always, that won them some peace and quiet.

When Smirsh—a half-giant regular—popped by, they slipped away from their desk, placed a few Big-sized shoes in the Giant-ish section, and got back to their regular busy-work with time to spare.

"Oh my!" They lamented in a long-ago perfected cadence when he came to pay for the most recent pair that he'd chosen to destroy. "I can't believe those didn't fit either! Maybe you should check out the Giant section next time. You must have the biggest half-Giant feel in the realm!"

Some of their regulars didn't come to *Interthrifter* for the clothing, after all, they did it for the experience.

They checked clothes in and out. When employees from the much more popular (and pricy) Kovienne location arrived to buy in bulk, they sent them off with a pile of new material and found that they weren't even all that bothered that they'd inevitably end up selling them for at least twice what they'd paid just because their location got more foot traffic. Even competition felt boring now that Nico had accepted that they'd be losing either way. General employees always did.

They ran through their tasks and scripts and busywork and then did it all over again.

"Still not cursed," they said. And "No I can't order that in for you, this is a thrift store". And "Cash only, I'm afraid we don't accept souls, favours, or entrails". And "No we don't have any more of that 'in the back room'. This is a thrift store."

And then, all at once, for the first time in over two years, they faltered.

"I'm sorry?" Nico snapped out of a work-induced haze, their customer service smile wavering for a fraction of a second.

The guest leaning over their desk looked human enough that they should have been the kind of stranger that Nico could get away with barely paying any attention to, but there was something slightly off about her. Eyes a little too wide, behind her glasses. Gaze a little too pointed. "Where," she leaned forward to repeat the question, long strings of blonde hair curling over the cash register. "is my skin?"

Chapter 2

The only word that could effectively describe what happened in the seconds after that was malfunction. Nico froze. Felt something catch then shutter then spark in the middle of their mind. They'd gotten so well practiced at their customer-service scripts, that they suddenly realized that the moment they stepped through *Interthrifter*'s doors every shift, they must have also been turning off the part of their brain that knew how to do anything but recite.

So, they leaned forward and booped the girl on the nose.

She jumped back, eyebrows shooting up in surprise as she swatted their hand away.

"Sorry," the girl said. Which is when Nico remembered that it was what they were supposed to be saying. "Wait, no," the girl remembered herself. She took another step forward. Looked Nico a bit too head-on once again. "I'm not... what did you with to my skin?"

"It's right there," Nico had the sense to only gesture this time though. They clutched the medallion hanging around their neck, trying to situate themself squarely back in the present. "Looks fine to me." Upon further examination they did find it a bit odd that she'd some how managed to acquire so many freckles while also looking like she'd never spent a day of her life under the sun, but they really didn't get how that could've possibly been their fault.

"Not my—" The girl clenched her fists. Sighed. "I left a pile of clothes here," she finally looked away again, studying the tiles. "There was a brown-ish cloak that must have gotten mixed in with it, somehow. What did you do with it?"

Nico couldn't recall any brown-ish cloak, but they rarely ever remembered any of the items that crossed their desk anymore. "All returns are final sale."

"That's not—" A foot-stomp this time, before the ensuing deem breath. "It wasn't supposed to be for sale at all."

"Sorry," they shrugged. "If it's not still here, it's probably already on a boat on its way to the Kovienne location by now. Not much I can do for you there."

The girl made some weird almost-choking noise and spun away from them. Then, just as quickly, she marched her way back. "I'd like..." Another fist clench. "I need to speak to your manager."

Ah. Nico's least favourite words. "He's not in."

"When will he—"

"He's never in. You'd need to set up an appointment and he's not going to do that because you're upset about some random coat."

The girl kept staring and pacing and fist clenching and she hadn't been absolutely atrocious yet (as far as these sorts of things typically went) so Nico decided to take pity on her.

"Look," they leaned forward. "If it wasn't interesting enough to catch my attention, I doubt it'll catch anyone else's, okay? If it's seriously that important just buy a ferry pass and go buy it back. Make a whole trip out of it or something."

"I can't just—" something shifted in her expression. She looked up again. "You do it."

Nico barked out a laugh. "Yeah, no thanks. It's not my job to—"

"It wasn't just a cloak!" The girl blurted. "It was my... I'm a selkie. It was my sealskin. I need it to change back."

Nico froze. They didn't know much about selkies (no one really did, they could only transform to come on land once every seven years, after all), but they did know that losing a sealskin was definitely a big deal. "Shit," they said. "Shit, sorry. Good luck umm..." they were suddenly filled with an overwhelming certainty that they were supposed to be doing something more here. More nose booping was out of the question though, so they redirected their energy to getting rid of her instead. "Hopefully you figure that out."

"You have to help me," she insisted.

"No," their eyes narrowed. "I don't."

"Stealing a selkie's skin is a big deal! It's... it's basically a declaration of war! It'd be custom to challenge you to a duel, you know. If someone took it and refused to give it back, I'd be honour bound to—"

Whatever sympathy Nico had felt for the selkie suddenly wore thin. They did not appreciate being challenged in their own workplace. "Good thing I didn't steal it, then." They leaned to the side to address the next customer in line. "Next, please."

The girl made another throat noise but then mercifully, she stormed off.

Nico shook themself off, slipped back into their customer service smile, and glanced at the clock. Only forty-five minutes to go. Almost the weekend.

They got through two transactions before the same frizzy blonde hair fell over their register again. They bit back a sigh and slowly looked up. "Listen. I'm sorry, but I don't know what—"

The selkie ignored them though. Instead, she turned around to address the man behind her in line. "You're watching this, right?" She asked. "Witnessing it, and all that?"

He gave a non-committal shrug that was apparently enough for the girl.

"Excellent," she clapped her palms together.

Then, she turned back to Nico and aggressively threw a single, fraying woolen mitten to the ground. It was the most anticlimactic customer temper tantrum that they'd ever seen.

They frowned at her. "You seriously got back in line to do... whatever that was?"

"That," the selkie stood just a little bit taller. "Was a gauntlet."

Nico's stomach dropped. Someone in line whistled.
Shit.
ed

14

Chapter 3

"You got challenged to a duel?"

Nico tried their very best to never bring work home with them, but that was a lot harder to do when 'work' suddenly involved a death match.

They threw their bag down beside the door. Where it landed on top of three other bags previously thrown down beside that door at various earlier points in the day.

"No third eyes in The House," Nico muttered, pointedly ignoring where Leif laid strewn out on the couch, waiting to eat up the time, attention, and affection of anyone who entered The House. They'd learned over the years that dealing with Leif was quite like dealing with a beachside seagull: both were prone to following you around eternally if given even a smidge too much attention, random bouts of annoying squawking, mind reading, and, of course, eating every scrap of vaguely edible material placed in front of them. So, for both of their sakes, Nico decided to let Leif stew for a while and went straight to the kitchen. Leif followed.

"You got—" Leif tried again.

"You," Nico shoved a bag of chips under their arm then popped onto their good foot to pull Leif's jar down from the top of the fridge. "Are not supposed to know that." They held out the jar, waiting. Kya had made them all a year and a half ago, after they'd first collected her. Leif's jar, like the rest of theirs, was a little bit of a mess. Kya'd had her vines punch out each of their names into old tin cans and then had tried to get them to press their flowers into the rest of the empty space to make them all a little prettier, but tin had apparently been difficult for vines and petals to shape. The result looked more like the vague reference of a name surrounded by a series of globby worms. They were perfect, though. A little big messy. A little bit The House.

"You slammed the door shut and dramatically sighed!" Leif whined. "You practically asked me to read you!"

Nico shook the can and waited. Despite it only being a couple of weeks into the month, there were already enough coins in the tin for them to clink together. Leif had been reading a lot of minds recently, apparently.

"Blindfold on," Nico commanded. "Now."

Leif rolled Leif's eyes—all three of them—before complying. Nico took a moment to check Leif's wrist as Leif did. Leif wore colour-coded beaded bracelets—also made by Kya, she was the only member of The House with any inclinations towards creation or nurturing—to let the rest of The House know which pronouns to use at any particular moment and though Nico had gotten pretty good at gauging what kind of day it was without having to check anymore, they always liked to make sure that they were using the right words to mentally curse Leif. Just in case. Today, Leif's wrists were bare. They'd been having a lot more 'no pronouns' days than usual lately.

"So?" Leif flopped back onto the couch, trusting them to follow. Being a few feet taller than The House's next tallest inhabitants, Leif took up almost all of their Middle-sized couch. Nico had to shove an assortment of clothing and half-emptied shopping bags onto the floor before squeezing in beside Leif. They *had* a Big chair. If Leif was on the couch, it meant that Leif wanted to be sat with. "You got challenged to a duel."

Nico rolled their eyes. "Shut up. It's not a big deal."

It was an exceptionally big deal. While duel challenges were rarely issued anymore, they were still technically binding. In fact, they were one of the only remaining ways to legally kill someone (a large factor into why fully getting rid of them was always met with massive protest). If a challenger had a valid reason for issuing a duel and provided a reasonable way for the challengee to get out of it, it was actually more legally and socially reprehensible to deny the challenge than to participate in an actual death match. That didn't mean that Nico had to like it, though.

"What'd you do to piss someone off that much?"

Nico started to answer, then frowned. "Don't you already know that?"

Leif shrugged. "It felt polite to ask."

Biologically speaking, Leif shouldn't have even existed. It wasn't supposed to be possible. Supposedly their mother was a cyclops who'd had a messy one-night stand with a human about twenty-one years ago, but that didn't explain how instead of the typical one- or two-eyed offspring that that should have produced, Leif ended up with three. The most annoying one sitting big and purple and swirling in the centre of Leif's forehead, filling Leif in on the innermost thoughts of anyone Leif pointed it at. Rule number one of living in The House (pretending that they'd ever gotten around to writing down official rules, that was. They'd talked about it over the years, but their planning and organizational skills were awful on a good day) was to never demand to know more about someone's backstory than they offered up unprompted, so Nico semi-politely pretended that anything about that explanation made sense.

They'd assumed for a while that Leif was the descendant of some long-forgotten god, but they'd since learned that that was absolutely not a secret that someone like Leif would've been able to keep bottled up. The demi-god card was the type of thing that Leif would've played constantly.

"It wasn't," Nico snapped. They sighed. "I'm not doing the duel, so it doesn't even matter. We don't have to talk about it."

Leif leaned towards them to try and nab a chip.

Nico pulled the bag shut.

"Does everyone else know?" Leif stage-whispered.

They froze. "Leif."

"If one of us is about to go battle someone, I think everyone else had better—"

"Leif!"

Trying to stop Leif was useless, though. It always was. Once Leif set their mind to something, it was inevitable. It was why sometimes, just slightly, they still found themself wondering if Leif was part god.

From the cracked then reglued then recracked pot in the corner of the room, a single vine twitched. Nico and Leif locked eyes.

"Don't—"

Leif was already grinning, leaping over the couch to whisper a message into its leaves. And, within seconds, every inhabitant of The House was on their way to the living room.

"Who has news?" Pat made it down the stairs first. He had just enough werewolf blood to assure that she was always the first to sniff out changes to The House's flora.

Honey perfume roses for gossip. Because they were sweet and thorny and lovely.

"Nico!" Kya floated down after her. She couldn't fly, but that didn't stop her from *acting* like she could. Kya'd gotten them to drill tunnels into all of The House's walls after first moving in just so she that could get her vines to dramatically deliver her from place to place. She'd offered, once, to use them to help move Nico around The House as well so that they wouldn't have to spend as much time putting pressure on their bad leg. Nico had only let her offer once. They'd known that she'd done it with the best of intentions, but there was something too embarrassing about letting some new kid two years younger than them carry them around everywhere. Even if she technically wouldn't have been the one doing the carrying. Presently, the nymph's vines were delivering her directly onto Pat's lap. This was both a recent and slightly disgusting development, but one that Nico wasn't about to protest against if it meant that they might all actually be able to sit down in the living room for once. Milo arrived last. Milo arrived to most things last. Being punctual would ruin that unbothered image that he'd spent years fussing over perfecting.

Nico crossed their arms over their chest as they waited for everyone to settle in. "I didn't say I had anything to share, actually."

"Booooo!" Milo pulled a wrapper out from one of his seemingly infinite pockets and lobbed it at their head. "Boring!"

"Nico got challenged to a duel," Leif (unhelpfully) supplied.

They reached up to elbow Leif's ribs. Leif ducked down to do the same.

"Leif read my mind!" They protested, hoping to turn all of the attention that was suddenly on them into outrage directed elsewhere.

It didn't work. Leif being annoying was too routine to merit much of a response.

"Against who?" Kya asked.

"What did you do?" Pat demanded.

"Can we watch?" Milo checked.

"Leif *read my mind!*" They tried again.

The tin can came whizzing in from the kitchen, safely enclosed in a tightly wrapped vine.

Leif put Leif's hands up in surrender. "I already paid."

"Oh," Kya said.

The jar was promptly returned.

Nico gaped. "We're all just okay with that?"

Pat shrugged. "Leif already paid."

"Who's the duel against?" Kya got right back down to business.

"Can we watch?"

"What did you do?"

Nico groaned, tossing a blanket over their face as they tried to sink into the couch and escape.

"Nico." A sliver of light snuck in as Leif lifted a corner to pretend to whisper to them. "Can I tell them?"

They waved a hand in their general direction and Leif disappeared again, leaving them to stew alone in their misery.

"It was a selkie," Leif revealed.

"No!"

"Shit!"

"Woah."

They'd gotten rid of their only cursed piece of furniture (an old kitchen table that Milo had *sworn* was an absolute steal) ages ago, but Nico couldn't help but hope that this one would suddenly gain sentience and swallow them whole.

"Yeah, some random girl comes in, leaves a pile of clothes up front to be evaluated, then goes to shop around while Nico goes through it. The Kovienne branch came in and bought a bunch of stuff in bulk, then poof! Gone! Except apparently said random girl wasn't a random girl, she was a shape-shifting sea creature who'd left the key to said shapeshifting in said pile accidentally and it's like, super ancient selkie tradition to challenge anyone who steals your skin to a duel. To the death."

"I didn't steal anything!" Nico protested from deep within their blanket cocoon.

"Of course you didn't, dear," Leif squeezed their shoulder affectionately. Or as affectionately as Leif could manage, with a palm four times the size of said shoulder. "You just slacked off a bit at work. Still unfortunately led to duel challenge, though."

They stayed hidden for a while longer. Nico loved their friendly dearly, it sometimes felt like they were all constantly competing to be the most entertaining person in the room. They didn't particularly feel like engaging in that when it was their actual life on the line.

(Not that they had any intention of actually dueling the selkie girl, obviously. But they could have all at least pretended to be even a smidge concerned.)

"No one's dueling anyone," they decided that they were ready to correct the rest of the room three minutes into a heated debate on whether or not beating the selkie girl up with their cane would technically be breaking the typical 'bring no weapons' duel stipulation since it was always on them anyway. "Selkie girl said that's only a thing if her skin isn't returned. It's literally on its way to another location right now and if I don't even remember seeing it, it was probably ugly as shit so it'll be there for a while. I'll just tell Todd to handle it."

Four pairs of eyes blinked at them. The room was suddenly filled with such a potent skepticism that they could practically feel Leif's third eye doing the same through the blindfold.

Nico had worked for Todd for three years. They were all incredibly aware that he had never handled anything.

"He'll handle it!" But he wouldn't and they all knew that he wouldn't which left Nico with four options: kill a stranger, be killed by a stranger, flee Bayside and change their entire identity, or take the time off work to go retrieve the skin themself. With an annoying mostly mer-person. None of that seemed particularly appetizing.

Pat shifted, uncomfortable. They were too frustrated to even take solace in the fact that it meant that he had to finally unentwined himself from Kya for a few seconds. Something about them being all young and hormonal and obsessed with each other never failed to make Nico feel incredibly old and hormonal and obsessed with themself. But Nico was happy that they were happy. Mostly. When them being happy didn't involve the audible exchange of saliva. "We could all go together," Pat suggested. "To get it back from the Kovienne location. It could be a fun little outing."

Nico rolled their eyes. "It's a three-day boat ride in both directions. We can't afford to all take a week off work just because I'll probably have to."

Milo—who'd been slouching back against their armchair, eyes almost all the way closed behind his eyelashes even though he'd obviously been paying attention the whole time—sat up a little bit straighter. "Technically," he said slowly. "I could—"

Nico winced. Rule number two of living in The House (pretending that they'd ever gotten around to writing down official rules) was to never, ever, ask Milo for any money beyond his share of the rent and groceries. They shouldn't have even brought finances up. "No one else is taking the week off work." They repeated, staring right at him.

Milo nodded slightly then leaned back, pretending to tune the rest of the room out.

"I could probably hunt down a temporary glamour or something," Pat suggested. "Leif can just pretend to be you and do the duel. Then no one has to waste their time on this."

Nico's eyes narrowed. "Oh what, just because I'm disabled I suddenly can't—"

Milo leaned forward to retrieve his abandoned wrapper and it was then once again tossed at their forehead. "Boooo," he crowed.

A different can (marked with something that vaguely resembled their own name) was instantly in front of Nico face.

Most of their friends' penalty jars were for magical eccentricities that they had to keep at bay to keep everyone else in The House sane. Nico's was for their constant onslaught of 'oh it's because I'm disabled, isn't it?' jokes. That was hardly their fault, though. Once Pat had finally come out and they could no longer blame every inconvenience on someone else in The House being transphobic, they'd had to find a work around.

Nico scowled. "That wasn't a joke! I am perfectly capable of beating up some random selkie and it was insulting to imply that—"

Kya's vine lightly knocked the jar against their forehead. "That being over two feet taller than you, twice your weight, and able to predict an attacker's every move might give Leif an advantage? Tithe. Now."

They sighed, digging through their pocket to drop a copper into the jar. The vine didn't retreat once the debt had been paid, though.

"Now apologize," Kya demanded, crossing her arms and leaning back against Pat.

"For what!"

"If you weren't joking then you were actually implying that Pat's an asshole which means *you* were being an asshole. Apologize."

Nico couldn't help but smile a little. The House was not the kind of place where apologies were ever really necessary (not because they didn't exist, but because they rarely ever needed voicing), but Kya was also normally not the kind of person who stood up to other people. If that cost them a couple of 'I'm sorry's and a bit of watching her swap saliva with Pat, then so be it.

"I'm sorry," they admitted. "She knows I know he doesn't actually suck."

They waited for Pat to nod in acknowledgement.

"But that's obviously still not an option," they regained control of the conversation. "We'd pay way more for a glamour than I'd even be losing if I went on the stupid errand. And then Leif would do what? Kill someone for me?"

"I absolutely would." Leaf leaned towards them.

"Yeah, well...obviously." They sighed. "It'll be fine. Annoying and a massive waste of time, but fine. Todd might even still handle it."

Pat frowned. "I don't think he'll—"

"Can you all stop fucking telling me what to do!" They exclaimed. "I said he'll handle it!"

Nico hadn't meant to yell, that was just the natural way that their voice came out when they felt backed into a corner. Still, the tone of the room instantly shifted. For the first time in a long time, The House was entirely silent.

"Nico..." Leif began.

"Don't." They got to their feet. "I'd better go get some rest." They tried to smile. Tried to fix it. Mostly though, they just tired to escape. They were not good at apologies. Especially when they were for their own emotions. "Might be beating someone to death tomorrow, after all."

Then they left them all to go upstairs. And soon they'd be leaving them all to go to Kovienne. It was a stupid thing to yell about. They'd travelled far longer distances before and it wasn't like anything disastrous would happen if *Interthrifter* didn't pay them for the time off. Ever since Milo had moved in, making rent had never technically been a thing that they'd had to worry about.

But something about the circumstances surrounding the trip felt a little too serious. A little too ominous. There was nothing daunting about a trip to a new town, but a trip to a new town that they were obligated to complete felt a lot more intimidating. Afterall, if someone did recognize the cloak for what it was and buy it before they got to it, they had no idea what'd they'd do from there.

They wouldn't kill anyone, obviously (probably) and they were fairly certain that the girl from the story wouldn't kill them either (probably), but one couldn't just be issued a duel, deny it, and then go about their normal life. If they somehow managed to mess this up, there'd be no coming back to Bayside or The House or the rest of the assholes that inhabited it. It wouldn't be their first time starting over, but Nico was startling to realize that it would be the first time they really didn't want to.

They slipped out of their binder and uniform and into their old, ratty pyjamas, crawled under their blankets, and stared at the ceiling.

There was no point in going to sleep, after all. They knew that someone would be popping in in no time.

And that—how absolutely, positively certain they were of that—terrified them a little.

Chapter 4

Pat came first. Nico had known that she would. Normally it would have been Leif if Leif hadn't been involved in the conflict since as the first and eldest inhabitant of The House, Leif had somehow become its de facto leader, but Leif always had to hide away for a bit after fights, even if the fighting hadn't fully been directed at Leif.

It was more of a reason that they should have been better at apologizing after they always inevitably exploded. It was more a reason that they couldn't.

So, when someone knocked on their door and then slowly started opening it before getting a response, Nico didn't bother looking up before saying. "I'm..." they winced. Pressed their tongue against the cracked molar in the corner of their mouth. Tried again. "Sorry." Breathy and fast and rushed, but it was as close to apologizing as they were going to get.

"Ewww." Pat sat down on their bed. "Twice in one day feels weird. Never do that again. It's freakishly of character."

Nico pushed themself up against their headboard. "You were being helpful. I shouldn't have yelled."

Pat rolled his eyes. "I don't know if you've noticed yet, but we're an incredibly yell-y group of people."

They smiled a little. "I bet she's going to come do some more yelling on your behalf, as soon as you leave."

Pat blushed, looking away. "She umm... did ask me to let her know as soon as we're done here," he admitted. "Just as a heads up."

Nico lightly nudged her shoulder. "She's obsessed with you."

"Maybe a little," Pat admitted.

"Nope. Absolutely obsessed and doing an awful job at hiding it. When did that happen and how the fuck did it take the rest of us this long to notice?"

Pat watched them for a second with an obvious question in her eye, but left it unvoiced. There was no need to say 'you're deflecting' or 'so we're ignoring it, then,' or even 'fine, I'll talk about how obsessed I am with my girlfriend for half an hour straight and we'll both pretend that we're not just talking about her to ignore how royally fucked you are right now'. Because even though there was technically only one mind-reader in their midst, The House rarely ever had to actually talk out loud to say things to each other.

So, Nico listened to Pat ramble about Kya and then acted adequately remorseful when Kya glided into their room a few minutes after he left until she believed it enough to sit down. They listened as she pretended to casually fill them in on all of the random hand-to-hand combat techniques that she'd learned about recently from a book that Nico was pretty sure didn't actually exist. Kya left their room covered in yellow roses. She almost always did. Milo accidentally came third because he was somehow still truly awful at pretending to be unbothered and brought with him stories about how exciting and hilarious and exhilarating his day had been and never once mentioned duels or selkies or Kovienne or even anything Nico specific at all because Milo's love—and only—language was talking about himself.

Leif came last which Nico had, of course, known would happen. Because The House kept having the audacity to be so endearingly knowable.

"Hello," She knocked against the doorframe. There was a blue bracelet on her wrist, this time. She'd avoided this particular conflict long enough to change it. "I fucked up today."

Nico snorted. "Yeah, no shit."

"I didn't know you were like…sad-worried-upset." She sat down at the edge of their bed. Leif's personal brand of conflict resolution was both Nico's most and least favourite. She was the only one who never even pretended to let them get away with acting like their problems didn't exist. "You seemed angry-upset. I thought we were angry-upset."

"I am angry upset," they said. And they were. They'd never been challenged to a duel before and were finding it wildly offensive and inconsiderate thus far.

"Well I," Leif fiddled with the bracelet, idly spinning around a few beads. "Was terrified=upset. But you obviously weren't so I couldn't say that I was without making it worse and I figured more people knowing would make me less terrified-upset. So... oops. I'm annoying."

Nico nodded. "You are." They crawled out from under their covers to sit with her at the edge of the bed. Leif was their only housemate that couldn't comfortably sit beside them against the headboard. "I'm not actually doing the duel thing, you know," they reminded her. "That'd be stupid. I'm pretty sure Selkie Girl also knows that no one in their right mind would do the duel thing. Declaring one is just an incredibly annoying way to force someone to help you get your shit back."

Leif swallowed. "You're definitely going on the quest, then?"

"It'll hardly be a quest," Nico rolled their eyes. "It's literally just hopping to the next closest store, buying the cloak back, and then going on with my life. It'll just be... annoying."

Leif just kept spinning her bracelet.

They frowned. "You did know I wasn't doing the duel," Nico realized. "Obviously I wouldn't... what am I supposed to be terrified of right now?"

Leif hesitated. "I'm older than you, right? So—"

"You're twenty."

"That's older!" She protested. "And wiser and more experienced and all that! Quests change people, Neek. You're already just barely tolerable enough to be around so don't..." they sighed. "Don't let it, okay? Change you?"

Nico rolled their eyes. "I promise a shopping trip that'll take like... a week tops isn't going to transform me into an entirely new person, okay?"

Nonymous

And it wouldn't. They were gone for far longer than a week.

Chapter 5

Selkie Girl had somehow found out where Nico lived. Their housemates had told them this, of course, but they didn't have to deal with it themself until they left for their Monday shift and found her waiting by their garden.

"Aye!" They yelled, waving their cane above their head to get her attention. "Person who wants to kill me!"

The girl jumped. Nico rolled their eyes.

"Don't trample the flowers," they muttered, continuing down the path. If she wanted to stalk them, they weren't about to make it easier on her. "They fight back."

Eventually, they heard her catch up enough to fall into step beside them. Nico kept their focus straight ahead. This girl did not get to waste any more of their time and attention than absolutely necessary.

"So, umm..." the girl said. Her voice was high. Light. Waspish. "I didn't get to introduce myself? The other day? What with all the..."

"Duel challenging?" Nico picked up speed.

The girl did too. "Well... yes, I suppose. That."

"Yet you somehow still figured out where I lived?"

"That was the easy bit," she said. "I had your name."

Suddenly there was a thin, pale finger against Nico's heart, pressing at their nametag. They let themself pause against it, but only for half a second. Then, they kept moving. They'd sooner let her finger impale them than willingly have more of their time wasted on this.

"I stopped by yesterday, actually," the girl continued, apparently completely nonplussed by Nico's very valiant attempts to escape her. "And the day before. But no one—"

"*Interthrifter* problems aren't my responsibility on the weekend."

"Okay," the girl said. "Right, of course. But a duel challenge is—"

"Not my problem until I've clocked in."

There was suddenly a face in front of Nico's. Or rather, above Nico's. It didn't seem fair that this girl had the audacity to both set their world off kilter *and* be taller than them. "I think it is, actually."

Nico had never met a selkie before—few people had, apparently, based on the hours of research that Pat and Kya had combed through the night before—so they couldn't help but scan the girl for any signs of magic. She was a boring thing, though. Hair so blonde that it was near white, frizzing all the way down to the small of her back. Skin too pale and freckly and eyes a green too dark to suit the rest of her face. But other then that, she looked entirely human. And, she had glasses. Thick round ones that made her too-green eyes look huge and buggy. If Nico had to get roped into an archaic death match, the universe could have at least set them up to fight anyone but some thin blonde in glasses. As things were, it all felt remarkably uncool.

"Look," the girl continued. Nico tried to step around her, but she moved to block them. "I'm not exactly thrilled about this either, but there's a proper way to—"

"You're the one who declared a fucking duel," Nico reminded her.

"Because you stole my skin!" The girl squeezed her fists shut in tandem with her eyes. She took a long breath. "We're not actually going to duel, right? That'd be..." she paused, considering. "Quite messy, I'd imagine. I'd rather avoid..." her eyes flicked to Nico's cane. "you know. That."

Nico snorted. "What? Didn't realize the person you were pulling into a public death match had a cane?"

"Well, obviously not," the girl said. "You weren't using it on Friday and you could hit me with it. Which hardly seems fair. But I also—"

Nico tried to escape to the right this time. The girl matched them.

"Would you stop that!" She stomped her foot. "I am trying to have a peaceful, civil conversation with you about—"

"The death match you challenged me to."

"You stole my actual *skin*!" She exclaimed. "I am not the one who did a terrible thing here! All I'm asking you to do is get it back for me so just..." she gestured vaguely. "Get in contact with this other store that you've apparently sent it to and demand that they—"

Nico rolled their eyes. "You declared war on the wrong person, if that's what you were after," they informed her. "I already told you that wouldn't work. Other locations don't give a shit about random employees and even if they did, you probably don't want to tell them that they have an incredibly magical object in their possessions right now. You'll just have to go rebuy it yourself."

"If you return a selkie's sealskin, you get a wish, you know. So you should—"

"I do know," they tried to step around her again. "That's the kind of thing you research when someone challenges you to a duel. Still not interested."

This time, the girl stuck out a foot to stop them. "You know we're going to end up having to go get it together, then. I don't see why you can't at least pretend to be polite about it."

Nico blinked. "Did you just try to trip me?"

The selkie's cheeks got a little less ghostly pale. "You—"

"Stole your skin," the waved her off. "After you fully left it in a donation pile. Yes. I've heard." They sighed. "I have a meeting with my boss this morning, okay? Let me talk to him. I'm sure any curses, challenges, or death-sentences incurred during shifts fall onto him anyway."

They didn't. Nico hadn't even finished explaining before Todd—a middle aged orc with a particular distaste for doing literally anything ever—said "well, sounds like you've got to either kill the thing or take her on a quest, then."

Though Nico would've normally been the first to protest that a few days' journey to the Kovienne was hardly a 'quest', the specific terminology was apparently important here. *Interthrifter* had a questing budget. They did not have a hyper-specific product retrieval budget. All that budget entailed was lost wages plus a travel and supplies fund, but if Nico was about to be exploited by some random selkie for the horrendous crime of doing their job, then they were going to exploit *Interthrifter* back as much as they possibly could. Todd was apologetic enough to give them the rest of the day off to pack but other than that (according to him), his hands were tied.

It did not surprise Nico to find Selkie Girl waiting just outside the door to the office, having apparently eavesdropped on the entire conversation. They hadn't even known that she'd existed a few days prior, but she was already becoming impossible to shake.

"When do we leave?" She asked, bouncing on her toes.

Nico glared. "I could still decide to just kill you instead, you know."

"Oh." The girl's face pinched. "Yes, I supposed that's... right."

Nico sighed, tapping to unfurrow their cane. Finally, the girl didn't breathe down their neck as they headed for the door.

"Be at my place an hour before sunrise tomorrow," they called back to her. "Bring money. I'm not paying your way."

They waited for the door to adjust to their size then exited into the sunlight.

"Nicole!"

Nico cringed when they heard her clomping after them. They would already have to spend the next week with this girl and her waspish voice. They didn't want her being any more involved in their last day of freedom than absolutely necessary.

"It's Mathilda!" She waved. "It's Mathilda! My name! I still hadn't given it to you!"

Nico continued out of the market district, pretending not to hear her. They wondered if an afternoon was enough time to finally join a witch's downline and learn how to curse someone.

Chapter 6

The House threw them a going away party. For the three days' journey that plenty of people made multiple times a season. For a journey much shorter than the ones that had gotten them all to Bayside in the first place.

Nico tried not to read too much into that. The House—or rather, one particular sixteenth-faery part of it—was a big fan of blowing money on parties whenever they could come up with the slightest excuse for having one, but something about the whole thing felt incredibly patronizing to Nico. Which made them feel guilty for feeling patronized.

Rule number three of The House (pretending that they'd ever gotten around to writing down official rules) was that all of its inhabitants were completely equal within its walls, regardless of magical ability, physical or mental prowess, or not-so-secretly rich asshole parents. Nobody in The House had ever patronized Nico in anything more than just jest, but they'd had the misfortune of spending the first sixteen years of their life outside of its walls. That could make a person suspicious of even the coolest of people.

Plus, if they weren't just being patronizing, then maybe that meant that they were also feeling this swirling thing buried deep in Nico's gut. And Nico wasn't ready to put any more validity into the thought that they might not actually be coming back. That this was a going away.

It was a ridiculous idea anyway. They'd go, grab the cloak, and be back. It would be mind-numbingly simple.

It was no big deal which meant that this party was no big deal, so they rolled back their shoulders, opened their door, and descended into the chaos that was their living room.

Only to instantly be intercepted by Leif.

"Okay," he said. "Don't kill me."

They frowned. "Why would I—"

And then, they saw her. Mathilda: standing awkwardly in the corner, pretending to drink from a very obviously empty cup. At least she looked slightly miserable.

"Why would you do that!" Nico hissed.

"Spying. I invited her this morning because I'm exceptionally clever."

"Leif."

"You're about to travel several days away with a stranger who's already made it extremely clear that she's okay with murdering you! I'm allowed to be cautious!" He dropped his voice. "We keep her here for a bit, I read her mind the whole time, and if anything spooky or murderous happens, we... I don't know. Do something about it."

Nico rolled their eyes. "She's a stick. I could take her."

"Let me be all protective and overbearing?" Leif pouted. "Please? It makes me feel useful."

"Fine," the relented. "Do what you must."

Leif skipped as they ran off to go secretly interrogate her.

Mathilda's presence might have technically made sense from a safety perspective, but it also meant that the party that was supposed to be for Nico was now even more miserable than they'd been worried it would be. Instead of just dodging sympathetic looks and poorly timed jokes, they now also had to avoid Mathilda's never-ending attempts to talk to them.

"So I was thinking we should—" She'd catch them at the sink, forcing them to turn up the tap to drown her out.

"Maybe we could—" she'd try every second she found them alone, causing them to initiate a conversation with someone else just to avoid talking to her.

They knew that it made logical sense to have her here, but surely any sleuthing that Leif was planning on doing couldn't possibly be taking this long.

Eventually, pretending to smile and laugh and joke around got too exhausting even for them, so Nico slipped up the ladder to the roof. Even their bedroom wouldn't guarantee them enough privacy. And there, leaning over the edge of said roof, staring at the garden, sat the last person that they'd wanted to see.

Maybe if they finally talked to her though, she'd finally leave. Maybe she'd actually been trying to get their attention to call off the whole pseudo-quest.

"If you're scoping out the place to rob us, we don't actually have anything all that valuable."

They realized too late that emerging out of the quiet darkness to say something to someone leaning over a rooftop was incredibly inadvisable. They had to lunge forward to grab Mathilda's arm before she went toppling over the edge. They hissed through the ensuing pain that shot up their right leg as Mathilda scooted backwards, hugging her knees to her chest.

"I've been trying to talk to you all night," she said, keeping her eyes locked on the place just below her shoulder where Nico had grabbed her.

"Yes." They sat down. "I noticed. Did you catch that part where I was trying to ignore you?"

"A bit," she admitted. "Eventually."

"Good," they nodded. "I hope you were horribly offended."

Mathilda sighed. She leaned back to stare at the sky, all fears of plummeting to her death apparently forgotten. "You could've told me I had your name wrong, you know."

Nico frowned. "What?"

"I've been using... the one on your nametag. Everyone else uses Nico, right? I didn't realize you were... not that I should have assumed you were a girl, of course. That was—"

"It wasn't wrong. The name part. Definitely not a girl. I wouldn't put the wrong one on my own nametag, though. Nico's for friends. Nicole is for strangers at work. And especially for strangers at work who con me into travelling days away with them after they fucked up and donated the wrong thing."

"Oh," she nodded. "Right. Well umm... you could use... I don't actually have a nickname yet, I don't think? I am a girl though. I'm pretty sure. Probably. But if you wanted to use a nickname in a non-gender way Mat's..." she frowned, scrunching up her nose. Her glasses slid down a bit and she had to push them back up. "No, I think I'd rather hate that, actually. Tillie would be fine, though. If you want. As a friendship thing, not a gender one."

"Good to know, Mathilda."

She sighed. "That's childish."

"Oh, is it?" Nico turned to look at her. "Am I supposed to act like we're fucking friends now just because you got my pronouns right?"

Mathilda just turned her attention back towards the sky. It was maddening.

Nico squeezed their medallion. "What are you doing on my roof?" They finally thought to ask.

"It was loud," she said. Like that was a perfectly valid reason for roof climbing up a stranger's house. "I needed a break."

"You don't actually live here!" They reminded her. "If you needed a break, you could've fucking left!"

She hesitated. "I really did want to talk to you, though."

"Yeah? How's that going for you?"

"I'm... okay," Mathilda finally got up, dusting invisible dirt off of her pants. "Alright. I'd better... see you tomorrow, then. I suppose." She waved. They flipped her off. Being childish, it turned out, could sometimes be incredibly cathartic.

They'd been expecting their friends to eventually realize that they were missing. It was inevitable that someone would come and find them up there. What they hadn't been expecting was Milo doing it first.

"Selkie bitch is gone," he declared, sitting down beside them. "You can come back downstairs now."

"Mmmm," they hummed, leaning against him. "Too sleepy. I live here now."

Milo shoved them away. They knew that he would. It was why they'd done it in the first place.

"You haven't opened the penalty jars yet," he unbuckled his satchel and started spreading them out on the roof. "Figured you'd forget. You're kind of useless, so..."

"Asshole," Nico smiled lazily.

"I can't help it. It's the faery blood."

They grinned, watching him pull out a copper and flick it towards them. At only one sixteenth faery Milo possessed no magical abilities nor inability to lie, but he pretended he did sometimes, just to justify any particularly asshole-ish comments. "I'm not a dick, just part faery" had been such a common excuse when he'd first moved it that the sentiment alone had warranted its own jar.

"I'm not going to need emergency money just to go to Kovienne," Nico reminded him. "It'll be like a vacation, remember? A paid one."

"It's also a quest," he pointed out. "Technically. Which definitely counts."

The money from the jars went first to personal emergencies, then renovations, groceries, and furniture, and then—if anything was left at the end of each month—to doing something fun as a group. Nico wasn't a fan of having to use them, but they flipped over Kya's and pocketed the few coins that slipped out regardless. If Milo hadn't forced the jar onto them, someone else would've eventually. They frowned before even checking his. It was far too heavy.

Nico looked a little closer and frowned. "Some of these are silvers," they pointed out. "Like... a lot of them."

"I had to convert a few," Milo shrugged. "To make them fit."

"The month's not even halfway over yet!"

"I've been particularly asshole-y then, I guess."

They sighed. "Milo, you can't..."

"I'll have you know, I said at least one rude thing for every single one of those coins."

They'd never doubted that. "And how many of them did you say since you found out I'd have to go?"

Milo looked away. "No comment."

"Okay. Fine." Fistful by fistful, they transferred the coins to their pockets. They'd have to pack a separate purse just for them in the morning. "Since I'm not gonna need it, I'll put it all back next week. Try not to fill it too much until then."

"I probably will," he admitted. "You'd might as well use it all."

"Thanks," they leaned against his shoulder, again. Let him gently shove them off, again. "I love you too."

"Ack, disgusting," Milo sneered, even as he failed to stop himself from smiling. It was why he was the easiest one for them to say it too. If he never accepted it, they never had to sit in how serious they were. "Absolutely not. I just pretend to tolerate you because you live here."

"Asshole," they whispered. Affectionately. It was the only affectionate thing Milo always let them get away with without protest.

"I can't help it," he mumbled. "I'm part faery." He handed them another copper then stayed with them to watch the sky until Leif came to take over.

"I have intel!" He announced.

He sounded so excited, that for a second, Nico let themself hope that he'd somehow figured out a way for them to just stay home.

Milo squeezed their hand before slipping back down the ladder, letting Leif take his place.

"Is she a secret outlaw I can just turn in for the reward money then never have to see again?" Nico asked, only half joking.

Leif shook his head. "Perfectly ordinary, I'm afraid. Minus the whole creature rarely every seen on land thing, obviously," he added.

Nico sighed.

"She's seriously not awful, Neek," Leif wrapped an arm around their shoulders. "She actually seems quite nice, all things considered."

"All things considered?"

Leif suddenly looked sheepish. "I mean, you did basically trap her in the wrong form."

"She's the one who donated it!" Nico reminded him. They didn't get how everyone seemed to keep forgetting about that part. "I was literally just doing my job."

"Okay," Leif relented. "You're right. You didn't do anything wrong. Just... play nice, maybe? She's not some nefarious monster trying to lure you out to sea to sacrifice you to some fringe god, she's—"

"I hadn't even considered that yet," Nico realized.

"Oh," he blushed. "Well... now you don't have to consider it." He sighed. "She's just some lost lonely kid, Nico."

"I'm pretty sure she's practically the same age as me."

"She is," Leif nodded. "Ergo, child. Just... try not to be so..."

"Me?" They raised an eyebrow. "Because as of a few days ago, I was apparently supposed to stay exactly the same."

Leif rolled his eyes. "I meant try to be maybe a little less defensively asshole-ish fake you. Playing nice for a week won't kill you."

Nico was pretty sure it might, actually, but they nodded against the dark and pretended to agree.

They didn't actually promise anything, though.

Chapter 7

In an attempt to pack light, Nico left the house with a single bag slung over each shoulder the next morning, their purse shoved in the bottom of the larger one for safe keeping. They always had to shift everything to their right arm they needed to use their cane so they weren't a fan of bringing multiple bags with them unless it was absolutely necessary.

Mathilda was waiting for them at the end of the path. With a single, tiny purse clutched in her fist.

"I thought I told you to pack," they said by way of greeting.

"I did," she smiled, nodding towards the purse.

Nico frowned. They hadn't even left yet and Mathilda was somehow already proving herself to be an awful travel partner. "It's a three-day trip," they deadpanned. "Even if you're planning on jumping into the ocean as soon as we get there."

Mathilda just kept nodding at them.

"And you're only bringing one change of clothes?" They finished spelling it out for her. What she had worn wasn't exactly sea-friendly either. A plain, stiff, off-white, pocketed dress reaching just past her knees. Nico had no idea what she'd been thinking. They'd packed two binders, four tee-shirts, three flannels, one pair of shorts, and two pairs of trousers. Being on a boat typically called for layers, not a single piece of short-sleeved fabric.

Mathilda's eyes narrowed, just slightly. "I don't exactly have a ton of them. I wasn't planning on being on land this long."

Nico paused, noticing for the first time that not only was she apparently planning on bringing the one dress with her, but that it was the same one they'd seen her in every time she'd inflicted her presence upon them. They sighed. "Give me a second," they turned back towards The House. "Don't follow me."

They crept up to their room and quickly shoved a couple of random shirts and slacks from the back of their closet into a satchel.

Mathilda smiled when they chucked the bag at her. It was a little too warm, for their liking. Uncomfortably genuine.

"Thank you," she said. "You didn't have to—"

"I did, actually," Nico stopped her. "You're already forcing me to spend the next few days with you. The least you could do is take care of your own basic fucking hygiene."

"Oh," her smile disappeared.

Nico started off toward the docks. Mathilda tailed after them.

"I'm sorry," she tried again. "I feel like I'm already doing everything wrong, somehow."

You are, Nico thought. Then, they realized how much more satisfying that would sound out loud. "You are."

Mathilda winced. She tapped her fingers against her side. "I know you don't want to be here," she said. "and I know it's not fair that you are, but I need... it's not like I had a ton of options, okay? And you might end up getting a wish at the end, so—"

"I don't want a fucking wish, Mathilda!" They yelled. "I want to still be asleep right now! I want to have never met you!"

They kept moving. Mathilda fell a few steps behind them. She was quiet, finally. And then, she was sniffly.

"Gods!" Nico spun around. "Are you seriously crying right now?" They demanded. "Because I what? Got a little mad at you?"

"No," she continued sniffing.

"Gods," Nico barked out a laugh at the sheer absurdity of it. "I'm the one who should be crying right now, Mathilda!"

"I know," she whispered. "I'm sorry."

Nico sighed, shifted their bags so that they could summon their cane, and tried their very best to leave her behind them.

Nico had spent the previous afternoon going through the effort of finding two ship workers to go along with their idea. It had cost them hours of begging and an unnamed future favour, but ferry rides to Kovienne were ridiculously overpriced, so they'd decided that it had been worth it. Mathilda, apparently, did not agree.

"We can't pretend to be other people," she argued when they met up with the crewmen that Nico had made arrangements with.

"She's kidding," Nico told them.

"I'm—"

They stomped on her foot. "She's kidding. Weird sense of humour, that one." They spun Mathilda away and tried to redirect her as far from the conversation as possible.

They crewmen turned to look at each other, suddenly a lot more skeptical. "If one of you blow this…"

"We won't," Nico smiled. "You guys know me, right? If I could handle *Interthrifter* for three year without getting fired, I can spend three days cooking bland fish for a few cargo-shippers. And you get a paid vacation. Win-win."

"Don't know her though," they nodded at Mathilda. Who was, currently, pacing in the sand and muttering to herself.

Nico sighed. "She's fine. Excellent cook. Great with fish. Awful with people, but I'll keep her in the cabin the whole time, okay?"

"If she's not on board…"

"She is. Just give me a second to talk to her, yeah?" They stomped off to collect her. Mathilda tried to say something when they grabbed her arm, but Nico couldn't risk her doing anything else stupid in front of the people that they were supposed to be using for a free ride. They linked their elbow around hers and pulled her further down the shore.

"I don't like tricking people," Mathilda said the moment they let go. She shook out her arm, as if even just them touching her was disgusted.

"It's not tricking, it's a trade. They still get their wages, we get a free ride."

She shook her head, clenching her fists. "No, not... the people on the boat. We'd be..."

Nico rolled their eyes. "It's a commercial cargo ship doing a supply drop. Half of the people on it'll be constantly revolving, no one's going to pay attention to a couple of random cooks unless we're ridiculously awful at it." They hesitated. "You can lie, right? That's not a selkie thing?"

"Well... yes, but—"

"Then it's fine."

"I can't really cook anything, though." Mathilda kept her eyes on the sand.

"No," Nico realized. "of course you can't. Great," they sighed. "it'll be stupid simple, okay? It's not like, fancy restaurant food prep, it's literally just making sure no one on board starves. And getting a free ride because of it. You're not fucking this up for me."

"I can't—"

"Do you have fifty silver?" They asked. "Because that's how much it'd cost to ferry the whole way there. Plus at least twenty five more to get me back. Or you can pay the twenty five to go yourself and leave me the fuck alone, but I'm not spending any of my actual money on this."

Mathilda was quiet. She definitely wasn't hiding fifty silver in her tiny little purse. "He gave you money though, right? They person at the thrift store? Specifically for the ferry? Surely he—"

"He gave me money that I'm going to be keeping as a bonus to make up for the massive fucking headache this is obviously going to be. It's my money. I'm not spending it on a pair of overpriced ferry tickets when I have perfectly good free alternative all lined up."

Mathilda hesitated. "You get a wish, though. You might be able to use it to—"

"No."

44

"I'll give you all the money I have on me, when we get my cloak back. I wouldn't need it anymore, so..."

"You haven't offered to buy ferry passes yet. It's obviously a lot less than fifty silver."

Mathilda licked her lips. Tapped her feet against the sand. "Okay," she breathed. "Okay, fine. I'm umm... I'm not good at lying, though. So—"

"Got it," Nico said. "Bad at lying and cooking. Great. I'm so glad we're doing this together." They considered for a moment. Their friends had found next to no information on selkies having any form of special ability, but it certainly wouldn't have been the first time a species worked to keep the true extent of their powers a secret. "Is there anything you are good at?" They asked. "You must have at least one useful skill or ability that we could use if we had to, right?"

"I can swim?" She offered. "Fairly well?"

Nico sighed. "Yes. Yeah. Figured that was kind of an implied thing. I can't," they tapped their cane against the ground to accentuate the point. "and unless you're planning on swimming all the way there, that's not super helpful anyway. Anything else?"

Mathilda considered. Then, she screwed up her face and considered even more. "I'm umm..." she said to the sand. "I'm quite good at magic, I think. Or... better than most people, I suppose."

Nico's eyes widened. "Holy shit!" Sheer muscle memory had them reaching out to whack her arm, but Mathilda squeaked and stepped away. They returned their fist to their side. "That's the kind of thing that would've kind of been important to know, Mathilda!"

Maybe they wouldn't need to sneak onto a ship at all. Whatever kind of magical abilities selkies had, they surely had something to do with the ocean. Maybe she'd be able to just glide them directly to Kovienne.

"What can you do?" They asked, perhaps a little too eagerly for someone who was supposed to actively be pissed at her. They couldn't help it. It had been years since they'd encountered new kinds of magic.

Mathilda sucked on her lip and reached into her pocket. Nico watched intently for some kind of wand or magical artifact but then, she pulled out a single creased box of cards.

"I can umm..." Mathilda froze, noticing their disappointment. "Oh!" Her eyes grew wide. "Oh, you thought I meant..." her cheeks flushed. "No umm... selkies can't do any actual magic, I'm afraid. Especially without our skins."

Nico turned around to return to the crewmen. They needed this to be done with as quickly as possible.

"I'm fairly good at close-up card tricks though!" Mathilda called after them. "If you wanted to see!"

It was going to be a very, very long trip.

Chapter 8

Mathilda had not been joking about having no useable skills. Not that Nico'd thought she'd been. Mathilda did not seem like the kind of person capable of humour.

The boat they'd gained passage on was small enough to not have a kitchen staff beyond the two crewman whose positions they'd stolen. This had seemed like a good idea, at first. It limited the chances that they'd interact with someone knowledgeable enough to recognize that they weren't supposed to be there. It also meant that they'd be able to remain relatively isolated from the rest of the ship and alone tended to be Nico's preferred state of being. Even after realizing that Mathilda obviously wouldn't know anything about fire or cooking or land-species food and likely wouldn't be able to pull her own weight, it had still seemed like a genius plan.

The problem wasn't that Mathilda didn't know how to cook; it was that she refused to learn how.

A basket of fish was dropped off almost as soon as they set sail, and when Nico sent Mathilda to retrieve it, she carried it back with shaking, outstretched arms. She wouldn't even look at the damned thing.

They sighed. "Is this going to be a problem?"

"I can't do fish," she said, depositing the basket and scurrying away from it as if its very presence was insulting to her.

They frowned. "What the fuck do you... you're a fucking seal!"

Mathilda looked away, her eyes already watering. Nico would quickly learn that it didn't take much to make her eyes water. "Yes, but they're... they're different, out of the water. Smellier."

"Then don't smell them?"

She shook her head. "I can't do fish," she repeated. Then, more quietly, "I'm sorry."

Nico sighed, pushing themself to their feet. "We're supposed to be making food on a fucking ship, Mathilda. Fish is pretty much all you do right now." They handed her the basket. "Clean them. I'll find the tools and teach you how to gut it."

They watched her face pinch in disgust as she made a dramatic show of holding the basket as far from her as possible all the way to the sink. Nico rolled their eyes and started rooting through the cabinets for tools.

When they returned to the counter to get started, they found Mathilda dramatically gagging. And crying. And rubbing a bar of soap against a fish's scales.

"What the fuck are you doing?" They exclaimed.

Mathilda jumped, dropping the fish into the thoroughly sudded up sink. "I'm... washing it." Her voice was even more pinched than usual. What, with all the crying.

"It's a fucking fish, not a dish!"

Mathilda frowned. "You said to clean it."

"You rinse it," they said. "Like any sane person would, to make it *less* slippery. You don't... why the fuck would you use soap!"

"You said to wash it! I did what you told me to!"

They sighed, nudging her out of the way. "Just... be not here right now. Be literally anywhere else."

Mathilda hesitated. It was so, so obvious that she couldn't wait to be as far away from the fish as possible, but at least she was aware enough to recognize how unfair that was. "I could wash them now," she said. "Now... now that I know. So you can chop them up and..."

"You obviously can't," they waved her off. She still didn't move. Nico looked up at her. She looked anywhere but towards them. "I'm not gonna force you to trade jobs, okay? I obviously can't trust you with a knife if you couldn't even fucking do this. Just... stay out of the way, yeah?"

And so, they did the washing and the gutting and the chopping and the seasoning all on their own. While Mathilda dramatically gagged and sniffled in the corner.

Then, they tried to give her easier jobs.

"Put the buns on, will you?"

Except then despite only being in charge of one thing while Nico did the job of two fully trained cooks, Mathilda had apparently been waiting for them to take the buns out of the ovens themself and by the time Nico'd smelt the burning, the bottoms were all destroyed.

"Put the spices away," they redirected.

Except then Mathilda had decided that it was necessary to ask them where each and every individual thing should go and it ended up taking more time than it would have had Nico done it themself.

They couldn't even trust her to do busywork.

"Organize the cupboards," they said just for the sake of distracting her then looked up from their work to find every single thing had been taken out and spread all over the kitchen, Mathilda having apparently taken it upon herself to sort everything by colour. For absolutely no reason.

Looking at that—at the mess of spices and preserves and utensils surrounded by the mess of flour and guts that Mathilda had also not been able to clean up—they longed for the ferry. They would've gladly wasted the coin, just to spare themself from having to put up with this.

"Can you do literally anything right!" Nico demanded.

Mathilda spun around from where she'd been comparing shades of brown cardboard. "I'm organizing," she said.

"How does it help anyone to have the salt with the fucking cleaning products!"

Mathilda blinked. "It... looks nice."

Nico almost laughed. It was so ridiculously that if they weren't in the middle of the most exhausting day of their life, they truly would have. "Get out," they said instead. They had no room left for humour.

She frowned. "There's still a lot left to put away. I can... I'll do it like it was before, now that I know."

Which, Nico was sure, would involve pestering them every two seconds. It would best to clean up her mess themself, before she found a way to make a new one. "I'll handle it. Just... go back to the cabin. I can't deal with you right now."

"I'm supposed to be a cook," Mathilda reminded them. "If someone walks in and I'm not here, they'll—"

"If someone walks in and you are here, they'll instantly know we're not supposed to be!" They screamed.

Her eyes welled again. They found that they didn't particularly care.

"You're fucking incompetent, Mathilda! There's no way you'll fool anyone!"

"I could—"

"No!" They pointed to the door that led to their shared cabin. "No just... don't do anything, okay? If you're going to be this useless, the least you could do is not make more work for everyone else."

Mathilda licked her lips. She stared at her feet and tapped them against the ground. She moved her jaw a few times before actually responding. "I'm sorry," she whispered.

This time, Nico did laugh. "Just... go be useless somewhere less destructive, yeah?"

She finally left.

Nico wiped the back of their hand across their brow and return to work. Dimly, eventually, they would feel guilty for snapping. Dimly, eventually, they would wonder if they perhaps had been a little too harsh. But it had finally gotten them a few hours of peace (or at least, as much peace as someone *could* get while rushing to singlehandedly feed an entire ship) and they still had two days of this left to go. If being a little too harsh was the only thing that was going to keep them sane through that, then so be it.

Chapter 9

By the time Nico had finally caught up on enough of the day's work to retire to their cabin, Mathilda was crying. Mathilda apparently cried at most things though, so they didn't let themself feel guilty about that.

Almost her entire plate of dinner was sitting by the door.

Nico tried not to look at her as they sorted through their luggage. They weren't a particularly big fan of having to be an asshole (despite any claims that anyone might make to the contrary), but they were also worried that being anything but right now might mean having to relive the chaos of today all over again tomorrow. They would just simply not acknowledge her at all.

Except, that was a very hard thing to do when she was actively doing a terrible job at pretending not to cry.

"Eat and get rid of your plate," they muttered. "I handled literally everything else. Do you think you'll be able to wash the one dish without somehow blowing up the entire boat?"

"I can do that," Mathilda hopped off of her cot. "I can do dishes, with gloves. Tomorrow I'll—"

Nico's mind was suddenly flooded with images of her somehow managing to smash every single dish on the entire ship. "Yeah, no. No touching anything I didn't explicitly tell you to from this point forward."

"Okay," she squeaked. And then, again, "I'm sorry."

Nico sighed. "Just hurry up and eat before you make the whole place smell even more like fish all night."

She crossed the room to grab the plate. "I'm probably just getting rid of it, actually. It umm... turns out I'm not really a fish person. On land. It's... it's too different when it's cooked. And I can't eat it raw in this body so..."

Nico made themself look at her. "We have two whole days left still. You can't just not eat."

"I had my bun."

"You'll be starving by the morning."

"I'll—" she tried to leave, so they got up to close the door. They took her plate. She watched their hands do it then her attention stayed there, head-bowed and eyes downcast.

And maybe it made Nico feel just a little bit like a dick, but at least they were a dick who wasn't going to have to drag around a malnourished selkie for the next few days. "Eat it," they shoved the plate against her chest.

"No thank you," Mathilda whispered.

"Wasn't a question. There's literally no other options. Now's not exactly a good time to be a picky eater." They forced a fork into her fist. "Eat it."

Still not looking at them, Mathilda lifted a shaking fork to her mouth. She chewed exactly once before spitting the whole thing out and shoving the plate back against them. "I'm sorry," she said.

And then, predictably, she started to sob again.

Nico was more than done with her sobbing. "You're nineteen!" They reminded her. "Why the fuck are you crying over fish!"

Instead of responding, she just whispered another meager, useless, "I'm sorry."

Nico sighed, clicking their cane. "I'll go get rid of this then, I guess."

"No!" Mathilda's eyes widened. She stepped forward to try and grab at it, but Nico had already turned around. "I can... I was supposed to..."

"I've got it." They slammed the door behind them, just in case she tried to follow. Hopefully, she'd at least get that hint. It had only been a day and they were already sick of the smell of fish, but they ate hers anyway as they looked through the breakfast plans. They brought half an orange back to the cabin with them and forced it into Mathilda's hand.

"Please tell me you at least eat fruit?"

"I..." Mathilda studied it. "Yes," she nodded. "Most of them."

"That'll have to be enough then," they nodded. "We have pretty exact numbers of supplies, so we'll have to go without fruit in the morning, but figured it's better than you just like, refusing to eat."

Mathilda frowned, staring at the orange intently. "It's... yours too?"

They sighed. "Yes, Mathilda, because you're apparently too fucking childish to get over yourself and try something you don't like."

"Thank you," she whispered. And "I'm sorry."

They waved her off. "Just... let me know ahead of time next time you're gonna force me to trade something, yeah?"

"Okay," she said. And "I'm sorry."

Nico rolled their eyes and grabbed their pyjamas. "I'm gonna go get changed," they grumbled. "Don't fuck anything else up before I get back."

They didn't realize how much of a problem getting ready for bed would be until they were already in their pyjamas. It wasn't like no one had ever seen them without a binder on. They hadn't started wearing them until after getting to Bayside and never wore them on weekends since they weren't exactly trying to fuck up even more of their bones. But suddenly, something about not wearing it around someone who wasn't used to them and the way that their body was supposed to look—someone who couldn't relate to their body sometimes needing to not match that—felt terrifying. They were even more covered up in their pyjamas than they had been in the shorts and t-shirt they'd been wearing all day but suddenly, they felt incredibly naked.

They slipped out of their pyjama top, put their binder back on, and finished getting changed. They weren't going to do anything dangerous. They weren't stupid enough to risk cracking a rib while on their way to a strange new city. But they didn't want to feel naked either.

So, they slid under their covers. Mathilda said good night. They did not. They were exhausted, but they made themself stay awake until her sniffling subsided and her breathing regulated. Finally, they climbed out of bed, took off the binder, quickly hid their body beneath the covers before they'd be forced to remember that it existed, and tried their best to get ready for what was certain to be an extremely exhausting second day.

At least after that was over, they'd be halfway to being rid of her. It didn't even matter how they got back to Bayside anymore, just that they did it alone.

Chapter 10

Mercifully, Mathilda gave up on trying to pretend to be helpful by the second day. She didn't even spend it haunting their cabin. She'd apparently managed to somehow entertain at least somebody with her card tricks over breakfast, and after triple checking that Nico wouldn't need her help with anything (which they enthusiastically assured her that they never, ever would), she decided to spend her day above deck entertaining the crew.

Alone time was exactly what Nico had wanted, but knowing that she was having fun up above them instead of wallowing in their cabin somehow made Nico even angrier. They weren't a cruel person, usually. Or at least, they'd never considered themself one. But they were exhausted and overworked and nauseous from the smell and taste of fish so knowing that the girl who had caused all of that was having a delightful time didn't exactly help.

At least now that she was in with the crew, Nico beat her back that night. By the time Mathilda slipped into their room, they were already changed and fully concealed beneath their blanket. They turned to look at her.

"Sorry," Mathilda whispered. "I hope I didn't wake you."

They didn't respond. Interactions with the selkie tended to go a lot more smoothly when Nico wasn't talking.

"Thank you for covering for me," she said. "Today. And... yesterday. And likely tomorrow too, I supposed." She sighed. "I'm so sorry, I know I'm the worst person you could've possibly... I promise I'm not being useless on purpose, okay? I was trying. I really was."

Nico closed their eyes and rolled towards the wall.

They heard Mathilda sigh. "Good night, Nicole," she said. "Sweet dreams."

And then, a few hours later, they were awoken by her aggressively shaking their shoulders.

Nonymous

Chapter 11

"What the fuck!" Nico hastily sat up, barely missing smacking their forehead against the selkie's.

Mathilda jumped back. Her eyes (always freakishly wide behind her glasses) were even wider than usual.

"They've been sounding the horn," she said. "You're an incredibly deep sleeper."

Nico swung their legs over the side of the bed. "What's happening?"

"Sirens, apparently," Mathilda sucked on her lip. "I umm... might have gone above deck and asked around before waking you. I figured you'd get up on your own. We're hitting siren infested waters in a bit, but it's an unavoidable part of the route so they're planning on going straight through it. Do you have earplugs?"

Nico tried to shake the final few tendrils of sleep out of their brain. "Obviously I don't have earplugs!"

Mathilda nodded to herself. "A few people are selling them. Could you umm..."

And they realized. Finally, they were awake enough to. "Would you have woken me if you hadn't needed money?"

"Yes?" Mathilda guessed. "Or... probably? If I'd remembered, definitely."

Nico rolled their eyes. "Gee. Thanks." They dug through their pockets. "How much?"

"Nine coppers."

They stared. "For earplugs? That's ridiculous. Whoever's selling them's obviously just using the situation to their advantage."

Mathilda didn't respond to that.

They sighed, counting out the coins. "Here,' they handed them to her.

Mathilda counted them. "I umm... would you mind umm..."

It clicked. "Gods, Mathilda."

"Tillie's still fine," she reminded them.

They ignored her. "I wasn't going to let you go overboard over nine fucking coppers. I just don't need any. I don't feel umm... the thing that sirens exploit in other people." They suddenly felt extremely embarrassed. Nineteen-years-old and too scared to say the word 'sex'.

Mathilda was frowning at them. Mathilda was staring at them like never having wanted to jump someone's bones was some kind unfathomable, rare disease. "You don't?"

"I'm still into people, obviously," they rolled their eyes. "Romantically, at least. Just not like..." they sighed. "Aren't you supposed to be running upstairs to get earplugs? I don't get why we're talking about..."

"I don't need them either, actually."

Nico frowned. "You're not... into people like that either?"

Mathilda's eyes widened. "No, what? Obviously I like people, I'm just... I'm a selkie. I'm immune. Similar mer-creatures and all that. There wouldn't be much of a point in trying to drown a selkie."

They watched her carefully. And hated her a little bit more, for that 'obviously'. Still though, they'd rather not have to feel semi responsible for someone drowning. "You sure?" They checked. "Because you didn't seem pretty sure a minute ago. And this is the kind of thing you need to be pretty damn sure about."

"I'm sure," she nodded.

And surely she wasn't stupid enough (or scared of them enough) to risk actual death just to save Nico nine coppers, right?

"Okay," They sat up, hugging their blanket to their chest as they did. "We'd better get dressed, then. Might have to go tackle a few people to keep them from going overboard."

When Nico got above deck though, everything was very quiet. There was just sea and wind and a couple dozen ear-plugged crewmen. They were almost disappointed. Few had ever heard a siren's song and lived to tell the tale. They'd thought that at least something story-worthy might have been about to come from this complete waste of time.

And then, all at once, that deafening sound. To call it singing would have been wrong. To call it screaming wouldn't have been right either. It defied definition and noise and human sense. It was beautiful and terrifying and all encompassing and terrifying.

And then, it was them: hurling themself over the rail and into the cool, dark water below.

Chapter 12

Nico technically could swim. They'd learned as a child, before their leg started limiting their mobility. They'd learned in crystal clear lakes with honeysweet biscuits filling their stomach. They'd learned between a pair of strong, tanned arms, waiting to catch them every time they'd faltered. They'd learned on day trips ending in celebratory campfires, between story and music and all that was light and good and honeysweet.

The first time they'd realized that whatever unseeable thing had made them start limping everywhere felt ten times worse beneath the pressure of even the clearest, sweetest waters, they'd pretended not to feel it. They'd wanted crystal clear lakes and honeysweet biscuits and story and song and music and campfires but more than anything, they'd been able to recognize that they were getting just a bit too old to overtly ask to be held by that pair of strong, tanned arms on land. They knew that the moment they gave up on the water would be the same moment that they gave that up forever.

So, they'd ached and they'd kicked and they'd splashed and they'd smile through the pain. They'd bobbed their head beneath the surface so no one could tell the difference between a face damp with tears or lake water.

Nico knew that they could swim. It would hurt and they probably would pay for it once they got back on land, but Nico had spent a long time knowing that no mattered how much their bones ached and protested, they could still technically swim.

They didn't even try. There was no space left in their head to remember that; only the crushing, impossible sound of that something that was both screaming and singing and neither.

That did not change the fact that Nico technically could swim. That did not change the fact that they remained limp as a leaf as they sank further beneath the water. That did not change the truth that swimming hadn't been worth the pain after all, in the end. The arms had given up on them long before Nico had given up on pretending that swimming was still enjoyable.

Chapter 13

The first thing Nico did upon coming to was grab their medallion, just to make sure it was still there.

The second was roll over to vomit up the entire contents of their stomach onto the sand. "Shit," they groaned, leaning back to try and remember how they'd gotten there. They were on a beach, that much was clear. It felt like their entire body was coated in sand and they could hear the waves crashing somewhere. The sky above them was dark and cloudy and the night air felt frigid against their water-soaked skin. They doubled over in a coughing fit just as they heard someone else begin to retch somewhere nearby.

"Hey," the selkie from the store, impossibly, appeared in front of them. She wiped her mouth with the back of her palm.

Nico jolted in surprise.

"It's okay," Mathilda raised her hands in surrender. "You're okay! You just need to... here." She dug through a black duffel bag that Nico didn't recognize and pulled out a small flask. She unscrewed and sniffed it. "This is water," she decided, handing it over. "I think."

Then, her cheeks puffed. She threw a hand over her mouth. "Sorry, I have to... I'll set up things over there," she jerked a thumb behind her. "Where it's a little less... vomit-y."

Nico waited until their throat was a little less raw and their brain was a little less fuzzy before getting up to find her. Their leg twinged as they did. Hopefully, it was just worse because of the cold.

They found Mathilda further up the beach, shivering near an incredibly unlit pile of twigs and leaves. They sat down beside her. "Want to fill me in on wherever the fuck we are right now?"

Mathilda flinched. "Sorry. I didn't... I should have..."

"Mathilda," they stopped her.

"Tillie's still fine."

"Sometimes I just swear because swearing's fun, not because I'm pissed. Unless you *did* intentionally strand me on an island in which case I definitely am pissed. Obviously."

She wound a dried leaf through her fingers before responding. "You jumped off a boat."

Nico winced. "Yes. Yeah, that's actually the kind of thing you tend to remember." Mathilda flinched again and they sighed. They had to get better at pretending to be nice. "What happened after that?" They asked, trying their best to sound gentle. Mathilda seemed like the kind of person who responded well to gentle.

"And I umm... rescued you. Obviously. After freezing for a bit," she added sheepishly. "But that means someone had time to get me an emergency survival kit so... that's good, right?"

They knew they had no right to be pissed that the person they'd spent the last couple of days screaming at hadn't instantaneously wanted to jump into siren-infested waters to save them, but Nico felt a little insulted nonetheless. "And you thought dragging us off to some random tiny island was smarter than getting back on the boat?"

"They didn't want to wait," Mathilda defended herself.

"Then you should've made them! Now what the fuck are—"

"You don't get to get mad at me for saving your life!"

Nico froze. "Mathilda..."

But she was already gone, pacing tight circles closer to the shoreline.

Nico was not used to the kind of person that required apologies (nor did they feel particularly enthusiastic about giving one to the girl who'd gotten them into this situation in the first place), so they dug through the duffel bag, found a fire starting kit, and fixed Mathilda's tiny pile of twigs to buy themself more time. Hopefully, she'd just forget about it and they'd be able to move on.

Mathilda did not move on.

"Mathilda," they carefully approached her. There was a fine line, apparently, between yelling to get someone's attention and yelling because you were pissed off. Nico didn't trust themself to navigate that properly yet.

She didn't turn around. Her pacing didn't even slow.

"Mathilda," they tried again, lightly touching her shoulder. She jumped in response, but at least she went still after that.

"You're soaked. You need to come dry off before you get yourself sick and start causing us even more problems."

The selkie didn't respond, but she did let herself be guided back to the fire. Nico'd had the fortune of having a flannel on when they'd gone overboard, so they took it off and spread it out to dry. They wished Mathilda had worn layers too, if only to give them an excuse to procrastinate for a little bit longer. But she was still just in that fucking dress. They adjusted their jacket two more times before sitting down beside her. She just kept watching the fire.

"I'm sorry," Nico said. The second their tongue began to form the words, the rest of their body tried to reject it. Shoulders tensing and hunching forward, as if to propel the sound further away. Eyes burning and squeezing almost all the way shut, as if not seeing would somehow protect them from having to hear it.

Mathilda's attention snapped towards them.

"You're right, I shouldn't have..." Nico sighed, stretching out on the sand. They let the fire warm their toes. "You were wrong, though. I wasn't mad, I was frustrated. And I feel like randomly washing up on a deserted island in the middle of the night after a bunch of evil mer-creatures tried to murder me is definitely a valid reason to be mad so... yeah."

Mathilda frowned. "That was... was that supposed to be an apology?"

"I just said I wasn't being a dick on purpose!"

"I've spent most of the last few days apologizing for things I didn't do on purpose," she said. It was light and casual though, not pointed and harsh like they would have said it. As if it was less accusation, more just her pointing it out to let them choose how to react.

And so, they reacted. "I'm sorry," they repeated. More intently, this time. Most of what Mathilda said came out that way and if she'd saved their life, they could at least try to match that for once. Even if it felt a little too much like peeling back an entire layer of their own skin. "You literally dove into monster-infested water for me. I get that. I shouldn't have blown up at you after that. I'm just... not super comfortable with that, I guess. Being rescued. But that's very obviously not your problem though so I'm sorry I acted like it was, okay?"

Mathilda nodded. "Understood. I promise I won't rescue you next time, then."

Their eyes widened. "That's not—" They spun to face her.

But her lips were curved upwards and her shoulders were shaking, slightly. She was laughing at them. And maybe they'd swallowed more seawater than they'd thought that they had, because Nico found that they didn't entirely hate that.

"Oh, so you're funny now," they grumbled.

"I can be," Mathilda licked her lips. "Occasionally." They thought she started shivering even harder, but then they realized that she was just swaying a bit. "Was that... are you okay with that?"

"What? Yeah, sure."

"It was a little mean though, wasn't it? I'm... I don't want to..."

They rolled their eyes. "I'm actually-mean pretty much constantly, Mathilda. I can handle a few barely-mean jokes."

"Okay," she nodded. "Good." She folded her knees up against her chest.

Something about seeing her sitting like that—body folded in on itself, hair blowing back in the wind, glasses slightly crooked on her nose—filled Nico with the inexplicable urge to drape something over her shoulders. Luckily, their flannel was still drenched.

"I'm so sorry," Mathilda whispered. "I'm so, so... I didn't think it'd be dangerous. If I thought it'd be dangerous, I wouldn't have—"

"Okay." They stopped her. If she kept talking, they'd have to remind her that not just taking a safer ferry route had been their idea. And if they had to say that out loud, they wouldn't be able to keep mentally blaming her. "Whatever. We'll figure it out. Did they... they know we're around here, right? They'll probably come back for us?"

Mathilda's eyes moved to them for half a second before returning to the fire. "They umm... we couldn't exactly talk, but we wrote notes, for a bit. Until I dove in."

Nico began to wonder how long they'd been left alone in the water.

"They said they'll be back in a week."

They swallowed. *A week.* And then after that, they'd still have to get to Kovienne, find the sealskin, and then get all the way back home. In an instant, their journey had doubled. And they had no way of telling anyone about it. Nico coughed into their arm and then kept their head bowed for a few seconds, just in case. They suddenly felt certain that they were going to be sick again.

They'd ferry back, though. Just to make sure they didn't get set even further behind. And Todd might have been a fairly lackluster employer, but they knew that he'd started caring about them at some point, at least slightly. He'd get *Interthrifter* to comp the extra questing time and he'd surely realize that them being gone this long might jeopardize their ability to pay their share of the rent. Their friends might worry about them for a bit, but surely at least one of them would be smart enough to seek him out and demand to get their pay directly. Nico's hand flew to their pocket. Their incredibly empty pocket.

"Did you pack our money?" They finally thought to ask.

"I... no," Mathilda frowned a bit. "It was kind of a fast-paced life or death situation, so—"

"You apparently had time to chat with the crew," they reminded her. "and you didn't stop to think we might need some fucking money?"

"They'll come back," Mathilda's voice began to shake. Because they could never go more than five minutes without making her cry. "I'm certain they wouldn't have just thrown out your stuff. I'm sure—"

"You think they'd what? Decided to save hundreds of silvers for some strangers that were stupid enough to jump overboard? Did you think they'd be keeping that safe for us?"

Mathilda frowned. "You had hundred of silvers on you? Why did we—"

"Fuck!" Nico groaned, running sand-infused fingers through their hair. "Fuck! Why can't you literally ever make a logical fucking decision!"

"I... I'm sorry," she whispered. "But I don't get how—"

"What did you think we'd do from here? How are we supposed to buy your stupid cloak back with no money, huh? Or even... you can just fuck off into the ocean after, but how am I supposed to get back home? Gods, have you literally ever thought of anyone but yourself!"

"I..." Mathilda started swaying faster, teeth chattering in the wind. "I'm sorry," she said. "I didn't..." she frowned. Slowed down a little. Her fingertips danced along her knees. "You're doing it again," she accused. "You're freaking out at me for—"

"I'm freaking out at you because this is your fault!" They screamed. "You were too fucking useless to keep track of your own skin and now I'm broke and stuck on an island! I'm freaking out at you because you ruined my life!"

She shakily got to her feet. "I'd umm... I'll give you space, then," she promised. "I'm..." her voice broke. "I'm so sorry. I'm so, so sorry." She wrapped her arms around her chest, whispered one final "I'm sorry," and wandered off.

Chapter 14

Mathilda had very clearly spent most of her life underwater and while Nico knew that that objectively wasn't her fault, it infuriated them nonetheless.

They loathed the way she seemed to just expect them to teach her how to perform every single task. Found themself infuriated that apparently underwater, 'I don't like the way it smells' or 'I'm used to that being cooked different' were valid excuses to refuse to eat things even when the alternative was starving. Couldn't stand her willingness to instantly and visibly cry the moment she got remotely uncomfortable. They knew objectively that she wouldn't have had the chance or need to train herself against any of that in a form where all tears were rendered invisible and pleas for help or refusals to comply weren't verbal enough to be grating, but that didn't mean that they weren't allowed to get frustrated at it. Partially, because pleading and refusing and crying were annoying. Mostly, because every time she did any of that, they were filled with an inexplicable jealousy. Mathilda had never had to learn to make herself less annoying for other people.

They flopped backwards into the cool sand. They wanted to cry or scream or destroy something, but their body wouldn't let them do any of that until Mathilda was far away enough that they couldn't hear her footsteps anymore. Still—even though they knew that she wouldn't possibly be able to hear them by that point—when Nico's tears did come, they still locked their fists into their eye-sockets to try and force them away. They'd gotten so good at never annoying other people that they were even embarrassed to cry around themself.

They shouldn't have brought the silver. It had been idiotic to bring the silver. They'd had their own money and what should have been enough money for safe passage from *Interthrifter*'s questing budget. They could have even let themself take the extra coppers from everyone else's penalty jars, if they were really that worried that they might need a bit more money for emergencies. Bringing the silver had been nothing but over-indulgence and paranoia and stupidity. And over-confidence. Because they'd been so, so certain that they were going to bring it back. They'd only accepted it in the first place so that they could triumphantly return it all and prove that they never, ever needed Milo's money.

And now, it was all gone. For nothing. Because they'd been too stubborn to buy a fucking pair of earplugs.

They cried until their eyes ached and their body felt completely empty and then they felt like an idiot for letting themself do that. They were stranded without food or a readily available water supply. They shouldn't have wasted their time and energy on tears.

They stumbled to the water and to try and splash any evidence of what they'd just done off of their face, if only to save themself from having to witness it. It stung. They felt their head for cuts or scrapes, but felt none. It still stung.

And then the air felt newly frigid because they were no longer dry because they truly couldn't seem to stop doing idiotic things, so they forced themself to return to the fire to warm up.

And then realized that Mathilda still hadn't retuned. And that she'd definitely have no idea how to start a fire.

They sighed as they got back up but really, they were relieved to have something to do. The illusion of productivity felt a lot warmer than the certainty of useless.

They clicked their cane out and wandered the island until the faint sound of snoring led them away from the beach and into the forest. They found her curled up between the roots of an old tree, somehow miraculously asleep despite the way her body was still shivering. They sighed again (it would be incredibly embarrassing to let themself know that they were relieved to be even further inconvenienced, after all), returned to their campsite to retrieve their now dry flannel. They draped it over her. Then,

Nonymous

they wandered around until they found enough rocks to hopefully limits the odds of started a forest fire, arranged them a few feet away from Mathilda so that they hopefully wouldn't set her on fire either, and built a fire. They left her with one of the few soggy pouches of cereal they'd found in the duffle and—for some inexplicable reason—the flint and steel, before returning to their own campsite and drifting off into a restless sleep.

Chapter 15

They awoke to blinding sunlight, the ashy remains of a fire, and sand that had somehow fused itself to every single inch of their skin.

Nico groaned, forcing themself to sit up. They'd gone to sleep starving and sore and too cold and they'd woken up starving and sore and too hot and they still had six days of this left. Whoever'd had the sense to pack the emergency supply bag had had the forethought to pack a few bags of cereal, but they knew that they'd have to save that. Something told them that even being stranded and starving wouldn't convince Mathilda to eat anything new. They'd catch themself a fish or something. Eventually. Somehow.

"Morning!" Someone called.

Nico winced against the sudden noise as they turned, and Mathilda's expression instantly fell. She took a step back.

Nico swallowed down a sigh. They knew that they'd been a dick the night before, but if she made them apologize again, it might actually kill them.

"Sorry," Mathilda said. "I umm..." she hesitantly approached them, arms outstretched. "I have your shirt?" She said. "I figured you'd need it back? I really can stay out of your way, though. Until—"

They rolled their eyes. "It'd make no sense to split up now. That'd just be double the work."

Mathilda stared at her shoes. "I umm... I am that, actually. Double the work. Most of the time." She flexed and unflexed her fists. "Which you've obviously already noticed. I'm sorry, I... I'm kind of the last person anyone would want to be trapped on a deserted island with. So... sorry. About that. Preemptively."

They barked out a laugh. "I'll keep that in mind."

Mathilda didn't end up being the one who couldn't carry her own weight though, that was Nico. She led them back to her camp where they learned that she'd apparently been awake for hours. She'd already scoured the island and collected a pile of fruits and nuts. She'd somehow even caught two fish for them ("I used a stick," she'd explained with a shiver. "It was gross"), though she'd kept them far from her camp, apologizing for not being able to prepare or cook either of them.

Nico spent the day boiling water to stockpile and cataloguing their supplies. And then doing that all over again because it turned out neither task took up that much time.

Mathilda spent it buzzing around the island, climbing trees and venturing deep into marshes and meadows to collect anything that might even possibly be useful.

They hated it. They'd thought that she was at her most unbearable when she wasn't helpful, but they were wrong. Nico was only ever comfortable when they were the most productive person in the room. Or, rather, on the island. But almost drowning and then sleeping on an uncomfortable beach had left their right leg even more useless than usual and even on their best days they wouldn't have been able to get to half of the places that Mathilda was searching for food. So, they boiled their stupid water and sorted their stupid bag and gave in to their own stupid uselessness.

Mathilda didn't stop moving until the sun was setting. It was as if she'd sucked up all of Nico's unusable productivity and stolen it for herself. By the time she sat down beside them, the back of her dress was coated in sweat. Her face was flushed with effort and her chest rose and fell rapidly as she caught her breath.

And Nico felt nothing but antsy.

"Hey," she breathed, handing them a grapefruit. They pulled a switchblade from their pocket so that they could focus on cutting it in half instead of on her. "How are you doing?"

"What's that supposed to mean?" Nico grumbled, spearing a slice and holding it out to her.

"I just... you did almost drown yesterday, after all. Are you—"

"Yes, Mathilda. Believe it or not, sitting here doing nothing all day didn't make me any more disabled."

She frowned. "I didn't... that's not what I said."

They rolled their eyes, shoving a slice of grapefruit down their throat. It stung their cheek on the way down. They still didn't understand why.

"How are you?" They tried to change the topic. And then failed to change the topic. "Done pretending you're some kind of fucking hero for the day?"

Mathilda's forehead creased. "I'm uncertain what... I don't think I understand whatever we're talking about right now."

They chuckled grimly. "No, no of course you don't." Nico returned their focus to the fruit.

They were both quiet for a bit. It was so all-encompassing that even apologizing started to feel like the less agonizing option, but then Mathilda said, "if my cloak's sold by the time we get there, it's not like I'd have any reason to return to Bayside, right? And I hope you wouldn't want to... I'm not planning on actually dueling you. And I'd hope that's at least slightly mutual?"

They just rolled their eyes.

"I suppose there'd really be no point in... there's an inflatable raft," she said. "And paddles."

"I know," Nico snapped. She must have known that they did, after all. They'd spent all day with nothing to do but stare at it.

"We could go find the closest inhabited shore," Mathilda said. "And then you can just go home, okay?"

They froze. They dropped the knife, suddenly not trusting themself to use it safely.

"I really didn't think it'd be dangerous, you know. I wouldn't have... I'm sorry. I'm still going to try and go get it back, but I supposed there'd be no sense in dragging you there with me, right? So you go home and—"

"Shut the fuck up." Mathilda couldn't be trusted to not burn bread when it was literally the only thing that she was supposed to be paying attention to. Mathilda broke down at the slightest indication of conflict. At something as insignificant as a smell. Mathilda was the kind of person who'd manage to lose her own head if it wasn't attached to the rest of her and the kind of selkie who actually *had* managed to lose her own skin the second it wasn't on her back.

And even she'd decided that they were too useless to keep pulling along.

"What?" She was saying. "I'm not... I'm saying..."

"Shut the fuck up!" They screamed.

"Okay," Mathilda nodded. "Okay. I'll..." she hesitated. "I umm... I don't know what I did wrong this time, actually."

They laughed. And then they kept laughing. Suddenly, it was the only thing that Nico was capable of doing. "You've done everything wrong!" They reminded her. "You don't get to act like you're the more capable person here just because you collected a few pieces of fruit!"

"I wasn't—"

"You can't cook," they started to count off her flaws on their fingers. "You can't clean, you can't... you can't even fucking eat food, Mathilda! That's a basic impulse. Fucking babies can do that!"

"I'm—"

"You can't go more than two seconds without crying and you just expect the rest of the world to cater to your every fucking outburst and eccentricity and that's ridiculous! You don't get to keep doing that! You don't get to keep being fucking useless and then expecting people to keep putting up with you anyway!"

She was not the person that they were yelling at. They were incredibly aware that she was not the person they were yelling at. But acknowledging that out loud would destroy them, so Nico watched her struggled to her feet. Looked down under the sheer weight of their own shame as she failed to wipe tears off of her face.

"I'm trying," she whispered, voice breaking as she did. "I'm trying so, so hard and you just keep... I don't think you're a very nice person, Nicole."

They laughed. Again. They'd thought that all of the oxygen in their lungs was long gone, but there was enough left for that. "You're just noticing that now?"

"No," Mathilda admitted. Still just light. Still just infuriatingly gentle. "I'm not... I'm not that oblivious, sometimes. I was just hoping..." she sighed, gesturing to her snot-covered face. "I'm not good at being upset. Obviously. So, I supposed I'd just been hoping... I think you might just be a mean person, though. I think..." she tapped her fists against her side, losing the end of the sentence. "I think I'd better keep my distance. For now."

"Good!" They called after her. "Great!"

But it didn't feel good. It felt like a thousand tiny flies, tearing Nico apart from the inside out. It felt like drowning, all over again. It felt as hollow and as useless as they did.

And they were. Hollow and useless. So instead of following her—instead of explaining or pleading or even just apologizing—they stayed at their campsite and finished off the grapefruit.

Chapter 16

Mathilda emerged through the trees late into the night.

"I can't start the fire," she said. "I need…"

It was their chance. They'd calmed down enough that the anger had all been eaten up by shame and regret. They were supposed to apologize. Even they weren't stubborn enough to hide that from themself.

But she was giving them a chance to feel like the useful one.

"Okay," Nico said, clicking their cane.

It was all that they said. It was all that either of them said. Nico started the fire, she sat down beside it, and they went back to being alone.

Chapter 17

And then she didn't say a word to them for a whole day.

Chapter 18

And then she didn't say a word to them for another day.

Chapter 19

On the fifth day—when Nico could no longer take the silence—they found Mathilda trying to blow up the raft.

"What the fuck are you doing?" They demanded. She jumped. Because that had definitely been the wrong way to open. They winced against their own idiocrasy.

"We can't stay here forever," she said, keeping her body turned towards the sea. "We'll run out of supplies. We should head out soon, while we have enough left to last the trip."

"That's stupid," they winced again. They didn't know why they couldn't get themself to stop doing that. Insults were practically muscle memory, especially when Nico was uncomfortable. Maybe it was the only language that they'd ever fully understood. "Who knows what other monsters are out there? And we have no way of knowing how close we are to land. I'm not putting myself in danger just because you're impatient."

"I'll go by myself then," Mathilda declared. "And then come back for you, once I find people."

"That's even more reckless. You can't—"

"What do you want me to do than!" She demanded. Her shoulders started to shake. She still wouldn't look at them. "It's my fault, right? So I have to get us out of this!"

"They'll come in a few days."

"And what if they don't! I can't *do* anything, Nicole! All I was good for was collecting food and I couldn't even do that right because I took too much too fast and now... you wanted me to be useful. This is the one useful thing I can do."

She returned to trying to blow up the raft. It must have been incredibly more difficult now. What, with all her shaking.

"Mathilda," they slowly approached her. The closer she got, the more they wanted to run away. The more impossible it was to ignore that she was crying. That they were an idiot. "Mathilda." They stopped about foot behind her. It was the closest they could let themself get. They waited. They weren't sure what for. The closed their eyes and prepared themself. They took a deep breath. Then, Nico took one final step and touched her shoulder.

She jumped. They let go.

"I'm... sorry," they whispered.

She didn't respond.

"Mathilda," they tried again. "Please don't... it's really not a good idea, okay? You can't just paddle off into who knows what all by yourself. Promise me you're not actually going to do that."

She kept blowing up the raft.

"Mathilda," they repeated. They caught themself just before yelling it, though. That would only set them back even further. They sat down. "Don't leave me alone, okay?" They were surprised to find their voice catching. They rubbed a thumb across their medallion. "At least promise me you'll warn me before you go."

She set down the raft, but not before pushing the stopper into place to keep air from escaping. "You want me to leave," she said.

"No," they shook their head, just in case she chose that specific second to turn around. "I don't."

"You should," she said. So lightly that the weight of it threatened to crush them. "I'm going to keep causing more problems. I'm going to keep making things harder on you. I'm—"

"Gods, Mathilda, you've been keeping us both alive for days now, okay?"

"Barely."

"No, extremely literally, actually." They sighed. "Could you look at me? Please?"

She slowly turned around, but her eyes didn't get anywhere nears theirs.

Nico swallowed. "I'm sorry I suck, okay? Which I know still isn't a proper apology, but I'm even awful at those, apparently. But you've been nothing but helpful since getting here, alright? I mean...Gods, Mathilda! I would literally be dead right now if it wasn't for you, remember?"

"You wouldn't be stuck here at all if it wasn't for me," she reminded them.

Nico paused. "Okay, maybe. I'm pretty sure I am still genuinely incredibly mad about that, but I'm the one who insisted on not taking a ferry and on not wearing earplugs and... don't get me wrong, this whole thing is definitely your fault but it's also a little.... Or maybe a lot..." they sighed. "I don't like feeling like I've fucked things up, okay? A lot of this is obviously on me and I've obviously known that the whole time, it just turns out it's a lot easier to get pissed at someone else instead? I'm sorry that I took that way too far like... so many times, but I really, really need you to promise me that you're not about to do something stupid just because I'm the worst, okay?"

Mathilda was quiet. "This is a thing I can actually do," she shook the half-inflated raft. "I want to... I can't do... most things."

Nico rolled their eyes. "You've been doing basically everything ever since we got here."

She shook her head. "That's one thing though. Collecting stuff and whatever. Because it's easy for me and it doesn't require any level of actual skill or practice. I can't... if I go, I'll finally be useful."

"I shouldn't have said that," they admitted. "Before. But it wasn't... that wasn't about you, okay? You're super useful."

She rolled her eyes. "I've pretty much collected all the fruit and stuff already. Name one other thing I'm good at."

They hesitated. They drew a blank. "You umm... magic?" They remembered. "You're good at card tricks, right?"

"An incredibly useful skill when you're stranded."

"It is, though," they lied. "We have food, heat, and water, right? Next basic necessity's entertainment. Could you show me?" They asked, just to make her stay a little longer.

She reached into her pocket, pulled out a thoroughly weathered deck of cards, then froze. "I umm... I had it on me," she said. "Just... for the record. I didn't leave you in the water to go look for it or anything."

Nico laughed. "Okay," they said, tapping the sand between them "Show me something. Entertain me."

Mathilda started to fan out the cards before stopping abruptly. "This is stupid," she said, starting to get back up. "You don't want to see a fucking card trick right now. I can—"

"Mathilda," they caught her wrist. "I do." (They didn't). "I love magic tricks." (They thought they were ridiculously corny and self-indulgent.) "Show me. Please." (They needed her to desperate.)

"Okay," she finally smiled a little, re-fanning the card. "I umm... pick one. Don't tell me which."

She guessed their card right. And then she did it again and again when they kept insisting that she repeat the trick so that they could figure out how she'd done it. They never did. She made cards disappear and reappear from sleeves and behind ears and beneath sand and it was overwhelmingly corny and self-indulgent but she was a person and she was talking to them and that was enough. And she was a person that they'd hurt who was smiling with them and that was a little bit wonderful.

"Okay," Mathilda eventually ruined their fun as the sun started setting, pushing herself to her feet. "It's getting late. Thanks for umm... we should umm..."

They grabbed her arm again. She flinched. They let go. "You didn't promise yet," they reminded her. "That you'll... don't go, okay? I swear I'll work on being less miserable of a person to be around, just..." their throat went thick, rejecting the request. They pushed on anyway. "Don't leave me alone here."

Mathilda frowned. "I shouldn't have... It wasn't nice to call you a bad person. You're not. I didn't mean that."

They rolled their eyes. "I was being a bad person. You absolutely should have called me out on that. Don't go anyway."

"Okay," she nodded. Light. Soft. "Okay. I promise. Not without you."

Nonymous

Chapter 20

Nico was setting up their camp for the night—wondering how they'd gotten to a point in their life where getting ready to go to sleep on a beach with no blanket or pillow had become routine, when they were startled by the sound of a twig snapping.

They jumped.

"Hi," Mathilda waved a little. "Hey, umm..."

"Gods, Mathilda!"

"Tillie's still fine, actually," she mumbled.

Nico ignored it. They lunged for their jacket and quickly pulled it around their body, despite the heat. It was always difficult to navigate the most comfortable way to sleep, with the temperature changing so drastically over night. "What the fuck are you doing here?"

They watched her blink. Take a step back.

"No," they kept one arm firmly wrapped around their chest and rose the other in surrender. "No, that wasn't... that was a me thing. Again. You didn't do anything wrong, okay?"

She watched them. They watched her.

"I umm... my fire went out. I need..."

"Of course," Nico made themself smile. "Meet you there in a second."

But Mathilda didn't get the hint and leave and they didn't know how else to phrase 'I've strategically been planning out how to only have my binder off when I'm alone', so they grabbed the fire-starting kit with their right hand, held their jacket closed with their left, and followed her.

"If I did something wrong," she said as they walked. "you can—"

"No."

Her fingers danced along her hip bone. That meant that she was upset. Nico didn't know when they'd first noticed that.

They sighed. "You didn't do anything wrong. I'm just... jumpy."

She frowned. "You don't seem..." she must have seen something in their expression though, because she stopped herself. "Okay," she nodded. "Thanks for letting me know."

Nico crouched down by her fire and started setting up their flint, steel, and cloth, before thinking better of it. "I can show you," they looked back at where Mathilda had stopped several feet away from the pit. "That'd probably be way more practical, right? Then you don't have to keep getting me."

She winced. "I'm sorry if—"

"You didn't do anything wrong," they repeated. And she hadn't. They just weren't ready to talk about what had made them so jumpy. "I promise, okay? It'd just be more efficient."

Mathilda blushed. "I'm umm... not certain that'd be a good idea. Trusting me around fire."

They rolled their eyes. "We're surrounded by sand, Mathilda."

Another impulsive, ignored "Tillie's still fine, actually."

"It's not like you'd even be able to set anything important on fire." Nico patted the sand beside them. "Watch."

She sat exactly where they'd indicated that she should, but it suddenly felt too close. Nico felt her hair against their neck.

"Oh, shoot," they realized. "We'd better umm... you should probably tuck your hair into your dress or something. That actually could be dangerous."

"Right."

It was a lot easier to think when Mathilda's hair was no longer tickling their neck.

"Okay," Nico readied the charred cloth and flint in one hand and grabbed the steel bar with their other. "Watch, okay?" They struck the two together and then quickly blew out the spark before the cloth was wasted. "Alright," they handed it to Mathilda. "Your turn."

She chewed on her lip. "I don't know if..."

"It's easy," they shrugged, already brushing together a small pile of kindling. "Promise. All you have to do is strike it, I'll put it in the actual fire this time. You'll only have to deal with a tiny spark."

Mathilda took a deep breath and hit the steel against the flint.

And nothing happened.

"I'm sorry," she tried to hand it back. "I told you, I wouldn't—"

"Try it again," Nico nodded. "We literally have nothing but time."

She tried again and nothing happened. And then a third attempt also yielded no sparks.

Nico frowned. "Maybe—"

But Mathilda was still trying, over and over again. Incorrectly, Nico eventually realized, though they still couldn't tell exactly how. Maybe it was the angle or the pressure or just the way that she was holding the charred cloth.

They sighed. "Mathilda, I don't think—"

That just made her go even faster. "I've got it," she insisted.

"You don't," they tried to explain.

But she kept hitting and swiping and striking, swaying in time with her own failed attempts.

"Mathilda," their confusion quickly morphed into concern. "Stop, you're going to—"

All at once she gasped, dropping everything to the sand. She hugged her hand to her chest, rapidly backing away.

"Are you okay?" Nico got to their feet to go to her. The swaying had picked up speed now, somehow. Without her flinty metronome. They sat down in front of her and tried to pull her arm away from her chest, but she wouldn't budge. "Mathilda," they tried again. "Are you okay? Are you hurt?"

She was humming something, they realized. They weren't sure if she knew that they could hear her.

"Let me see," they tried to adjust their tone. Tried to be a little bit more light. "Please?" They held out an open palm.

Slowly, Mathilda extended a fist. She still wouldn't look at them. Her knuckles were bleeding.

"That's not so bad," they pulled their sleeve over their other hand before pressing down on the cut. They didn't know why. It wasn't like it was any cleaner than their hand. "You must have just caught yourself on the flint. It's barely a scratch, though. You probably won't even feel it by the morning, okay?"

"I'm sorry I couldn't do it," she whispered.

"You just need more practice," they shrugged. "If you wanted to practice more. It's totally fine if—"

"You said it was easy."

"Exactly. So you'll get it eventually if—"

"It's not, for me," She told her own stomach. "Nothing's ever... it won't be. I'm sorry, I shouldn't have let you think... it's never going to be easy for me. I never do anything right."

Nico wanted to hit something but that clearly wasn't a viable option so instead, they made a decision. Got up. Held out a hand. "Let's go try again."

Maybe it was shock alone, but Mathilda finally looked towards them. "I told you," she sniffled. "It's not going to work."

"Bullshit. I'm actually an incredibly good teacher. I just fucked up this time."

"Nicole..." she cautioned.

They sighed. "Please, Mathilda?"

"Tillie's still fine," she said, even with snot dripping down her chin.

They rolled their eyes. "I think... I need to show you that you can do this, okay?"

She frowned, confused. "But... I can't."

Nico considered. "Then," they said slowly. "We'll make a bet, okay? If you do start a fire, you have to..." they paused, unable to think of something low stakes enough to trade without freaking her out. "You have to start mine too. Until they come for us. If you're right and you can't, I'll start them forever, okay? But no failing on purpose. That's cheating."

She swallowed. "Okay," she agreed.

Nico grinned. "Prepare to lose."

They took it slower this time, not even grabbing the charred cloth as they set up.

"Okay," Nico smiled. "What do you know about fire-starting?"

"Pretty much nothing," Mathilda admitted, studying her hands. "I umm... didn't spend much time on land, before this."

"Right." They nodded. "Obviously." They held up the striker. "This is steel right? It's umm... metal. It..."

Mathilda smiled a little. "I do know what steel is, actually."

They felt their face go hot. "Right, umm... you're just going to hit it, okay? Like this." They demonstrated. "If you do it right it makes a little bit chip off and it gets hot enough to spark." They held it out to her.

She didn't take it.

Nico didn't let themself sigh. "All we're doing is trying to figure out how to get it to spark, okay? You're not wasting anything but time and we have a disgusting amount of that right now."

She reluctantly swiped the two objects together. Nothing happened. She tried handing them back. "I can't—"

"Try again," they wrapped their hands around hers. "Or I win by default, okay? Which would be really inconvenient considering you still don't actually know how to start a fire. Try keeping the flint still and moving the striker instead."

She went again. They suggested an adjustment. She went again. They suggested a new one. And, eventually, the steel sparked.

Nico gasped. "Mathilda."

"I know." She smiled then bit it down then smiled again.

"Mathilda!"

"I know." She grinned. She went again and again until she was making a spark almost every time.

"Okay," Nico pulled out the cloth. "You're going to do the exact same thing except hold this against the flint this time, alright?"

"Why?" she asked. Then, she blushed. "Sorry, I guess that's less important than—"

"It catches the spark," Nico stopped her, pulling the pile of kindling closer. "It won't spread that quickly though so when it happens, all you have to do is put it in here, let it spread a little, then wait until it gets big enough and add it to the actual fire, okay?" They also finished with 'easy', but caught themself just in time.

Mathilda hesitated. "I thought you were doing that."

"I could," they nodded. "Do you still want me to?"

She considered for a moment before shaking her head. She took the cloth. And, in only three attempts, it caught.

"Holy shit," she whispered.

They laughed. "You still need to put it in the kindling, Mathilda."

"Tillie," she corrected. "I mean.... Right. I mean..." Luckily, she managed to pull herself together enough to press the cloth into the pile.

"Lift it and wrap the kindling around it a bit more," Nico instructed. "Just a bit though. You don't want to smother it. Leave it open on your end." They waited for her to adjust her hands. "You're going to gently blow on it, okay? Fires need oxygen so gently..."

Mathilda was already doing it. They smiled as the pile began to catch.

"Holy shit," she whispered again, dropping the kindling into her firepit. Nico laughed, grabbing a stick to prod it until it was positioned better. When they turned around, Mathilda was on her feet, jumping up and down in the sand.

"Holy shit holy shit holy shit!"

Nico hated jumping. It was one of those things that usually made them irrationally angry. A needless reminder of what they could no longer do that no one else ever seemed to even think twice about. But as they watched Mathilda do it, all they could do was smile.

"I did that," she eventually calmed down enough to say. "I..." she gestured frantically towards the fire. "Did you *see* that?"

Nico bit down on their lip. Mathilda's emotions tended to always be big and fast-changing and they refused to risk laughing and ruining this one. "I did," they grinned. "Incredibly cool. You're celebrating way too much for someone who just lost a bet, though."

She stopped jumping. "I'm sorry," she sucked on her lip, staring at the sand. "I'm overreacting. I don't know why... sorry. That was obnoxious."

They rolled their eyes. "You're a mer-creature who just mastered fire, Mathilda. That's definitely the kind of thing worth being obnoxious over. You weren't actually... it suits you, being all happy and hoppy and giddy or whatever. Don't stop on my account."

Slowly, her smile returned. "It makes everything bigger, kind of?" She tried to explain. "Like instead of just your brain being excited your whole body gets to be? It makes it last longer."

"Cool," they nodded.

"You should try it," she suggested. "Unless that'd make you feel stupid. Next time you're happy or excited or..." her eyes widened. She stared at their armlet. Nico prepared themself. They would not fuck up again. Not tonight.

"I'm so sorry," she sat back down. "You've been being so nice to me and I had to go and..."

Nico forced an exhale. "I definitely wouldn't call it nice. You're fine. Believe it or not, I actually am aware that I'm disabled even when it isn't actively making other people uncomfortable."

They felt it right away anyway, though. The thing in their stomach beginning to unfurrow. Something mean and dark and vengeful. Knowing that it was there didn't stop it from slithering up their throat.

"We'd better go to sleep," Nico mumbled, pulling their jacket tight around their chest. "Big day of doing nothing to look forward to, so—"

"Nicole," Mathilda said.

They ignored her. If they stayed, they would blow up at her, again. And she would take it too seriously, again. They did not like being the kind of person that made other people hate themselves. "Night. See you in—"

"You could stay?" Mathilda blurted.

They slowed down. Slightly.

"I'd... it's just a waste of resources at this point, right? Having two different campsites if we're not still actively fighting? Unless we're still..."

"We're not," they said, a little too forcefully. "I just... I don't want to."

"Oh," Mathilda said. "Okay. Sorry, I thought... I shouldn't have..."

They sighed. The thing in their stomach went back to sleep, just for a moment. "It's not your fault, Mathilda."

"Tillie's still fine," she whispered. More hushed impulse than actual declaration though, so they ignored it.

"It's a me thing," Nico insisted. "Again. I have a lot of those, apparently."

Mathilda looked towards the water. "Could I... we could talk about it?" She offered. "If you—"

"No."

"Right," she nodded. "Of course. Good night." She was just so willing to be understanding and accommodating at every single turn. It was infuriating.

They took a deep breath and sat back down on the other side of the fire. "Okay, but you can't look at me while I tell you, okay? Because then you're inevitably going to impulsively stare and then you're inevitably going to feel guilty for impulsively staring and then I'll have to comfort you until you stop feeling guilty and I don't feel like doing that right now."

She smiled a bit. "I'm umm... very good at not looking at you, actually," she whispered. "You're a little overwhelming. A lot overwhelming, actually."

Something stabbed a stake through the thing in their belly. Pins and needles ran through their whole body.

Mathilda didn't notice, though. She craned her neck uncomfortably towards the sky. Her glasses slid halfway down her nose. "Ready," she declared.

They sucked in the sea-touched air. "I'm wildly insecure, right?" They said. Like it was a given. Because by that point, it probably already was. "About a lot of things, but especially about... I don't like knowing that people spent most of my life thinking I was a girl. I hate having to remember how fucking bad at pretending to be that I was so I keep my chest bound whenever I can because somehow I keep convincing myself that if I don't see any proof of that I'll be able to forget it which is stupid because I obviously don't and other people obviously still know but it's..." they sighed. "It's not safe to wear my binder all of the time and it's not like I'd risk messing up my body even more just to protect myself from having to see that or whatever, but apparently I'm still way too insecure to have it off around strangers? So I can't... I think I'd better head over now, actually? Before you look down because now that you know to look for it it'll be harder not to... it's not your fault." They winced. They should have just left it at that. She didn't need to hear their entire life story. They didn't know what they were doing. She made then feel too exposed. "Good night," they got up. "I umm... have a good sleep."

They took a step. Another. Then, "Nicole?"

They froze. They didn't turn around. Even just the thought of turning around made them want to crawl out of their skin.

"It's umm..." she started. "That's only dangerous if you sleep in it?"

"And if you wear it too long or for too many days in a row without taking breaks," they admitted.

"Have you been doing that?" She asked the sky. "Taking breaks?"

"I normally do," they shrugged. "For a few minutes at a time throughout the day and on weekends when the only people I have to worry about interacting with are my housemates. And for a while yesterday because I was pretty sure I wouldn't randomly be running into anyone, but that wasn't why... I didn't hold off on apologizing just because it made it easier to secretly take my binder off, or whatever," they promised. "I'm just stubborn." Which was, they realized, possibly worse.

"That doesn't sound super safe," Mathilda (unhelpfully) pointed out.

Nico rolled their eyes. "We're stranded on a teeny tiny island. I think we've been being exceptionally safe, all things considered." They took another step. "I'd rather not keep doing the whole 'million questions about my identity' thing, okay? It's late. I can explain more in the morning if you need me to but—"

"I can take off my glasses!" Mathilda shouted.

They stopped moving, in confusion more than anything. "I don't... good for you?"

"I can barely see without them," she explained. "You can check them yourself, if you want."

They didn't have to. You only had to look at how big they made her eyes to know that they must have been a strong prescription.

"And it's not like I sleep in them anyway, right? So if you wanted to stay, I swear you'd look equally like a blobbish, blurry smear of colour whether you're binding or not. And I could just keep them off in the morning. Until you wake up and get changed or longer if it'd be safer for you to not get changed for a bit. I could—"

They almost laughed. "Mathilda, you can't just stop seeing every time I need to have it off. That'd be ridiculous."

"Maybe," she acknowledged. "But would it help?"

They frowned, considering. "I... yeah," they admitted. "Yeah, it... I'll go put out my fire and get the rest of our stuff, then."

Chapter 21

True to her word, Mathilda was blindly milling around their camp when Nico woke up the next morning. In fact, they were pretty sure that the sound of her tripping over her own feet was what had woken them.

They bit their lip to smother a laugh, pushing themself up. "Mathilda."

She whirled around to face them. Or rather, their general direction. "Hello!" She waved. "Good morning!" And then caught her foot on a rock.

This time, they couldn't help but laugh out loud.

"I umm... you might have to help with breakfast? Sorry, I tried, but—"

"I can just go get dressed, Mathilda," they stopped her.

"Tillie" she said. "And... no. Not until tomorrow. Or in a few hours. Or..." she frowned. "I don't actually know when it's safe to, but... not until then, okay? And I'd rather have you nearby than hiding off somewhere so... stay, okay? Please?"

And how could they say no to that, after begging her for the exact same thing just a day before?

"Okay," they smiled. "Sure. I can make breakfast."

Mathilda beamed, clapping her hands together and popping up onto her toes. "Excellent. I put—" She turned to find their bag, overshot its distance, and went toppling to the ground.

Nico sighed, retrieving her glasses from beside the fire. "Here." The sat down in front of her, holding them out.

She frowned. "What?"

"Glasses, Mathilda," they carefully directed her hands. The last thing they needed was her somehow managing to crush them.

Mathilda shook her head. "I'm fine. I'll get used to it. I already pulled you into all of this. I can't also—"

"I'm genuinely worried you'll manage to set yourself on fire if you don't put them back on right now, yeah?"

She sucked on her lip. "I'm not... I don't want you to get hurt, because of me."

"I won't."

"You almost *drowned*, Nicole," she reminded them. "Because—"

"Because I felt like being cheap and clearly didn't know enough about myself to deal with sirens. I'm fine. I'll be more careful about it, okay? I promise."

"I also don't..." she went quiet, wringing her fingers together. "I really don't want you to have to avoid me," she whispered. "Which I know is awful and selfish but..."

"Mathilda," they stopped her. "I'm not going to get mad just because you think I'm overwhelmingly cool and awesome and delightful to be around, okay? It's fine. I'm not exactly going to be able to carry you around all over the place when you inevitably fall and break something though, so that won't be. Put them on. I'm over it."

They were absolutely not over it and they both knew it. Still, it was incredibly more difficult to mentally spiral that someone was constantly thinking about their chest when that same person had been eager to just not see at all to avoid looking at it. She took the glasses. Her fingers brushed against theirs as she did. They tried not to think about how much they were thinking about that too much.

Mathilda put her glasses on, processed how close Nico was, and quickly looked away. "I'm sorry," she whispered.

They shook their head. "You didn't do anything wrong yet today. It's too early for apologies."

Now that she could actually see it, Mathilda unzipped the bag and started rooting through it for fruit and what remained of their dried cereal collection. "Here," she handed Nico a banana, still not looking anywhere remotely towards them.

They smiled. "Thank you." It felt like it was for more than just the fruit, but they still weren't brave enough to make that more clear.

"We're running out," Mathilda reminded them again. "Maybe we should leave. I'm sure there must be somewhere nearby that—"

"We're not leaving. They still have one more day to get here. Leaving now would be just about the dumbest thing we could possibly do." They hesitated. "I mean umm... no offense." They were really trying, at this whole niceness thing. It was just taking a while to get used to.

But that night (after restarting their fire, as per the bet), Mathilda still finished blowing up the raft.

"It'll probably be more comfortable than just sleeping on the floor, right?" She pointed out.

And Nico felt stupid for not thinking of that earlier.

"You take it," she insisted. "You obviously need it more." She said it as lightly as she always did. As if it was just an objective fact. Because, technically, it was. Mathilda did not need to worry about sleeping in some mysterious slightly-wrong position and waking up with an even more dysfunctional than normal leg. Mathilda was not the one who woke up every morning with an increasingly more noticeable limp. They knew that she said it like an objective fact because to her, it was one, but they also felt their stomach churn in response.

"Okay," they spoke through dried lips and a drier throat. "Thanks. Good night."

And then they awoke to the feeling of water splashing onto their face.

Chapter 22

"What the fuck!" Nico tried to sit up to better orient themself, but something pressed back against their chest.

"Slowly," Mathilda cautioned. "You'll tip it."

Their head whipped around frantically. It was dark. Night. And, notably, they were no longer on the beach.

Less than a foot away from it, but still.

"I'm..." they sat back up, more slowly this time. "What's happening?"

"Oh," Mathilda sucked on her lip, looking to the side. There was a paddle in her hand. "Yes, well, I suppose I should have... I'm kidnapping you. Or... I was trying to. If that's alright with you."

"You..." Maybe they were still asleep. That felt like the only possible explanation for whatever was currently happening. "I'm sorry, what?"

"Dang it!" Mathilda hit her side. "This would've really been a lot easier if you hadn't woken up. I didn't realize it would splash like that, when I finished getting it in the water. I just... shoot!" You can get mad," she offered. "You probably should. But please... let me finish kidnapping you first?"

"Mathilda!" They exclaimed.

"You can still use Tillie," she mumbled.

"What's going on!"

Mathilda sighed. "They're not coming for us," she admitted. "No one is. I'm so, so sorry I know I should've told you right away, but I couldn't... I couldn't. I was scared... I don't know how to take care of myself and I was scared... and then it was just far too late to possibly bring it up and... I tried to get you to agree to go and you wouldn't and I knew that once the week was up you'd just go back to hating me and then it'd be harder to... you weren't supposed to wake up until we got somewhere safer! You weren't..." She slammed her fists against the raft. Nico felt the whole thing ripple. "Ugg! Why couldn't I even get this one thing right!"

Nico blinked. Processed.

"The water shouldn't even be knee deep yet," Mathilda mumbled, staring at her hands. "You can... you can go back or I can even steer you back but I really, really don't think that's a good idea, Nicole. Let me—"

"Yeah," they tried to shake the confusion out of their head. It didn't work. "Yeah, obviously. We have to—" They were stranded in the middle of the ocean, but their mind was too busy running in a million different direction to be appropriately freaked out by that. "There was another paddle, right? Give me..."

"It's in the bag," Mathilda whispered. "I'm sorry."

She was audibly crying by the time they figured out how to unfold it.

"Nicole," she sniffled. "I'm so sorry. I'm so—"

"You should have told me," they stopped her, gritting their teeth. "I have people waiting for me, Mathilda. You made me waste a week for nothing. And drastically increased the chances of someone else buying your cloak for absolutely no reason. This was a bad decision."

"I know," she whispered. "I know, I—"

"You're fine," they lightly touched her knee. It didn't help. If anything, it made her even jumpier. "It's not like I've been the easiest person to..." they grimaced. "You still should have told me, though. That wasn't fair."

"I know," she quietly repeated.

They started paddling towards who knows where.

"I took out umm... cloths," Mathilda eventually said. "From the fire starting kit. Just in case? The odds of running into sirens again are pretty small since they move around a lot and you shouldn't keep them in your ears all the time or they'll get all black and burn-y but if we come across any, I'll be ready."

"Okay." They nodded. "Smart."

"I'd keep you safe, you know," she squeaked. "If we did come across any. I wouldn't... we won't so you don't even have to worry, but I'd keep you safe."

"Okay," they repeated. "Good."

They kept rowing in silence. Neither said anything about where they should have been steer, because neither had the slightest of clues. Or rather, in relative silence. It took over an hour for Nico to notice, but Mathilda was jumping and hissing every other second. It had been way too long for her to still be crying over them.

They sighed. "What's wrong?"

"What?" She looked up at them. "Nothing."

They rolled their eyes. "Mathilda, you're freaking out."

"No, I'm not."

"Gods, can you stop lying for two second!" They regretted it as soon as they'd said it, but being gentle had never come naturally to Nico.

Mathilda tapped her fingers against her paddle. Her swaying—Mathilda was almost always swaying, Nico had realized—picked up speed. "I'm umm... it's the water," she explained. "I'm used to water, obviously. But when it's constant and everywhere, not when... I'm not used to feeling each individual drop splashing onto my skin. I'm fine though," she sat up a little bit taller. "I'll be fine."

Nico sighed, balancing their paddle across their lap to make it easier to shrug out of their flannel. "Here." They held it out to her.

Her eyes widened. "No," she said. "No, I can't... that wasn't me trying to..."

"It'll just make me overheat when the sun finishes coming up," they shrugged. "It's fine."

"I'm..." she hesitated but then splashed herself again and relented. "Thank you," she whispered, pulling it on.

They nodded.

They both kept paddling. Mathilda kept crying.

"Okay, give me your paddle," Nico finally gave up.

She froze with it still in the water. "I'm... I don't..."

"You're freaking yourself out Mathilda. Pass it and like... I don't know. Try to stay as close to the centre as possible so you don't get splashed as much."

She tapped her knee with her freehand. "We'll be slower," she told the raft.

"Well now you're just doubting my upper body strength." They flexed their fingers. "Come on. Pass it."

She sucked on her lip. "Are you sure?"

"Positive."

"You can give it back and I can take over if... we can take turns. If that's easier. I'm seriously not—"

"Okay." They nodded. "We'll see how long this takes. We might have to start taking shift at some point."

Mathilda surrendered her paddle and quickly pulled her body in around itself. "Thank you," she said.

Nico just kept nodding.

Mathilda started swaying again. Her breathing picked up. But she wasn't crying again yet, so Nico didn't mention.

"When are you going to get mad?" She finally whispered.

"What?" They frowned, almost breaking rhythm with the paddles. "I was. I told you. It was fucked of you to not tell me the truth day one."

"I know, but..." she shuddered. "Your money was on that boat, Nicole," she reminded them. They faltered. They definitely could have done without the reminder. "And your stuff. And because of me, now you can't—"

They rolled their eyes. "Mathilda. You're not the one who launched themself overboard."

"I'm the reason they wouldn't let us back on though," she whispered. "If one of them had gotten you they would have... I did jump after you," she admitted. "Right away. And then tried to follow the boat so they could pull us back up. That's why... they freaked out when they realized I wasn't affected. That..." Her eyes welled. "I'm so sorry. I'm so, so sorry. I should have pretended to be normal. Then they would have... they started screaming at me to stay away and I'm pretty sure only tossed in the supplies so I wouldn't keep following them and... I'm so sorry. If I'd just pretended... I should have..."

They touched her knee. Again. She jolted away. Again. "You saved me," they reminded her. They couldn't believe she just kept glossing over that part. If their roles had been reversed, Nico would have held that against her for the rest of eternity. "I'm not going to get pissed that you were able to save me, obviously. I've known you were a selkie the whole time, Mathilda. It actually worked wildly in my favour for once that night."

"They were scared of me," she whispered. "Because I was immune to it. If I'd acted like I wasn't..."

"If you'd acted like you weren't, I'd be at the bottom of the ocean right now with some creepy mer-monster feasting on my flesh, yeah?"

"Someone else could have—"

"They wouldn't have. I don't know if selkies are naturally more brave or heroic or reckless or whatever, but jumping overboard for someone you barely know—especially when every interact you've had with them had been absolutely horrible, by the way—isn't exactly a thing that most that land people would do. I'm not angry about that. I'd have to be the world's biggest asshole to be angry about that and, despite everything I've said or done that might point to the contrary, I promise I'm not actually the worst."

"I don't think you are," Mathilda said. "The worst. I think you're... you gave me your shirt. And didn't get mad that I didn't want to row. That's sweet. You're sweet."

They almost choked. "Gross. I absolutely am not."

Her eyes widened at that though, so they took a deep breath, held in their nausea, and swallowed.

"Thank you," they whispered. "You're not half bad either."

Chapter 23

A few hours past daybreak—long after Nico's arm had started to feel more like noodles than appendages—they spotted light off in the distance.

Nico steered into a mostly isolated section of beach, got Mathilda to hop out and pull the raft onto the shore so it wouldn't float away, and then instantly rolled over to catch their breath on the sand.

"Sorry," Mathilda winced. "I should have... I didn't know you were tired. I'm sorry."

They raised an arm to dust sand out of their hair. "Not like I told you," they shrugged. "You'll have to deflate it though. I'm..." They fell back down, rendering the dusting completely useless. "I think I'll stay right here for a little, actually." They stared at the sky and let the sun slowly bring the feeling back to their flesh. Mathilda draped their flannel over them, at some point.

"Okay," they eventually forced themself to sit up. They had to figure out next steps. They'd returned to civilization, but what that civilization was was still an unknown. They had a home to get back to. They couldn't waste any more time lazing around on some random beach. The raft and paddles were gone by the time they did, presumably packed away in the bag once again. Mathilda was sorting through it. "We'd better do... something, right? We umm... any idea where we are?"

She shook her head.

"Right." They clicked their cane and got up, looking around to try and decide which direction to head in first. "We'll ask around until we—"

"Nicole!" Mathilda stopped then. "I umm..." she stared at her feet. "It's not like you have to or I think it'd be better if you did but you might want to..." she nodded towards the bag. "You're binder's in there?" She reminded them. And all at once, they felt completely naked. "If... before we head into town? If..."

"Right," they nodded. "Thanks. You can umm... turn around, please."

They quickly got changed.

"Okay," they smoothed down their shirt. "Let's go figure out what the fuck we're going to do next."

They grabbed their cane, Mathilda grabbed the bag, and they headed into town together.

They'd washed up on a town called Harper. It was small, touristy, and—based on the fact that Nico had literally never heard of it even once before—nowhere near either Bayside or Kovienne. Which was less than ideal. Mathilda trailed them around as they asked questions and searched for maps, jumping any time they actually succeeded in getting a stranger to talk to them. Nico ended up doing all the talking.

It'd be a little over a day's ferry ride to get to Kovienne and a three days' journey to Bayside. Which also meant that it would be a lot of money. That they didn't have.

"We could sell things," Mathilda suggested, following after Nico as they trudged back towards the water. "There's no way we'll be able to paddle all the way there but if we sell the raft and the other stuff we have, then—"

"Then what, Mathilda?" They whirled around at her.

"Tillie," she whispered, unhelpfully.

"We'll get dozens of silver by selling a few bruised pieces of fruit and empty flasks?" They didn't know why they'd let themself think that this was any kind of progress. They were still broke and stranded. The only difference was that here, all resources were commodified. "We're fucked! We're so fucked!"

A passing elven family out walking with their children slowed to glare at them, but Nico found that they couldn't care less about judgey strangers right then.

Mathilda's eyes followed the family until they were out of sight. "We'll figure it out," she lied. "We're getting you home, okay? I never should have... we'll figure it out. We could... we could work again?" She suggested. "On a boat? And I swear I'd actually... I'll be better, this time. I swear. We could—"

They scoffed. "No one here knows me enough to convince them to trust me," they reminded her. "And we both look like messes. There's no way anyone would want to make a trade like that. Especially since neither one of us would actually be coming back to give them their wages. Fuck!" They kicked the sand. "Fuck!"

They would have to start over. With nothing but the dirty sun-worn clothes on their back and a few useless survival supplies, they would have to start over. Again. They squeezed their medallion. It made their fingers too hot. They shoved their fist into their pocket.

"It can't hurt to try though, right?" Mathilda gently suggested. "I'll go find a market or something, you go talk to people around the docks, then we'll meet back here at sunset and see if anyone's figured anything out, okay?"

Nico didn't want to go talk to people at the docks. They wanted to lie down on the ground and curl up into a ball and wait for someone to come solve all of their problems for them. But that would be impractical.

"Okay." They nodded. "Fine. Whatever."

"Nicole!" Mathilda called after them as they tried to escape. She must have forgotten whatever she was going to say though, because when they turned around expectedly, she remained silent.

Nico sighed. "I'd better—"

"You'll come back, right?" Mathilda finally said. "You'll... I'll see you again? I get you have no reason to—"

"I will." They nodded. "I wouldn't have let you take everything with you if I was planning on running."

"Oh," Mathilda said. "Right. Good. I... good luck."

Nonymous

And so, Nico set off from one impossible situation to another.

Chapter 24

No one trusted Nico to take over their job for a couple of days. Nor did anyone want to hire a random, dirty, disabled teenager in exchange for free passage. They knew that they were supposed to keep trying until sunset, but if they had to go through one more rejection, they'd lose it. They milled around for a bit, checked their meeting spot in case Mathilda had also given up early, and then headed out in search of the market.

It was a terrible idea. The market was full of the smell of actual cooked, seasoned food. The colours of actual produced, material goods. And they could afford none of it. They ignored peddlers and tried to keep their attention limited to the space right in front of them as they searched for Mathilda.

After passing rows and rows of beautifully decorated tables of wears, they found her sitting cross-legged at the edge of the market with their meager belongings spread out in front of her. Barely even looking up at anyone that passed by.

"Hey!" She smiled and waved when she noticed them. "Have any—"

They shook their head. They didn't feel like reliving that particular embarrassment.

Mathilda's expression flickered, but she was quickly back to smiling. "I sold the raft!" She declared.

"For how much?"

"Six silver."

Nico sighed. Six silver would get them absolutely nowhere.

"I'm sorry," Mathilda's expression instantly fell. "I should have—"

"You did great," they stopped her. "That's great. Seriously. It's not like anyone would've bought it for much more."

They sat down beside her and tried to wave over a passing family. It didn't work.

"I'm kind of awful at this," Mathilda leaned towards them to whisper.

They laughed. "It's not you, it's the stuff."

"And me not knowing how to talk to land-people."

"Okay, a little," they relented. "But," they nudged her shoulder. "You got six silver. That's better than I did. That's huge."

"And now we have pretty much nothing sellable left."

She was right, of course, but if Mathilda was done being the optimistic one, then Nico would have to be. They decided to stay until sunset after all, just to keep themselves from wallowing in self pity. Nico waved over every passerby. Attempted to start up conversation with children to pressure their parents into buying things. By the time the sky started turning purple, they'd only managed to sell a single grapefruit. To a man who'd clearly only bought it because they'd waved him over with their cane and made him feel guilty.

They found that this particular pity was one that didn't disgust them as much as usual, though. It was harder to get annoyed at pity when it was also the only thing keeping you from complete destitution. They'd given in and started packing up when a woman cleared her throat.

She did not look like the kind of person who would stop at a non-official half-stall in an entire market full of wears. She wore a sleek, full length, ruby studded cloak that contrasted against her pale skin. Her purse was bedazzled. Her sunglasses were bedazzled. Even the black umbrella attached to her head was bedazzled.

Rich vampires were a whole other level of rich. They'd had the time to horde disgusting amounts of money, if they'd played their cards right.

And rich people were exploitable.

"Hello!" Nico smiled. "Is there anything I could—"

"How much is that?" She tapped their armlet.

The frowned, instinctively moving it behind their back. "It's not for sale."

"It's a cane!" Mathilda (unhelpfully) explained. "It shapeshifts!" As if that didn't make it all the more intriguing.

The woman's smile grew. "Could I see?"

"No." They were being stupid. They could get another cane made of something cheaper. They could sell this one for enough to get them back home and then still have a ton of money left over.

But this was the first big thing that they'd ever bought themself. This was independence.

"Three gold." They decided. Because this was clearly the kind of woman who just carried gold around with her.

The vampire laughed. "That's ridiculous."

"Two gold and five hundred silver."

She considered. "Twenty-five silver."

"It's gold-plated!"

She shrugged. "It's a lot less valuable, when it's already been turned into something. Can't make that official currency." She looked them over, the disgust in her eyes evident. "It seems like you could use the silver, though."

She was using them. She was exploiting them. It was supposed to be the other way around.

"No," they crossed their arms over their chest. "I could get more for it at a pawnshop. Absolutely not. It's not—"

Thin fingers reached out to tug on their medallion. They froze. "Two silver then," she offered. "For this."

"That's... you can't..." They stumbled back. They clicked out their cane. They needed her attention back on that.

And all at once, they hated themself.

They were prioritizing a piece of the life that they'd left years ago over the first sign of their new one. Over getting home to their new one. The pendant went hot. They wouldn't have been surprised to find their skin burnt beneath it, if they'd been brave enough to check.

"Five," they whispered.

"Four."

And then, it was done. She gave them the money. They gave her the necklace. And it was over, forever. And they felt naked, again.

"We're packing up," they muttered. "I'm tired."

Mathilda hesitated. "Are you—"

"I'm tired!"

She nodded and got to work. "We could umm... probably afford a room, somewhere," she suggested. "Now that—"

"Are you trying to waste even more of my time?" They demanded.

Mathilda blinked. "I... no! I just..."

"We sleep on the beach. We sleep on the beach and we find a way to save up more money then we get the fuck out of here."

"I could—"

"Shut up!"

She did. They trudged back to the beach and threw their stuff down in the first semi-tucked away alcove that they could find in the rockface. They ripped off their shoes and socks. They tore their shirt off then on again. They limped down to the shoreline to splash water through their stiff, dirty hair.

"Nicole..." Mathilda started again when they returned to the alcove.

"Don't." They threw themself down onto the sand and rolled away from her. It was still warm. They'd probably need a fire, eventually, but Nico could wake up later and handle that. They just wanted to stop being awake.

"You seem... are you okay?"

They rolled their eyes. "I'm fine, Mathilda. Just go to sleep."

"I don't..." She touched the small of their back. Lightly. Everything about her was always just so fucking light. "I'm sorry, if you didn't want to sell that. You didn't have to—"

"I didn't have to what, Mathilda?" They sat back up. "Get enough money for fucking food? Because that's all that was. By the time we... if I *ever* have enough to get back home again, all of the money from that's already going to be long gone!"

"I don't..." Mathilda stammered. "I wasn't—"

"So I didn't have to what, huh? Make sure we could fucking eat? Sell one of the only things I actually fucking cared about to do it? Spend over a week already and who knows how much longer constantly hungry and cold and exhausted because you were too fucking stupid to hold on to the most important thing you owned and then decided that that was somehow my fault?"

"I said I was sorry," she whispered. "I said you could go home."

They laughed. "With what! After I've suffered for weeks and destroyed everything I care about? It wasn't even my *fault*, Mathilda! You fucked up and then decided to exploit some stupid, archaic tradition to force me into this mess with you because you knew there was no way anyone would ever spend time around you voluntarily and now I'm going to have to lose everything just so you can maybe get back the thing you fucking willingly gave away!"

Mathilda tapped her side. "That's not... you don't... I just didn't know anyone on land. I-I'm sorry. I was scared and—"

"You're so full of shit," they rolled their eyes. "You know what I think, Mathilda? I think whatever mer-community you're from is probably fucking thrilled right now. And you know it too."

"That's not—"

"You can't do anything!" They reminded her. "You know that! You told me that yourself! And yet I'm supposed to believe you decided to come on land all alone? They didn't want you, Mathilda. They couldn't *stand* you. Maybe they pretended they did for a bit because you were young or shared blood or it would look bad or whatever, but they obviously didn't want you and you obviously knew that, so you decided to get away for a while and give them a break but you were so fucking incompetent even on land that you accidentally did them a massive favour and trapped the rest of us with you instead. Congrats."

"That's not true," she sniffled.

"Yeah?" They raised an eyebrow. "Then why haven't you tried to get in contact with anyone for help, huh? We've been surrounded by water this whole time. At Bayside and on the boat and the island and..." they gestured towards the water. "Go. You can swim. Find someone to talk to and get a message to them."

"I'm... I can't," she whispered.

They rolled their eyes. "Of course you can't. Because you know they wouldn't come. You disappeared without a trace and you already knew that no one out there would come looking for you so you trapped me in this instead. No one gives a shit about you so you thought you could what, force me to? You thought I wouldn't realize why they didn't want you around? I bet they're celebrating, right now. I bet they're—"

"You're being mean!" Mathilda had her hands over her ears and her knees pulled to her chest. She swayed against the sand. "You're... you're just trying to be mean! Because you—"

"Because I'm sick and tired of tiptoeing around your next fucking meltdown." They lied back down. Rolled away just before hot tears started to roll down their face. "Night."

"I'm sorry you had a bad day," Mathilda whispered. "See you in the morning."

Nico snorted. "I hope not."

Chapter 25

And then they woke up alone.

Chapter 26

They woke up alone.

School stopped being required once children reached sixteen.

Nico'd known that their entire life, but it didn't start feeling significant until they were about thirteen. That was when everyone started counting down. To their futures. To freedom. To whatever came next.

Not with Nico, of course. Even the beginning of a new era wasn't enough to entice anyone to try to do that. But still, they knew.

Limping into the kitchen at fourteen, past the post where their mother had marked their height every first-day up until they'd reached eleven.

(they'd been leaning too much for it to be accurate, she'd said. They were getting too old for it anyway, weren't they? Unless they could get over it and stand a little taller, that was.)

"Two years left," they tried to smile. Their parents didn't look up from their breakfasts as they nodded. Nico made the walk alone. Their parents hadn't enjoyed being seen with them out in public for a while, by that point.

Returning home after the last day at fifteen. They'd made a cake to celebrate.

(the baker had made a mistake, they'd said. Putting only their little sisters' name on it)

Their father had been top of his class. Nico wouldn't be. Their parents had known that since they were little. Nico had always been a more athletically gifted than academically successful child. Their father would let them play with his medallion sometimes though, back before.

"Not just best in my school," he'd remind them. "Not in the town, in the entire province." They'd wrap their tiny fingers around it, revelling it its calm, cool, smoothness. He'd smile and tap their nose. "And you will be too, Nic."

(Nico was not academically gifted and they both knew it. They'd been something better, though. Something more visible. Something easier to brag about.)

The medallion was going to be theirs, after they graduated. They hadn't talked about it for years—only ever in the before—but it was going to be theirs. Not because of some grade or ranking or accomplishment, but just because Nico was his.

He'd known. They'd all known. Nico had returned home after their last day, assuming that they'd just forgotten. They were busy, after all. With their sisters. Their last days. Not graduations, but still. Busy. The medallion lived on their father's bedside table, so Nico went home to retrieve it.

He'd bought a lockable case. He'd been so sure that they would come looking that he'd made certain they wouldn't be able to take it.

They were sixteen and they were done with school and their future was ahead of them. They were sixteen and they were done with school and their future was supposed to be ahead of them, and their own parents couldn't even trust them to not steal an heirloom.

Nico proved them right. They threw the case to the ground and when it didn't shatter, they slammed their fists against it until it finally did. They slipped it around their neck and it was no longer as cold as they'd remembered it, but they didn't care. It was around their neck.

Then, they left. The case in pieces. The carpet covered in bloodied glass. Their bed made and their closet full. They were too full of too many thoughts to have space for material possessions, so they left with their clothes and their malfunctioning body and a stolen medallion.

And, luckily, the coins in their pocket.

They couldn't get far, at first. They didn't even bother trying to. They walked until their leg wouldn't let them anymore then too a buggy to the next village over. It was a terrible escape plan, because it wasn't an intentional escape or plan. It was just them, sixteen, lashing out.

They didn't know where to go. They couldn't afford a hostel. Hiding anywhere private felt more illegal, somehow. They waited for the public square to empty out then fell asleep beside the fountain with their heart pounding and their palms slick. It had been a stupid idea. They'd barely gotten anywhere at all. Their parents would just find Nico instantly, drag them back home, and be even more disappointed in them than they'd already been.

Nico fell asleep imagining officers waking them up in the middle of the night, already in contact with their parents. Maybe even their father himself, come to collect them to save their family even more public embarrassment.

They woke up alone.

And then the next morning, they woke up alone again.

They waited two whole weeks. Two whole weeks of odds jobs and spare change in a town within walking distance (for most people) from their own front door. Two whole weeks of barely hiding.

Then, they got on a boat, sailed away, and never looked back.

Chapter 27

They bolted up, twisting their torso to try and gather their bearings. They were alone. No Mathilda, no bag of supplies.

No money.

Shit.

They'd fucked up. They should have known that they would, eventually. They couldn't believe that they hadn't already. They'd pushed her away, finally. They'd practically begged her to go.

Nico felt very small, all of the sudden. Or maybe the rest of the world just got bigger.

This was what they did. What they'd always done. They found somewhere to stay—someone to stay around—and they pushed and pushed and pushed until everyone there gave up on them. Until it was time to start all over again, somewhere where no one knew enough about them to run away.

Maybe it was good, then, that they'd left Bayside before that happened. Maybe it'd be easier, now that they'd be able to spend the rest of their life pretending that The House hadn't wanted them to go.

They put their binder on. It was the only thing left on the beach, since Mathilda clearly hadn't wanted it. They could feel themself about to fall apart. They needed something to hold their chest together, just for a little while longer.

They would be fine. They'd done this before. They would be fine, eventually. For a bit. Until they fucked it all up again.

Their vision went blurry. They rubbed at their eyes. Even those wouldn't do what they wanted them to. Nico's body was made up of a collection of traitors. They held their fists there anyway, as if that was fooling anyone.

They should have insisted on keeping the silvers in their pocket. They should have remembered to be more careful.

They would have to get up, eventually. They would have to figure out their next move. But right now, they could blame the tightness in their chest on their binder and the water on their face on the not-too-distant waves and they needed to keep lying to themself, for a while longer. They squeezed their eyes shut. They leaned back to let the sun dry their face. They tried their best to remember how to breathe.

"Okay, before you get mad, I didn't spend any money on it."

They froze. They squeezed their eyes further shut. They couldn't let her see them like this.

"Nicole?" They heard her sit down beside them. "Are you umm... sleep-sitting? Because I'm fairly certain that's not a common human thing. Or... if you don't feel like dealing with me right now, that's—"

Their eyes flew open. "Hey, Mathilda," their voice came out hoarse. They hoped she didn't notice. "Morning."

They didn't have to worry, though. Mathilda, like always, was looking nowhere near their water-logged eyes.

"I didn't spend any money on it," she repeated, handing them an omelette on a paper plate. In her freehand she balanced a deconstructed one. Bits of ham, mushrooms, and cheese carefully separated around a couple of fried eggs. "I promise. I umm... I was going to because we're kind of running low on options, but... sorry. I didn't though."

Nico winced at her panicked, flustered tone. "Okay," they tried to smile. Tried to be light. "Thank you," they accepted the plate. "But even if you did, I'm not going to..." They sighed. "I'm sorry. About last night. That wasn't about you. I shouldn't have made that about you."

Mathilda just shrugged, but her expression flickered a little as she did.

"Mathilda," they tried to hold her attention. "Seriously, that was so, so... I'm really sorry. You didn't deserve that. That was really fucked up."

"It's okay," she nodded. "You were stressed. I get it."

They frowned. "Mathilda, that doesn't—"

But she was already stretching out her legs in the sand, moving on. "We can't stay here, though," she said. "Sorry. They're apparently not fans of people camping out on beaches. Or... anywhere, I think. The officer who told me seemed super nice, though. She bought these." Mathilda nodded towards the plates. "But we... if we don't want to start getting fined, we'll have to waste a bit on a room somewhere. Sorry. She gave me a list of cheap ones though, so..."

"Okay," Nico said. "That's fine. We'll figure it out. Thanks for handling that."

She smiled a little. "You're a ridiculously deep sleeper. Which would have come in handy like a day ago, but... you know." She cut into her eggs, raised the fork to her mouth, then grimaced. "Do you like egg yolks? I think I can handle the whites but the yolk's too slime. And the mushrooms," she shivered. "I can't stand mushrooms. Figured I shouldn't turn them down though in case you liked them."

Nico was lost. Last time they'd spoken, they'd completely blown up at her. Now, she was casually talking about breakfast foods. "I'm... yeah. Thanks. You need to eat though, Mathilda."

Her eyes widened. "I know," she said. "I know. And I will. I'm not... I'm not stupid. I know we need to be saving up I'm not going to waste money on replacing it or anything, I just can't..."

They leaned forward. "I'm not mad that you're giving me extra breakfast," they said gently. "But next time, let's go for something you'll actually eat, yeah? Could you take some of mine?"

She sucked on her lip. "I... I don't think so. My body's not used to things being all mixed up like that. When I'm a seal everything's pretty separated."

They nodded. "Okay. We'll just get them both separated next time, alright? So we can trade."

"That's not fair to you," she whispered.

They rolled their eyes. "I can survive with a bit less cheese on my eggs. Promise." They hesitated. They were supposed to keep apologizing. They were supposed to make sure she knew that they had been *wrong*. They just didn't know how to even start.

"Look, Mathilda," they tried anyway. "I—"

"Oh!" She reached into her pocket. "I can't believe I didn't... here."

They froze. They stared. "Gods, Mathilda," they whispered.

"I didn't spend money on it either," she rambled. "I promise. Obviously. It's not like she would've sold it back for less than it cost. I just—"

They reached for the medallion with shaking fingers then kept reached, wrapping their arm around the back of her neck. They pulled her into a hug, trapping the necklace between them. Mathilda went rigid, then slack. Noodley. "Thank you," they whispered. They knew that they'd probably ruined their whole charade by crying against her neck, but they were too overwhelmed to care. "I don't even know how... thank you," they repeated. "So much."

"Oh. Yes. Well..." Mathilda gently wriggled out of their embrace. "You seemed upset and she seemed... not very nice... so I figured..."

They slipped the medallion back over their head. It instantly made them feel more balanced. "When did you..."

"Last night. I waited a bit so she wouldn't remember who I was and get suspicious, but she seemed like the forgetful type so..."

"And you just took it?" They exclaimed, utterly flabbergasted. "And she didn't even notice?"

Mathilda blushed. "I told you," she shrugged. "I'm good at magic tricks."

"Magic—" Nico laughed. "Mathilda! Pickpocketing's not a magic trick!"

"It basically is, though," her blush deepened. "And it... I don't think it counts as stealing, right? If the person doesn't seem like they'd miss it and is also kind of a bitch?"

They grinned. "That's some extremely sound reasoning. Did you take anything else from her?"

She started tapping her side. "I... no. I should have... I'm so sorry, I can't believe I didn't..."

"Mathilda," they pressed down on her knee. "You did more than enough, okay? I promise." They sighed, tracing slow circles around the ridge of their medallion just to remind themself that it was still there. "I was awful last night," they whispered. "I was... I've been horrible to you. This whole time."

She smiled a little. "You're not so bad," she gently touched their shoulder. "You're—"

"No, Mathilda. I'm serious. I am. I... fuck! I'm sorry, okay? I'm sorry I'm an asshole, I'm sorry I know that and still can't stop myself from being an asshole for more than like, ten minutes at a time, I'm sorry you clearly think you have to keep being ridiculously nice to me despite all that, but you don't, okay? You can get mad. You should."

She cocked to her head to the side. "I don't think..." she looked away, tapping her fingers against her hip. "I'm not a fun person to be around," she said. "When I'm mad. I'm not... I can't, actually."

They rolled their eyes. "I don't know if you've noticed, but I'm not either."

"No." She shook her head. "It's different, though. It's... I don't do it right. I don't..." She took a deep breath. "I can... understand. Being out of character when you're mad. I can... it's fine. And I literally did trap you in all of this, so you're allowed to..."

"If I say I'm not mad about that anymore, will you stop letting me walk all over you?"

Mathilda frowned. "Are you actually, though? " She checked. "Not mad?"

"I'm... I don't know," they admitted. "I'm really good at being angry, apparently. But it's less every... ask me tomorrow, okay? Hopefully I'll be sure tomorrow. But," they sat up a bit straighter. "I am sure that I don't want to be, okay? And that I shouldn't be. At this point I've fucked up so many times that it's definitely at least equally my fault and I mean... fuck, Mathilda, I'd be back home already if we'd done things your way."

"I don't... I don't think I want you to lie about being mad."

Nico sighed. "I'm always mad," they said. "But I shouldn't be mad at you or maybe you should be madder at me or maybe it's both or... whatever. Can we just decide that we're even right now, though? So that next time I fuck up—because there probably will be a next time and I don't want there to be one but it's almost definitely going to happen—you can be all like 'you're clearly being an asshole right now and I'm going to yell back or walk away or do whatever I need to do until you calm the fuck down' instead of just acting like it's somehow your job to just take it?"

Mathilda sucked on her lip. "I'm not... I don't want you to have to see me mad. It's seriously fine, it—"

"Well now I'm just super intrigued and desperately do need to see it, actually."

"No," she looked up at them for half a second. "You don't."

"I'm..." Nico frowned. "Okay. Then I won't. Then next time I fuck up you don't have to get all nice and apologetic or loud and angry, okay? You just walk away." Their pulse spiked. "And umm... hopefully, eventually, you decide to come back. And I promise to not get mad at you for needing to walk away, alright? As long as you come back."

She smiled a little. "I can... okay. I can do that."

Nico hesitated. "We're in this together now, you know that, right? For better or worse. I'm not... if you do ever lose it at me—or even if you don't, even if you just decide you need to take a break from being so overwhelmingly sweet and accommodating all of the time—I'm not leaving. I mean... I'm wildly annoying, okay?" They made themself smile. "So if I take something too far, even if you take it further back, even if I need to be the one to walk away for a bit, I'll come back too, okay? I promise. I'll stay."

Mathilda's fingers touched theirs. Lightly. Like always. "Okay." She whispered. She yawned because of course she was tired. She'd stayed up longer and woken up earlier. For them. "That's..." she slouched down and rested her head against their shoulder. Lightly. Like always. "Thank you."

Chapter 28

There was, unfortunately, still the little matter of figuring out how the hell they were going to get out of Harper.

They relocated to a park further inland and set up base on a bench, just in case a more fine-happy officer went looking for them at a beach.

They went over their meager set of belongings. And found it to still be incredibly meager.

"You know," Nico suggested, trying their very best to sound casual. "if you're good at pick-pocketing—"

"Sleight of hand," Mathilda corrected.

"Okay," they nodded. "Of course. Sleight of hand. Then umm... *sleight of hand*-ing people would be a really easy way to—"

"No." She stopped them.

Nico nodded. "Okay." They tried to think of something else. "Right. Well then, maybe we could—"

"I'm sorry," Mathilda blurted. "I know... I get it would be..."

"You don't need to apologize," they rolled their eyes. "It's not like I was gonna force you to do something illegal. We'll just see if anyone's hiring anywhere. We should probably umm... blow a bit on our budget on less sweaty, sea-stained clothes before that, but then..." They stopped.

Mathilda was tapping and swaying again.

"Hey," they put their hand in the middle of the table. Not to grab hers, just to have it there. "It's seriously fine. It was just a suggestion."

She shook her head. "That's not... you saw me try to work, Nicole. Remember?"

"So we won't have you look into kitchens," they shrugged.

"That's not—"

"I can't work *anywhere*," she said. "That's not... I'm not trying to get out of it or make you do all the work or... I'll try, I

125

swear, but it won't... there's no way I'll be able to pull my weight," she admitted. "I'm sorry. You're going to end up having to do basically everything which isn't fair at all and... we'll get you home first, obviously. Obviously. But then... could you wait?" She asked. "Which isn't fair to ask, but just until I have a bit to work off of? I don't know how I'll... nowhere's going to hire me, Nicole. I can't do anything."

Their throat went tight. This was too familiar. This was their fault. They'd done this. "Mathilda, that's not... holy shit!" they realized.

"What?"

"You're good at magic," they remember. "Card tricks and sleight of hand and—"

She sighed. "I really, really don't think I'll be able to keep pickpocketing people, Nicole."

"No!" They slammed their hands against the table.

She jumped.

"Sorry," they smiled sheepishly. "Excited hitting, not angry hitting. You're... we're in the middle of a small little touristy town, Mathilda. Tourists *love* spending way too much money on street performers. We'd probably make way more doing that than in any temporary job willing to hire either of us. We could—" They were expecting her to get excited but instead, her shoulders slumped.

"I'm not good at audiences," she mumbled. "Land-people ones, at least. I don't think... I won't be able to do that. I'm sorry. It was a good idea. I'm so sorry."

"Oh," they said. Then caught themself. "Or... that's okay, I mean." They considered. "How long did it take you to learn?" They asked. "Magic."

"A umm..." She stared at her lap. "A while."

"Do you think you'd be able to teach me?" Nico asked. "Enough for it to look impressive to people who know nothing about it? Or would that just be a waste of time?"

"It would probably take a couple of days to figure out a whole routine," she admitted. "And if we have to rent somewhere to stay, by the time we're ready we'd probably be out of..."

"Oh." They deflated. "Right. Shoot."

Nico hesitated. Maybe it was because they were worried about how she'd answer. Maybe it was their body trying to stop themself from practically begging to learn *street magic*, of all things.

"It's super okay to say no if you don't think it'll work," they started. "But what if we just try and see if you could run a stand? Just for a bit," they quickly added. "Just as long as you're comfortable with. And then you teach me more basic stuff and I take over as soon as it's physically possible."

Mathilda chewed on her lip. "I don't want to get your hopes up."

"Okay." Nico nodded. "Understood. Hopes all the way on the floor then. In the politest most supportive way possible."

"There's a chance we set up then I freak out instantly and have to... it might not work."

They shrugged. "Then at least we'll know we've tried, right? If you're... I really, really think we should try."

Mathilda took a shuttering breath, reached into her pocket, and pulled out her cards. "Okay. Let's try, then."

Chapter 29

The room that they ended up in was objectively a shithole, but it was a shithole with a roof, so Nico instantly decided that they were in love with it.

It was one room with no closet, no windows, and no furniture beyond on tiny bed. There was no sink or toilet—though they apparently had permission to use the communal washroom and kitchen a building over—and no light fixtures, so they'd have to buy their own candles if they wanted the luxury of seeing after sunset. Luckily, there were so many cracks and termite holes in the roof though that the room at least wasn't pitch black during the day.

Nico fell onto the bed instantly. They were going to take a long nap. They were going to take a long nap and then celebrate with another long nap.

"Okay," Mathilda sat down at the edge of the bed, pulling out her cards. "Ready to keep going?"

They groaned, rolling over to bury their face in the pillow. "I know magic now," the mumbled, voice muffled by the feathers. "You taught me a trick at the park."

"Yes, *a* trick," she said. "That you pulled off exactly once."

Nico sighed, sitting back up.

"Was that too mean?" Mathilda leaned forward to whisper. Nico had no idea who she was whispering for. "Or..."

They bit their lip. "It was perfect. If you're gonna be teaching me stuff, you should probably know that I respond best to people being slightly rude, actually."

"Oh, excellent!" She clapped her hands together. "I can do that!"

They laughed.

Mathilda didn't though. She was slow and cautious and patient. She would show them a step then wait patiently as they did it over and over again until they got it exactly right. She never said, "what are you doing?" or "why the fuck would you do it like that?" or even just "that wasn't right", Just "ooh, getting better" (even when they weren't. Especially when they weren't) and then she'd curve her fingers around theirs, remodel how they should have been moving their hands, and wait to repeat the whole thing all over again.

"We'll have to get there early tomorrow," she announced over an incredibly sparse dinner of bread, butter, and more bread. "so we can get a good location."

Nico hesitated. "Mathilda, I don't think I'm ready to..."

"You're not," she agreed. Then blushed. "Sorry. No offense. You're doing really well, actually. I can... I'll try. I said I would, right?"

"Okay," they nodded. "Thank you. You'll crush it."

They never did go out to buy candles so when the sun set far enough that they couldn't see the cards anymore, they decided to call it a night.

Mathilda took the floor without question.

"Okay," Nico pulled the thickest blanket off the bed and handed it to her. "Right, I guess we're... we'll take turns," they decided. "You get the bed tomorrow."

"That'd be ridiculous. Only one of us is disabled, I don't need—"

Nico's breath caught. A little too loudly.

"Nicole?" Mathilda called through the darkness. "Was that... I'm sorry, I didn't mean to... I thought that was the word you used. I didn't mean to—"

"It is." They swallowed.

"Oh." She was quiet. "I feel like I did something wrong."

They winced. They were not going to let their own bullshit ruin two nights in a row. "You didn't," they promised. "I'm just... I'm weird about it still, I guess. Weirder than I'd thought I was. That was right, though. I'm not ashamed of..."

They sighed. "I like to act like I'm not ashamed of it, I guess. I don't want to... can we not talk about it? Can we just go to sleep?"

"Okay," Mathilda's voice was small and tight but she didn't apologize again, so at least they hadn't messed up that badly. "Good night."

"Sweet dreams."

Chapter 30

Watching how completely enthralled full adults were by Mathilda's card tricks made Nico feel a lot better about themself. If they were still insistent on preserving their own dignity by pretending that they thought close-up magic was lame, them being actually confused and mystified by some of Mathilda's tricks would have made them even lamer.

But if everyone else was equally impressed, then maybe they could just tell themself that Mathilda was the best and only non-lame street magician on the planet. That was a much easier pill to swallow.

They hadn't wanted to buy any bigger crowd-pleasing props until they were sure the act would work, but even just working in small groups with her deck of cards, Mathilda quickly amassed a crowd. Nico stood dutifully by to collect payment and donations as she blew minds, one group of five by a time. By the time the market had been open for an hour, they'd summoned one of the longest lines in the place. By the time the market had been open for an hour and ten minutes, Mathilda was abruptly and shakily declaring the show over, abandoning the table, and sprinting out of the market square.

"Alrighty folks!" Nico swept themself behind the booth, trying to regain the line's attention. "Watch out for us back here again next time! Any donations to help us improve our act would be greatly appreciated."

They went for the old people first. It was always easier to guilt them into giving money to a young-ish girl-ish looking person. They managed to wring a couple dozen more coppers out of the crowd before cleaning up Mathilda's cards and heading off in the general direction that she'd disappeared in.

They found her on the beach, sitting and swaying at the edge of the water. It was the first place they'd checked. Mathilda was supposed to be aquatic, so of course that would be where she'd return to.

"Hey." Nico sat down beside her. She'd chosen a spot so close that the waves were practically nipping at their toes so Nico carefully tucked their feet behind them. They didn't feel like spending the rest of the day in wet socks. "If it isn't the magician of the hour."

"I'm sorry," she whispered.

They frowned. "Don't be. You killed it. Everyone was wildly impressed."

"I gave up, though."

"Yeah, after making more than I probably could have working for hours. You were great," they lightly nudged her shoulder. "You were amazing, actually."

She licked her lips, watching the waves. "You're being nice to me because you're worried I'll start crying if you're not," she accused.

"Mathilda. Respectfully. I'm pretty sure that's going to happen at some point no matter what. Respectfully."

She snorted. "Gods, I'm a mess."

"Ditto," Nico nodded. "But you're a mess who just did something super impressive and got us a lot closer to getting out of here. That's really cool."

"I swear I tried," she insisted. "I swear I'm not... I'm not just awful at everything because I'm lazy, alright? I know it seems like... I tried."

"Okay." They carefully put their hand on top of hers. "I—"

"I don't want to be useless!" she flung their hand off, kicking her heels against the sand. "It's not like I like this! It's not like I'd choose this! It's just so, so—"

"Mathilda," they knelt down in front of her. Ignoring the way it made their leg twinge. Ignoring the sand that flew into their face and the waves that lapped against their heels. They watched

132

her: chest heaving and shuttering. Fingers tapping away. Nico swallowed. "I'm so sorry."

She rolled her eyes. "It's not your fault that—"

"No," they stopped her. "It is." Nico got up. Held out a hand. "Can we walk somewhere?" They asked. "Anywhere? It seems like... I don't know, you just seem like you're supposed to be moving, right now. Would that help?"

Mathilda nodded. "I think it's... in water I'm basically always moving, right? So..."

"Okay," they shook their wrist. "Let's walk, then?"

Her eyes flicked to their armlet. "I don't actually need to walk around. We don't—"

They concealed a grimace. "I'll be fine. I'll tell you if I'm not."

She didn't take their hand as she got up, but then, she hadn't been looking at them, so maybe she just hadn't noticed.

Chapter 31

It was a lot harder for Nico to use their cane on the sand, so they slowly led Mathilda to a park. They'd walked circles around it three times already before they finally managed to force themself to talk.

"I'm not good at apologies," they admitted. "Like, at all. Like, I don't think I've literally ever actually given a good one."

"You don't have to apologize," Mathilda shrugged. As if it was perfectly normal for someone to ask to talk to you and then spend the better part of an hour not talking.

"I do, though. I... fuck." They squeezed their eyes shut to try and collect themself better. "I don't like being all mushy and emotional and... I'd quite rather do literally anything else than talk about this kind of stuff, actually."

"Oh," she said. "Umm... okay? We don't have to—"

"No," they stopped her. "Don't let me do that. That's basically the whole problem. I'm..." they sighed. "I shouldn't have called you useless. Or anything else shitty or awful or... it shouldn't have happened at all, but I was never once actually talking to you, okay? I need you to know that."

Mathilda sighed, but even that was light. "It's fine," she said. "I was never offended. Especially on the boat. I'd just roped you into all of this and I wasn't exactly being—"

"No. You... okay yeah, you shouldn't have trapped me in a duel and I should have been mad about that but it wasn't... I didn't know it would do this. I didn't know you would take it so seriously." The tried to turn to her but she just kept staring ahead and walking, so they did the same. "You were in a whole new biome and trying your best and instead of explaining how to fucking do things I just kept exploding and I shouldn't have..." they swallowed. "That wasn't at you. That wasn't about you. I just..." they laughed a little. "I think I have some kind of complex? I definitely do, actually, that's just another thing I like to pretend doesn't exist. Because... complex. People see me and assume I can't do things which means if I mess up ever, even once, I don't have room for second chances. Either because they swoop in to try and rescue me or because I start freaking out about them swooping to rescue me or even just about them thinking that they should and... that fucking sucks. And experiencing that or feeling like that or even just remembering that makes me feel like shit but when you're disabled and let yourself look upset around people they get even more convinced that you're incompetent so I've stopped myself from doing that. But apparently that just means that I force all of my hurt and shame and bullshit onto other people which I know is so, so much shittier than just letting myself be sad but I can't do that. Yet. Maybe ever. But that doesn't mean it's ever actually been about you, okay? Ever."

An older couple walked by them. The man's shoulder touched Mathilda's. She jumped. "Okay." She nodded. "Thank you for letting me know. I'm... sorry. That you have to feel like that."

"Don't let me convince you you're useless just because I'm bad at dealing with all of my own bullshit, okay? Don't—"

"Oh." She blushed. "That's not... you're definitely not the first person to point that out, Nicole. I can't do... most things. It's not like no one else has noticed that. It's fine, it... you didn't transfer you're complex to me or anything. I already had it. You're fine."

"That's not... Mathilda, that's not fine!" They scrambled for a way to contradict her. "You did basically everything when we were stranded, right? All of the scavenging and exploring and—"

"That was easy."

"I couldn't do it," they reminded her. "Does that make me useless?"

"I... no!" Her eyes widened. "I wasn't..."

"I know," they smiled a little. "Of course you weren't. Because you're ridiculously nice, to everyone except yourself. But that's hypocritical, Mathilda. You can't say you're a fuckup for not being able to do the things that you can't then act like its totally fine that I can't do a ton of things either."

"That's different, though," she mumbled. "You physically can't. That's not your fault. I just... I don't know why I'm the way I am, but it's not... it's different."

They considered. "Could you have stayed?" They asked.

"What?"

"Did you feel like you could've actually stayed at that booth?"

"I... no."

"Then I hate to break it to you," they dropped their voice. "But you're a massive, ginormous hypocrite." They leaned to the side, tapping their arms together. "We're going to make a deal, okay? Because we're stuck working together for a few more days, at least, and I'm wildly dysfunctional and you're wildly hypocritical so we have to figure out how work around that. So I'm going to pretend to understand that not being able to do things doesn't make me any less awesome because when I fall down that rabbit hole I start treating you like shit and you're going to pretend that you know the same thing about yourself because when you spiral about it, it makes me feel like shit. And we're going to hold each other to that, okay? Until we maybe start to actually believe it at some point." They held out their hand. "Deal?"

She shook it. "Deal."

They kept walking. There was little else left to do. Eventually someone—maybe them, maybe her, maybe the both of them simultaneously—started steering them back to their hostel.

"I'd stay too," Mathilda said abruptly as they started turning in for the night.

Nico slowed down, already half-way under their sheet. "What?"

"If you... obviously if you have to get mad too, but you already know that, right? If you need to get sad though, I'd stay too. Not... not panderingly or pityingly or even helpfully at all, unless you'd want that. I'd just... I'd stay and I'd wait and then we'd never have to acknowledge it again at all after if you didn't want to, but I need you to know that I'd stay."

They smiled, rolling over to face the other wall. They knew that it was probably too dark for her to see them, but being caught crying right after she'd told them that they could would feel ridiculously uncool. "Thank you," they whispered. "I know."

Chapter 32

Nico walked back to their room alone. They'd been doing that so frequently those last few days that even the tourists had started to accept it as part of their routine. Mathilda would perform for a bit, abruptly disappear and leave them to declare the show over. Then they'd mill around talking to potential customers for a while before heading back to join her. Mathilda was almost always asleep when they peeked in on her—land-people were their own particular brand of exhausting, apparently—but Nico always did before continuing on with their day, just in case she was awake.

Partially because they knew that no matter how well shows went, ending them almost always led to her spiralling down the same train of thought they were now honour bound to prevent, but mostly, because they just liked it when she was awake. With each passing day, they found themself a little less eager to leave Harper.

Which felt like betrayal. Which felt pathetic. Which felt ungrateful.

But it also felt like her calm gentle hands wrapped around theirs as they ran through more complex tricks, open and ready to catch them when they inevitably messed up.

They were expecting to find her asleep again, but she stirred as the door squeaked on its hinges.

"Hello," she smiled, eyes still half-lidded and voice dripping with sleep.

"Sorry," Nico said. They were getting better at doing that, slowly. It almost felt natural now. "Didn't mean to wake you."

Mathilda rolled her eyes, sitting up. "It's not even noon, yet," she pointed out. "You shouldn't be worried about letting me stay asleep."

"Aye!" They pointed an accusatory finger at her. "Illegal. Bad. We have literally nothing else to do until tomorrow, if you need to rest, you rest."

She blushed. "I'm umm... I think I'm getting up now, actually. So if you wanted to keep practicing..."

Nico sighed. They wanted to. They really, really wanted to stay in all day with her, listening to the light, gentle way she always walked them through everything. But they had other things to do. "I was gonna go shopping, actually," They admitted. "See if I can find more things to use in the act. If we use something bigger and showier, we can get through more customers more quickly."

"Oh," Mathilda nodded. "Right. Smart."

"You could come?" They added, a bit too eagerly. It was Nico's turn to blush. Something about Mathilda made them want to be honest though—perhaps it was some kind of selkie ability she'd neglected to inform them on—so they pushed forward. "Please come, actually. We'll explore the shopping centre together. Could be fun."

She grinned, getting to her feet. "Of course."

It was not fun. Despite the town's small size, Harper's Small-ish to Big-ish range shopping centre was a goliath. It ascended up past the clouds, possibly just for the sake of doing so. Based on the directory on the ground level, the shops up there were few and far between. Nico tried to scan through it to find anything remotely magic adjacent, but that was a task made much more difficult by Mathilda jumping beside them every couple of seconds.

"Hey," they leaned towards her, wrapping their fingers around her wrist to try and keep her on the ground. And just to have their fingers wrapped around her wrist. "You okay?"

She nodded instead of actually responding which they should have recognized was probably a less than good sign, but they were too overwhelmed by the sheer amount of options ahead of them to notice. They'd go to stores likely to carry magic-props and essential supplies and only stores likely to carry magic-props and essential supplies. Nico was a retail veteran. They would not let themself be swayed by flashy signs and deceptively phrased sales. They had a ferry pass to save up for.

"Okay." They pressed a finger against the directory. "I think we hit everything on the first floor first—I'm not a super big stairs person, obviously—then work our way up? I'm not really sure what kind of stuff would work best though, so it's up to you. Preferably the cheaper the better."

They turned to her.

"Mathilda?" They prompted. "Ideas?"

"Oh!" She hopped. "Yes. I'm... that sounds good. Excellent."

Despite being the more mobile of the pair, Mathilda started lagging behind so drastically that Nico had to grab her arm with their free one and pull her around. They bought non-magic specific props first. Cups. Rope. A bedsheet that they could cut up and repurpose as needed. Nico wasn't sure how helpful any of it would be, though. Mathilda had gone quiet the second they'd stepped into the building so it was mostly just a lot of them asking if things would be helpful and her grunted her displeasure or assent. They'd expected her to get more enthusiastic once they reached an actual magic-trick store—Mathilda was never not enthusiastic when talking about fake magic—but instead, she whispered a breathy "sorry", ripped her hand out of Nico's grasp, and sprinted down the hall.

"Mathilda!" They followed after her. She had a head start and two fully functional legs though, so it really wasn't much of a chase. "Mathilda!" They called anyway, already knowing that they'd just have to wait for her to stop.

And she did, eventually. They found her down a dimly lit hallway leading to nothing but bathrooms, curled into a swaying ball.

"I'm sorry," she repeated again as they eased themself down beside her.

They smiled a little. "You were supposed to stop doing that, you know."

A sink started up. Mathilda curled even further. Nico had no idea what they were supposed to do here. They'd dealt with shoplifting faeries and scheming witches and incredibly nit-picky werewolves, but never with a selkie so deeply terrified by the sound of water.

"Mathilda," they scooted around to face her better. They decided to go for honesty. "I don't know what I'm supposed to do here."

Mathilda didn't seem to know either, though. She just kept struggling to regain her breath. Nico figured that that must have been hard, what with her knees pressed against her diaphragm.

"Mathilda," they tried to gently press down on them. It worked, a little. Only slightly. "I'm sorry, I don't fully know what's going on, but if I can help at all, I—"

Her hands flew out and wrapped around their wrists. She pulled them over her ears and then left them there, so Nico carefully cupped them and tried their best to keep up with her swaying. Mathilda had pulled them close enough that it was impossible to look anywhere but her face. It was red and snot streaked. Her glasses had slid almost all the way down her nose and Nico desperately wanted to fix that, but they were too afraid to move. "Mathilda," they whispered. The world felt so incredibly quiet, this close to her. "Umm... glasses."

She reached out to push them up then wrapped her arm around the back of Nico's neck to pull them even closer. She pressed her forehead against theirs. The only things in the universe were suddenly Mathilda's buggy, waterlogged eyes.

Then, they closed. Lightly. Fluttering. She pressed her free palm to Nico's chest just before closing them and for a while, they just breathed together.

"Don't pull back right away," Mathilda eventually whispered. "I need... please don't pull away."

Nico wouldn't have dreamed of it.

Slowly, her eyes reopened. She inhaled snot. "Hi," she whispered.

"Hey." They brushed their finger along the skin behind her ear.

She shivered. "I don't... I'm not ready to see everything else, quite yet. I don't—"

"Okay," they nodded. Slightly. Lightly. Because now, they were attached to her. "Can I help?"

"You are," she whispered. "Just... keep being the whole world. For a little bit. Until I'm ready for the rest of it."

"Deal."

They watched her. She watched them. And they both breathed. Slightly. Lightly.

Mathilda licked her lips. Pushed away more snot. "I don't suppose I can just stay here forever, huh?"

"I don't think the shopping centre people would be super happy about that, no."

They felt her breathing pick up again before they heard the difference.

"Can I get you home?" They asked. "Can I take you home?"

"I'm... we're shopping. We still didn't—"

"I can do that on my own. I was going to anyway, remember?"

"I'm... okay," she took a deep breath. "Please. I..." her eyes overflowed, yet again. Maybe that was a selkie thing. That she never seemed to fully escape the water. "I want to go home."

"Let's do it then," they smiled.

They both got to their feet: clumsily and shakingly. Neither seemed ready to let the other go.

"We can walk just like this," Nico offered. "Not all the way, but at least to the doors. You'd have to be the backwards one, though." They definitely didn't trust their leg to carry them that far backwards.

Mathilda rolled her eyes. It shook more tears free. "That'd look ridiculous."

"Maybe," Nico agreed. "But would it help?"

So, entangled, they stumble their way all the way out of the shopping centre. Nico would have brought her the rest of the way home, but Mathilda refused to let them.

"We're holding each other accountable, remember?" She smiled through chapped, enflamed lips. "No pretending walking that far twice back-to-back wouldn't be a big deal. I'll be fine."

"Are you sure?" They tried to hold on, just a little longer. "I could—"

"I can do this. I need you to pretend you believe that I can do this."

They swallowed. They might have been terrified of letting her go, but that was a struggle that they were all too familiar with. "I believe you," they promised, pressing their forehead to hers, one last time. Then, they kissed her. Right where their head had just been. When some fae did that, it meant good luck and protection. They wondered if they knew stuff like that under the sea or if faeries were as elusive to Mathilda as selkies were to them. "Seriously," they added. "I'm just clingy." They made themself let go. Stuffed one hand into their pocket and summoned their cane with the other. "See you in a bit?"

Mathilda smiled. "Sure."

They watched her until she'd completely disappeared into the distance.

And then, as they walked back into the shopping centre, they were finally forced to admit it. Not to her, not even quite to themself (they were a judgemental asshole, after all. Much too sarcastic for these kinds of confessions). But, to some unseeable, unknowable, unjudging other, they thought about how desperately they'd needed to see her alright and how incredible they'd felt just sitting across from her, even as she self-destructed, and admitted that at some point, maybe, they'd started to fall for Mathilda.

Chapter 33

"Hey," Nico tried their very best to act normal when they returned to their room and found Mathilda going over card tricks on their bed. They weren't sure if they were doing it right. It had been ages since the last time they'd had a crush, so their experience with pretending that they didn't was lacking, to say the least.

Mathilda jumped, quickly sweeping the cards back into the box.

They frowned. "How—"

"I'm sorry I was such a mess."

Nico sighed. "Mathilda, no. Not allowed. You were fine."

"I was being ridiculous."

"You were scared. That's—"

"Of what?" She demanded.

"Huh?"

Mathilda got to her feet. Her arms started to tap. "There was nothing scary there! It was a fucking shopping complex! I was just being an overdramatic, overemotional mess and I don't need... I don't want you to make up excuses for me. I don't... I'm not actually that fragile, you know. You're allowed to be upset when I do something ridiculous because if you don't let yourself be upset then you're going to get sick of me and I don't want... that'd be worse," she whispered. "Than you being mean or mad or whatever you need to be. That'd be worse."

Nico's brow creased. They sat down on the edge of the bed. "I'm not mad, Mathilda," they said carefully.

She snorted. "You could be. You should be. I ruined—"

"Absolutely nothing," they shook the shopping bag before putting it back down. "You didn't do anything wrong."

"I was *terrified*. Of nothing! And I made you take care of me and—"

"No one knows what's wrong with me!" They cut her off, wincing even as they did. It was their deepest secret. None of The

House even knew (minus Milo who they'd told after one too any not-so-casual attempts to give them money for a treatment that wouldn't even work and Leif, they supposed, who'd likely accidentally read it out of them at some point) because it just wasn't the kind of thing that they ever wanted to talk about. And because it was a little bit terrifying to talk about. But if there was one thing they wanted to do even less than tell Mathilda the truth, it was let her keep spewing self-hating bullshit about herself.

Mathilda froze. Turned to look towards them. "What? Nothing's wrong with you. You're perfect. You're—"

They couldn't help but smile. "My leg, Mathilda," they prompted lightly. "The one that I kind of have a whole cane for?"

"Oh." Her face flushed. "Right. I umm..." she sat down beside them. "Have you been to a healer, yet?" She asked.

They winced. It wasn't her fault. They knew it wasn't her fault. It was a perfectly reasonable question to ask. They tried to swallow down the serpent in their stomach. They could not let it out again here.

"Yes," they nodded. "Lots. And tried just about every kind of spellwork possible, but no one could figure it out. Back home—not home," they corrected themself. "Back where I grew up, it was this big scandalous thing, actually? Small towns are really gossipy like that, you know?" They paused. "Sorry, I forget you spent most of your time as a seal, before this. It's just... trust me, they are. And I didn't used to be disabled. I could run faster than kids twice my age and climbs trees like it was nobody's business. And when I was little, everyone acted like that meant something. Like I'd *be* someone." They took a long, slow breath. The room suddenly felt entirely too quiet. "And then, one day when I was like ten, I just woke up and walking hurt. But subtly, you know? Like if I wasn't paying much attention, I wouldn't even know it was there. So I kept running and climbing and playing and competing but it kept getting worse until I couldn't hide it anymore and I just... I hadn't *done* anything! I knew all the safe ways to exercise. I'd never done anything dangerous or reckless and legs aren't supposed to randomly stop fucking working, but we assumed I must have just hurt it and not realized it and for a while everyone was super sweet and accommodating but then one healer said nothing was wrong. And then another healer said nothing was wrong. And then by the time I turned thirteen I could barely fucking walk, but it wasn't like we could get something to help with that because there technically wasn't anything wrong with me." They tapped their fists together. They would not get mad. They would even let themself get upset, if they had to, but they would not let themself freak out at Mathilda again while she was already on edge. They took another breath. Breathed in tears and frustration and rage before any of it could escape and make things even worse. "And people started... they'd act like I was lying? Like I'd just gotten tired of being good and loved and acclaimed and had decided to throw that all away for what? A little bit more free time that I didn't even get to fucking enjoy because no one would ever stop fucking pestering me about it or accusing me of faking or trying to catch me in a lie?"

They put their hand over hers, just to keep themself in the present. Mathilda pressed back against it.

"So, I don't... I don't know why you were scared. It didn't make sense to me. But I know that you were and I know that that means that even if it didn't make sense to me—even if it never will—it was real, okay? It was real and it was hurting you and even if I never know why—even if you don't fully understand it either—you were feeling it which means that it was. Which means that nothing about the way you reacted to that could have possibly been ridiculous because you were the only one feeling it so you're the only one who knows how you're supposed to react to something like that. I'm not... I don't need to see something to know that it's really affecting you, okay?" They finished. Mathilda was still quiet though and the room was just so fucking quiet, so they quickly added. "Because I really am disabled, okay? You know that right? Even if it doesn't technically make sense and people can't explain it, that doesn't mean—"

"Of course," Mathilda stopped them, tapping their good foot with hers. "I believe in you," she whispered. "More than anyone I've ever known, I think. So I'd never... that means all of you. Every single bit. Obviously. And I'd..." she swung her legs. "So umm... I've never been good at physical activity stuff," she admitted. "Like, even when I'm in my seal form, but if you're ever stuck dealing with someone who doesn't believe you ever again, I'd umm... I'd help you," she said. "Fight them."

They burst out laughing. It gave them the perfect excuse to let a single tear slide down their cheek. "Gods, Mathilda! You're quite possibly the most duel-happy person I've ever met."

She blushed. "That wasn't... I never actually..."

"I know," they tapped her foot back, leaning against her. "Thank you. I'd love to kickass and defend our honours together. Sounds fun."

"Well, good." Mathilda nodded. Then, she frowned. "We're not actually going to fight anyone, right?" she whispered. "Because—"

"No," they chuckled, shaking their head. "Don't worry, I'm not actually holding you to that."

Her shoulders relaxed. "You're umm... you're not mad, then?" She studied the floor. "You're sure?"

"Positive," Nico nodded. They hesitated. "But it might help...you don't have to, I don't actually have to know, it might just help me help you if you... do you know why?" They asked. "You got scared? Could you try to tell me?"

She squeezed her eyes shut. Flexed her fists.

"Forget it," Nico said. "It's seriously no big—"

"I need you not to touch me," Mathilda said. "While I explain. Or... or talk or... I need to be able to pretend I'm the only person in the room."

They frowned. "Mathilda, you seriously don't have to—"

"I want to," she insisted. "I'd like... I want you to know everything about me, okay? We're going to be stuck together for a while longer, so you really should, right? I just don't know if I'll be able to explain it properly."

They nodded. They slid away from her to give her space. "Okay," Nico said. "Whenever you're ready."

Mathilda took a deep breath, flexed and clenched and flexed her fists again. "It's like... you've been underwater before then, right? It's like... that's what it's supposed to be like all the time, for me. Quiet—but not normal quiet. That's too much too, sometimes. This incredibly specific quiet that's also full of pressure and motion and well, noise, I suppose, which doesn't make sense, but it's that. Having your head underwater. And it's nice and cold and solid and it's holding you tight from all sides and never actually touching you and... it's perfect. And if you give into that long enough and keep your head under long enough, you get used to it, right? But then you surface to take a breath and it hurts. It doesn't, somehow, underwater but then you come up and for some reason that's when it hurts and everything suddenly feels too loud and too bright and too cold or too hot and for most people, I guess, the ones who didn't spend their entire childhoods underwater, they adjust. But it feels like... I suppose I've spent so long under at this point that my body's forgotten how to adjust. I'm just stuck there, all the time. Which means it still hurts to breathe pretty much all the time but especially in places like that where there's more people and noise and... I can't do it, Nicole," she whispered. "I've tried everything. I want to adjust. I want to get used to it so I can enjoy things that are too loud or too quiet or too bright or too dim like humans can, but I don't think I'm ever going to get there. I'm..." slowly, she looked towards them. "Does that make sense? Does that—"

"Perfect sense," Nico nodded. "I'm sorry. That sounds awful."

She smiled slightly. "It's not umm... I do like some of it," she said, scooting a bit closer to them. "The human stuff. But sometimes—most of the times—it's just so, so much."

Nico swallowed. "You're not... you knew that already, didn't you?" They realized. "The first time we met. You knew... that's why you needed me to come? Because it might be too overwhelming to try and get the cloak back yourself? You weren't just trying to inconvenience me because you were in a mood, or whatever?"

"I... yeah," she admitted. "I'm still so, so sorry. I never should have... I never would have..."

"Okay," they nodded. "I know." Then, they kept nodded. "Alright," they decided, pushing themself back up. "Okay. I'll come."

"I... what?" Mathilda scrambled to follow them to the corner housing their supplies. Nico retrieved the coin purse they'd been storing their profits in and sat back down on the bed.

"It must be cheaper, right?" They started counting it out. "Going to Kovienne? Obviously we'll have to make more there to get me back home, but—"

"Nicole, I didn't—"

"It'd be smarter to go there first, right? Just so we wouldn't have to keep worrying about someone else buying it. Then—"

"No!" Mathilda jumped up.

They frowned.

"You can't... I wasn't trying to get you to do that! I can't— that's not fair! This already wasn't fair! I can't ask you to do that!"

"I know," Nico nodded. "You didn't ask. It's okay."

"No, it's... you're supposed to go home! You're supposed to be happy."

They sighed. "I won't be though, alright? Unless I know you're okay again, back in the skin you're supposed to be in, I'll have to spend the rest of my life worrying. So just... it'll add what? A day or two to my trip? I've come this far; I might as well see it through."

Mathilda's eyes welled. "I'm so, so sorry," she whispered.

"Don't do that," they reminded her. "Nothing to apologize for."

She shook her head. "This isn't your mess. You were right, I was just too irresponsible to keep track of it. This isn't—"

"You are absolutely my mess, Mathilda," they told her. "You know, in the nicest way possible."

She smiled a bit, tears still streaming down her face. "Tillie's fine."

They laughed. They couldn't help it. "Okay, yes. Of course. Tillie, then."

Her jaw dropped. She kicked her feet back and forth against the bed, grinning ear to ear. "I mostly just say that out of habit," she admitted. "You didn't have to—"

"I know you do," they stopped her. "That's why I didn't switch earlier," they smiled sheepishly. "I'm umm... I'm pretty sure I've been tuning it out for a while now. Oops. Sorry. Tillie."

She kicked her feet even faster. "No one's ever actually called me that."

Nico laughed. "Yes. I remember. It suits you, though. As long as you think it does."

"I do." She nodded. "Keep using it."

"Okay," they agreed. "I guess um... you might as well switch over to Nico too then, right? If we're going to be spending more time together."

Her eyes twinkled. "The name that's just for people you like."

"Yes, Tillie," they sighed.

"Because you like me," she poked their arm. "So much that you're following me all the way to Kovienne."

Nico rolled their eyes. "See, this is exactly why I wasn't going to tell you."

Tillie laughed. "Can I say it?" She asked.

"I literally just said you could."

She bounced to her feet. "Nico, Nico, Nico, Nico, Nico," she hopped around the room.

150

They groaned, flopping back onto the bed.

"Nico, Nico, Nico, Nico, Nico!" Tillie began to sing. Eventually, she fell down beside them. Rolled over to face them.

"I like you too," she said. "Just so you know."

Nico blushed. "Well, duh."

And they weren't under any blankets but finally, they felt warm.

Chapter 34

Nico was nervous for their first shot at running their own magic show. They wouldn't tell this to anyone, of course (that would have been incredibly embarrassing) but Tillie, maybe, had gotten used to them enough to not need to be told.

"You'll be great," she insisted as they set up. "Perfect. Better than me."

"Liar."

"Well... okay, maybe," she admitted.

They snorted.

"But you'll be really, really good, okay?" She promised. "I just have more practice. You're going to be way better at the showmanship part though. They'll love you."

They did not love them. Not at first. Their tricks were a little more repetitive. A little less mind-boggling. But after several hours of basic card tricks and minor manufactured illusions, they'd made almost as much as Tillie normally did. They considered that a win. Tillie hadn't been able to stay for the whole show, but she jumped up and down in a rapid applause when they went to find her by the beach.

"That was amazing!"

Nico rolled their eyes. "You didn't see the end. I might have completely flopped."

"Nope," she shook her head. "You didn't. I know it."

What could they possibly do but blush at that? "Okay. Maybe it was mostly fine."

"Yay!" Tillie clapped again. "We should celebrate! We should get ice cream or cake or—" She froze. "Sorry. Bad idea. We're saving money. I shouldn't have..."

But Nico had just done an entire magic show when they hadn't known a thing about fake magic a week ago. They didn't particularly feel like being frugal. "We could make a tiny one ourselves?" They suggested. "They're pretty basic, before all the decorations and stuff. We have most of the ingredients anyway and they have mixing bowls and stuff in the communal kitchen. We shouldn't do it all the time, but once won't set us back much. Totally up to you, though. We're going after your thing first."

Tillie considered. "I... yes. You deserve it. We should celebrate." She glanced towards the water. "Does it still count as celebrating?" She checked. "If you make the cake yourself? I'm fine with spending more to—"

"We can do it together," Nico shrugged, already heading back up the beach. "Then it's not technically doing it myself. It'll be fun. I love baking with people."

Tillie was no longer beside them.

"Tillie?" They turned back. "You still in?"

She sucked on her lip. "I'm umm... I don't know if you remember, but I don't exactly have a great baking track record."

They rolled their eyes. "That's just because I have a shit teaching track record. I'll be better this time. I promise."

"I don't want to waste our supplies. I'd... I'll find a way to mess it up. I'll—"

"Tillie," they grabbed her hand, briefly pressing their forehead to hers. "You won't. I'm the one in charge so if something does go wrong, it's on me, okay? But nothing will."

She stared at the sand.

"Trust me?" They tried. "Please."

Tillie smiled. "I... okay," she said. "Of course. Always."

They found the communal kitchen relatively empty when they got there, so Nico got to work filling a counter with the bits of ingredients that they'd acquired over the week. They had to step out to grab baking powder, but they'd already had pretty much everything else.

"We'll have to skip vanilla," they regretfully informed Tillie. "And icing it. Which might make it a little more bland, but it'll still technically be a cake, right?"

She nodded her assent, so they got to work.

"Okay," they pulled over a bowl. "We're going to mix the dry and wet stuff separately first. You do that for a lot of baked stuff."

"Oh," Tillie said. "Why?"

"I... don't know," Nico realized. "There's probably a reason, I've just never really thought about it. We'll have to figure it out later, maybe. Here." They handed her the flour and told her how much to measure out, watching her carefully add it to the bowl.

"I don't know if—" Tillie backed away from the counter once she'd finished that first step.

"You're doing great, Tillie," they lightly nudged her back into place. "I don't particularly feel like eating a disgusting cake either, okay? I promise I'll tell you if you're about to mess up."

And she didn't. They went step by step, ingredient by ingredient until it was done. The only thing that gave them issues were the eggs—Nico absentmindedly just said "crack them and put them in" which led to eggs shells swimming amongst of the other wet ingredients—but they'd just fished out the shells, modeled how to do it properly, and kept going. Nico made a point of trying to get Tillie to do as much of it on her own as possible. It felt important. If they'd been part of convincing her that she would be terrible at this, then they had to also help her prove that she wasn't.

Even if that meant a potentially burnt cake.

"Okay," Nico smiled once they'd put it in the oven. "I actually need to go buy a few things, if you wouldn't mind watching it? Just put on gloves and take it out to cool once the top's raised and browned, okay?"

Tillie frowned. "That... didn't go so well. Last time."

"Because I didn't properly tell you what to do," they insisted. "I did, this time. Or... I hope I did. That made sense, right? You don't have any questions?"

She considered. "Brown as in..."

"Right. Light brown. Like sand." They hesitated. "I don't have to go," they offered. "if it'll freak you out. But you've seriously got this, okay? I don't think I need to stay."

Tillie thought about it. "Could you... stop being so mentally supportive, okay? Convince yourself that it's horribly, irreparably burnt so you won't be upset if you get back and it is."

They laughed. "Deal."

Nico went back out to the market. And then stayed in the market long after their shopping was done, just so she'd be able to do it entirely on her own. When they returned though, the kitchen was empty.

Nico rushed back to the hostel with their heart in their throat.

And found Tillie sitting on the floor, humming to herself as she finished decorating a perfectly-unburnt cake.

They froze in the doorway. "What the fuck," they whispered.

"Oh!" She spun around. "Hello!"

"How did... where did..."

"Don't just stand there with the door open!" Tillie hissed, moving around them to pull it closed. She clicked the lock shut. "People might see!"

Nico blinked. "You stole cake decorations," they realized.

Tillie looked away, cheeks turning pink. "Only the tiniest most unnoticeable bits and only from vendors who seemed particularly rude so it's barely... it hardly even count, really."

They laughed. "Tillie!"

"We're celebrating!" She stomped her foot to accentuate the point. "You deserve an actual celebratory cake!"

They grinned. "Thank you. Very heroic thievery."

Tillie added the final few sprinkles before plating two pieces and joining them on the bed.

"Mmm," Nico hummed, taking a bite. "Holy shit, it's been so long since I've had anything sugary."

Tillie laughed, though she clearly shared the sentiment. Within minutes, the entire cake was devoured.

"Nico," she said. Icing under her nose. Eyes twinkling.

Their heart pounded. "Tillie."

"I made an entire cake."

They smiled. "I know. Very cool."

Her expression flickered. "It's not really though, is it? Most people can—"

"Tillie," they put their hand over hers. "It was your first time doing it and you crushed it. Very cool. Extremely exciting."

She grinned, biting her lip. "Yeah. It....yeah." She nodded towards the bag. "What'd you get?"

"Oh," Nico reached into it, suddenly inexplicably embarrassed. "Just... ideas? You don't have to use them, if you wouldn't want to. They were super cheap so it absolutely wasn't a loss." They pulled out the first item: a flimsy black piece of plastic. "I figured sunglasses might help?" They explained. "With the whole 'world being too bright above water' thing. But the guy said the normal ones wouldn't work with actual glasses so gave me this to layer over them instead. They're supposed to be temporary but, you know. Don't really have the budget for new prescription ones right now. And these," they pulled out the next item. "Are earmuffs? I don't know if you've been anywhere cold in your land-form but people normally wear them to keep their ears warm there. I figured it might also block out a bit of sound though? We could go earplugs too, but I figured those might be too quiet." They'd picked a fuzzy, dark-green pair. If they were going to suggest she cover her eyes, they'd need another reminder of them.

Tillie hesitated. "People don't wear them though, when it's not cold. Or these, on top of their normal glasses. I'd.... it'd make me look ridiculous, wouldn't it?"

"No," they said. "And if they'd genuinely make it easier for you to be in this skin, then anyone who thinks there's anything ridiculous about them is just a stupid asshole."

She slipped the plastic over her glasses and one end of the earmuffs into her pocket. "Thank you," she smiled. "For thinking about me. You... that was really sweet."

Nico looked back into the bag even though there was only one item left. They needed to conceal their expression.

"Look!" They pulled out a new, beige binder, just to change the topic. "I'm extra thinking about you, actually. Because now I can stop wearing the same disgusting sweaty, sea-watery one all the time and actually be tolerable to be around."

Tillie scrunched up her nose. "You're not that bad," she lied. "You know, when you're far enough away."

They laughed.

Tillie swung her legs. "Is that umm... there's spellwork people use for that, right? Instead of having to wear one all the time? Not that you'd have to, obviously, but why haven't you..."

They sighed. "There is and I've looked into it, but it's ridiculously expensive because everyone who knows enough complex spellwork to offer permanent body transformations like that is also smart enough to know that people would pay ridiculous amounts of money for it."

"Oh," Tillie studied her fingers. "Was that why... on the boat you had..."

"No." They stopped her. "I wasn't even going to use that, okay? And again. Absolutely not your fault that I lost it. I just..." They sighed. "It was from this friend I have, right? And he'd also... I'm not even one hundred percent sure if I'd want my boobs gone or if I just don't want any kind of gendered chest. Maybe I just hate them because they're the thing I got stuck with and if I got rid of them, I'd instantly be dysphoric in the other direction and want them back. I don't know. But this friend of mine does know and he has for a while and he could definitely afford to do it but he can't... his parents don't know he's a boy? They're the ones with all the money, technically. He's not. And if they knew he was a boy they might stop giving him money so even if I did want to make a chance I couldn't..." Nico sighed. "It would be way too much for me to pay for myself and I know the second I started saving up he'd try to help, but there's no way I could ever let him do that, right? Because then me getting to look the way I might want to comes at the cost of him looking the way he's supposed to and I couldn't... I can't put him in a position where he thinks I need his money because that's too close to letting him think I need him to keep presenting the way his parents want him to, which is bullshit. It's just... that wouldn't be an option for me. Right now. But it's absolutely not a money thing so don't you dare try to feel guilty about it."

Tillie nodded. "You're a good friend."

They rolled their eyes. "Barely. He is too, though. A really good one. He'll just never admit it." They rolled their shoulders. "That's why I freaked out at you about money, okay? Not because I was actually mad or because it was at all your fault, I just... I'd taken some from him and I fucking hate that I won't be able to give it back. I hate that me getting back home and admitting that what kept me away for so long was money-based means that he's probably going to feel extra pressured to keep pretending to be a girl for his parents."

Tillie considered. "You could lie?" She suggested. "Say my cloak wasn't actually there and that I was a terribly, horribly, overbearing duel-challenger who pulled you all over the continent with me until we found it?"

They wondered if she knew that that probably wouldn't entirely be a lie after all. With each passing day, Nico became less and less convinced that her sealskin would be waiting for them in Kovienne.

"We could... we'll do more shows," Tillie decided. "In Kovienne. After we have my cloak so no one else takes it, obviously. If you go home with extra money, he'd have no reason to suspect you ever ran out."

They frowned. "We?"

She rolled her eyes. "You're going on a whole extra ferry ride for me, Nico. Obviously, I'd stay on land a bit longer if it made things easier for you."

"You don't have to—"

She poked their shoulder. "Hypocrite!"

Nico grinned. "Alright." They agreed. "Thank you. It's a plan, then."

Chapter 35

Nico only got through two performances before encountering every busker's biggest rival: a slightly inebriated heckler.

"It's fake!" He slurred when Nico made their deck of cards disappear beneath a cloth. "It's in her sleeve!" (which it was, but that was hardly the point).

They did their best to ignore him. They really did.

"That's fake too!" He laughed when they pulled a coin from mid air. "It was between her fingers!"

The audience was on their side. A few adults in his area tried to shush him. All Nico had to do was keep going.

"Booo," he crowed. "She's a fraud! It's all—"

They snapped. They rounded their table to confront him and the crowd parted to let them. "If you're sure it's fake, then—"

But the man just smiled, pointing a long, boney finger towards where they'd left their cane resting against their table. "Guess that was fake too then, huh?"

And they saw red. They knew he was just trying to aggravate them, but they saw red anyway. "Fuck you," they hissed, keeping their volume down to try and preserve their family-friendly image. But that wasn't enough. That didn't make them feel better. "Fuck you!" They screamed. "No shit it's fake, it's a fucking magic show! If it was real there wouldn't be a point, idiot! Get out before—" Nico froze. The audience was no longer on their side, they were spreading out and rushing away. They'd fucked up. Because of course they had.

"Show's over," Nico returned to the booth, grabbed their cane, and left as quickly as they could. Tillie could gather their props, if she wanted to. Clearly putting them in charge of the table had been a stupid idea. Without looking back and as quickly as their leg could handle, Nico ran away. Again.

"Hey!" Tillie sprinted after them. It wasn't fair, how hard it always was for Nico to run away from people.

"I already left," they muttered. "You don't have to worry about me cussing out our revenue source anymore. Go home, Mathilda."

She frowned, sliding in front of them. "I'm not... I'm worried about you. Not—"

Nico rolled their eyes. "Don't be. I'm not you, I don't need constant fucking comforting."

Tillie's brow creased. "You're upset," she realized. "This is you... you're upset."

"I'm fine!" They made themself laugh. "Gods, Mathilda! Just because you're pathetic enough to break down after every fucking—"

She caught their hands. You're upset," she repeated. "Tell me... how do I help? Tell me..."

"I don't need your help!" They exclaimed. "How the fuck would you even... you are the last person anyone would ever want in a crisis! You're—"

She wrapped a hand around the back of their neck and pulled them closer, leaning down to press her forehead against theirs.

Nico's breath caught, for a moment. Then, it came out a little less frantic.

"Tell me what you need right now."

They scoffed. "I need him to fucking pay! I need you to stop fucking following me around everywhere like some pathetic little—"

"Okay!" All at once, Tillie's skin was no longer on theirs.

Nico blinked against the sudden cold.

"You go home, I'll go clean up."

They glared. "I said—"

"And *I* said you need to go home right now before you cuss out more of our extremely child-heavy audience." She patted their shoulder. "Go home. I've got this. Trust me, okay?"

"I literally just said you—" they tried to yell, just to be yelling.

"Right," Tillie stopped them. "Right well then go home because you deserve a break, okay? If I fuck things up even more, that's on me."

They wanted to fight. Her or the man or *something*. But suddenly, all at once, they realized that they were exhausted. Their every bone felt heavy. "Fine," Nico pulled away. "Whatever. This shouldn't be my problem anyway."

By the time they got back to the hostel, Nico's anger was no longer solid enough to carry them. It always happened like this, whisps of smokes they had no business ever attending too that they'd fan into flames just for the sake of doing something. An all-encompassing inferno that ate quickly and desperately and brutally and then all at once, ate up all the oxygen and left them alone, gasping in the cold.

It had been a stupid comment. It had been a stupid comment in a sea of stupid comments that they should have gotten used to years ago, but they'd let it push them to self-destruction anyway.

They shoved the door to their room open with their shoulder and clicked their cane away. Then, in the cool of their own isolation, they tried to summon the anger back.

"Fuck!" They yelled. But it was a feeble thing. Shaking and questioning and as lame as their leg.

"Fuck!" They tried again, slamming their fist into the pillow.

Nothing happened. Nothing sparked. Nico rolled onto their back, stared at the ceiling, and waited for their chest to reinflate.

They felt like shit. They'd freaked out at her again and now they felt like shit about it and yet they already knew—as they lay there gasping for air—that the next time they got upset they'd do the exact same thing.

How fucked was that? How much of a fuck up could one person possibly be?

The worst part was, they didn't even have to worry about her not coming back. Tillie had their money. It had been her job to collect it, while they performed. Tillie had everything they'd saved up and Tillie was the one that was actually talented enough to get to Kovienne. Tillie could have been gone in a matter of days if she decided she wanted to be and the fear of being left was woven into every overgrown purple strand of Nico's hair, but they didn't consider for even a second that she was gone. Because she was Tillie and she was nice and sweet and good and open. The kind of person brave enough to hand out tears and smiles in equal measure. And a little bit broken too, maybe. By them or by someone before them or probably both. So, Tillie would come back no matter how awful they were to her because she was Tillie and Nico would keep fucking up again and again even though they knew that because they were Nico, and they would both never get to escape.

They stared at the ceiling. They tried to breathe without screaming. And then, eventually, the door opened.

"I am so, so sorry," Nico threw their legs over the edge of the bed, propelling themself upright.

Tillie looked like Tillie. Hair blonde and wild and eyes big and distorted and clothes wrinkled from spending too long in the absence of an iron. They had screamed at her for doing nothing but worrying about them and yet here she was: still Tillie.

She frowned. "You didn't do anything—"

"Tillie," they stopped her. "I did. We both know I did. I'm sorry."

"Oh," she said. "That's alright, then. We're fine."

"No," Nico protested. "We shouldn't... we don't have to be. We shouldn't—"

Tillie rolled her eyes. "We were supposed to stop each other from apologizing, remember? That's—"

Nonymous

"That's only a thing with you," they argued. "Because you do it way too much, for someone who rarely ever actually fucks up. Not..." Nico sighed. "I should probably do it a lot more, honestly."

Tillie frowned, sitting down beside them. She watched their hands. "I'm not mad," she said quietly.

They shook their head. "You should be. You can't just let me hurt you, Tillie. I don't want to be able to do that."

"You didn't hurt me, though."

"I didn't mean physically. I—"

"I know." She nodded. "You didn't. I'm seriously fine."

"You don't have to..." They sighed. "I was trying to, you know that, right? I got my feeling hurt and I wanted to hurt the world back so I..." they didn't know how to explain it. That at some point, the line between Tillie and the entire world had become too blurred for them to navigate. "I didn't mean any of it, okay?" They promised. "I just knew it was what was mostly likely to work. Which I know is extra fucked up, but—"

She pressed their knee. Lightly. Obviously. "I don't know if you've noticed, Nico, but it's actually incredibly easy to tell when I'm upset, okay? I don't think I've ever once been good at hiding it. Did I look upset?"

They frowned, remembering. Her eyes shaded and buggy and too close and incredibly, obviously clear. "I'm... no."

"Then I wasn't." She smiled. "I think... I would have been, I suppose. If you'd said any of that a while ago. But... you told me you do that, right? When you're upset? So I knew you were upset and that obviously took precedent over anything else."

They shook their head. "I shouldn't have lashed out like that, Tillie."

"You shouldn't have," she nodded. "I'd prefer if you didn't, obviously, but I promise you did not hurt me, okay? I think... that's why it was so easy to tell that you were just upset. Because it was obvious that you were lying. Because I know... you've decided that I'm fairly tolerable, I think. Unless I've seriously misread that. So I didn't have to even consider that you meant any of it because I know you think I'm..."

They squeezed her fingers. "I think you're fucking awesome, actually."

She blushed. "Well... yes. That."

They laughed, leaning against her.

She stiffened. Because they still weren't okay, not really. Tillie was just too nice to admit it.

"I'm still really, really sorry," Nico whispered. "I hate... I don't know why I do that. You don't deserve that."

Tillie shrugged. "I'm way too emotional all the time. It's—"

"This is different."

She chewed on her lip. "You still haven't seen me mad," her voice shook a little "I don't... could we drop it? Please?"

Nico swallowed. "Okay. But—"

"Excellent!" Tillie clapped her hands.

They sighed and actually dropped it.

"Now." She twisted her torso to face them better. "Ask me what I got."

Nico failed to smother a laugh. "What did you get?"

Tillie dug her hand into her pocket then presented her fist to them. "Ta-da!" She uncurled her fingers.

And revealed three silver coins.

Nico stared. "You kept the booth running by yourself?"

She blushed. "Oh, no. Absolutely not. That would've been incredibly too much attention, even without the heckler. I umm... took it."

Their eyebrows shot up. "From who!"

"The heckler!" She sounded slightly exasperated, like it should have been obvious. "You told me you wanted him to pay!"

They threw a hand over their dropped jaw, but that didn't stop laughter from escaping. "Tillie!" They exclaimed. "I didn't mean you actually had to rob the guy!"

"Well obviously I knew that," she grumbled, rolling her eyes. "But he..." she looked around. "He made you sad. So he really ought to have paid, right? It was just... easiest to do that literally."

They fully gave into their laughter. "You're amazing," they smiled, shaking their head. "I think I'm actually obsessed with you."

"Oh," Tillie said. "I... thank you? I think? Me too. With you, I mean. Anyway I..." she cleared her throat. "Would it be smart to keep doing that? The umm..."

"The stealing?"

Tillie's eyes widened. "The... profitable sleight of hand! I just..." she tapped her fingers together. "We need to get to Kovienne quickly, right? It alright might have gotten sold to someone else. We need to—"

"Tillie," they stopped her. "It'll be there, okay? Don't worry about it."

"Right," she lied, still tapping away. "Of course."

"But," they added. "Getting there a bit faster couldn't possibly hurt."

Tillie grinned. "Here's what I'm thinking."

Chapter 36

Tillie was morally above robbing innocent strangers.

Nico absolutely wasn't, but that didn't particularly matter since they wouldn't be the one doing the stealing. They might have been getting better at magic, but not the kind that would let them lift coins directly from someone else's purse without them even knowing that they'd touched them. If Tillie was going to rob people for them, there had to be rules.

1) Never too much from one target
2) Never a large enough portion of whatever was in someone's purse that they'd miss it
3) Only ever from assholes.

Tillie was morally above robbing innocent strangers but, evidently, she possessed no such qualms when it came to less than innocent ones. So, Nico started providing more opportunities for people to show their true colours.

Tillie could be among crowds for a lot longer than she was alright standing in front of them for (especially with her glasses-shade and earmuffs on), so Nico would run the show while she slinked round in the audience, waiting for targets. Sometimes, it was easy. Someone would boo or yell out something rude and Nico would have to pinch themself under the table to stop from beaming at it, knowing that they'd be adding more to their savings momentarily. Or someone would figure out a trick and loudly explain it to the entire audience and then moments later, there'd be long, thin, unseen fingers dipping into their pockets. Tillie almost always took more from the hits who ruined tricks than the ones who overtly booed Nico. They were trying not to take that too personally. Apparently, there was no bigger crime to her than disrespecting the sanctity of a magic trick.

Sometimes though, during particularly pleasant shows, Nico would make a mistake. Let the card in their sleeve fall to the ground. Twist their wrist just enough that people could catch a flash of fabric. Rude assholes always got a lot bolder once they'd decided that they were no longer being tricked.

Once—for an especially insufferable heckler—Nico even got cocky with it.

"For this next trick," they announced once they caught sight of Tillie's now familiar frame sliding in behind him. "I'll need the entire audience to close their eyes and count to ten, please!"

They watched her hand dart in and out of his purse and had to press a fist to their mouth to keep from laughing. Tillie added the coins to her own bag then flashed them a big, toothy grin and a quick thumbs-up before bouncing back off into the crowd.

And just like that, Nico decided that that would become a regular part of their routine, just to buy them more chances to watch her smile like that.

It only took two days of Tillie being lured into ethical robbery for Nico to realize that they officially had enough for one ferry pass.

It wasn't awful of them not to tell her. She could have counted it out herself. Maybe she had, already. But still, each time she mentioned something about hoping her cloak would be there, guilt threatened to choke them.

It would have been smarter, to go on their own. Tillie might not have been able to, but Nico could have easily. Leave her here for a bit, grab the cloak, and then work odd jobs on their own until they could get back. It would have been safer.

But they didn't know exactly what selkie skins looked like (there was a library downtown) and they didn't know if Tillie would be fine on her own (she was both the more functional and profitable of the both of them) and they didn't want to leave her. They didn't want to rush her leaving them.

Every night, after Tillie was already softly snoring, they'd promise their conscious that they'd tell her when they woke up.

Every morning, the thing in their belly would slither up their throat and smother any chance of confessing.

They were getting close now, anyway. Another few shows, another few assholes, and then they'd be able to bring her to Kovienne themself. They'd be together, until she got her cloak back and disappeared into the ocean for another seven years.

That made it worse, somehow. That they were potentially destroying her life just to buy themself a few more days.

But it would be there. If it hadn't been bought yet, no one was going to buy it these next few days. It would be there.

And if it wasn't, they could always pretend that it wasn't their fault.

So, they ran their shows. She robbed their adversaries. And afterwards, they'd go home and laugh together about any uniquely cocky hits or go to the communal kitchen and make dinner together or just be together: somewhere doing something. Until, after a week, it became easy and comfortable and routine and Nico started to get dangerously addicted to it.

And then Tillie got caught.

Chapter 37

It was shaping up to be a fairly normal—if not slightly anticlimactic—show. Nico had their routine down to an art by that point so even the rowdiest of audience members no longer phased them (unless they decided to act phased, of course) so when a more rambunctious group started watching from near the edge of the crowd, they didn't spare them anything more than a quick glance before continuing with their current card trick. If anything, hopefully, Tillie would decide that they were being a bit too loud and get them some extra money.

They decided to test it. They were so close to having enough to get two tickets to Kovienne. If they played their (literal) cards right this one performance, then they wouldn't have to keep feeling guilty for not insisting on going on their own.

"Could I get a volunteer, please?" They asked.

None of the louder group raised their hand. Plenty of other onlookers did.

"Umm... you!" They pretended to scan the crowd before pointing in their general direction. "One of you lot! If you're going to insist on being so loud, you might as well be a part of the act, right?"

There was a low, excited "oooooh," from the audience. For a moment no one moved and they were worried that their bait had been useless, but then an orc peeled off from the group. And Nico got even more excited.

He was old, but not too old. Probably somewhere in his forties. He had long, curly pink hair, a gold chain around his neck, and an actual cape on. Red. With a gold trim, of course. He looked like money. Hopefully, that meant that his friends had a lot too. And that they were about to do something stupid.

"How can I be of service?" He curtsied a little once he reached them.

Nico kept their smile frozen in place. Years of retail had trained them for exactly this. "Pick a card," they fanned on their deck. A new, shiny, slightly larger than normal one. Mathilda was incredibly attached to hers, but it had a lot less audience appeal.

The man started to reach for one but Nico pulled back, tutting loudly. "Bad choice. Pick another one."

His group snickered, but the man seemed entirely nonplussed. He picked another card and presented it to Nico face down. "This good enough for you?"

They nodded. "Much better."

They continued on with the trick now that they were certain they'd captured his group's attention, getting him to show the card to the audience before placing it back in the deck. This time though, while they pretended to shuffle, they made sure that their back was in full view of the rest of his group.

"Aye!" One of them yelled. It didn't matter which, after all. Nico was already mentally planning their next scheme. "They're cheating!"

They tried their best to look sheepish, sent the man back into the audience, and moved onto their next trick. And then all at once, the group in the corner got even louder.

Nico sighed dramatically for the audience's sake before turning to them. "What's—" They froze. The group suddenly seemed a lot more sober. Their shouting was a lot more refined. And in the middle of their circle—and all of that shouting—was a single selkie, caught in the act.

Shit.

"Thief!" Someone was yelling. "Thief!"

Nico was pretty sure that there was no attention on them anymore, but they still kept their smile locked in place. They had years of training at it, after all.

Even if someone was grabbing Tillie by the wrist. Even if Tillie was already shaking and crying and terrified.

Someone ran to get an officer. They had no idea how they were supposed to stop someone from getting an officer. They tried their best to calm the crowd back down, but they had no idea what they were supposed to do here at all.

And then, once she was already in cuffs—still shaking and crying and terrified—they did.

"Aye!" They quickly rounded their booth. "Is that my fucking purse?"

Attention was back on them. That was good. Surely someone had seen them with it earlier. They'd figure out how to get Tillie out of wherever they were taking her later but as of right now, all they could do was assure that they wouldn't lose all of the money they'd gotten so far.

"Holy shit!" They reached her. "It is! You were going to what, ruin my show and steal my livelihood?"

Tillie didn't challenge them. But then, it didn't seem like Tillie wouldn't been able to challenge anyone, in that moment. She was staring at her feet, rocking from head to toe and tapping her side frantically. They couldn't tell if she had any idea what was going on around her at all. Still, just in case, as they raised the purse over her head to reclaim it, they allowed themself one quick, fleeting, squeeze of her shoulder.

They were going to fix this. They were going to fix this and everything was going to be alright. "If anyone's missing anything," they called out to the crowd to try and improve their own credibility. "Please, let me know. Show's over for the day."

Nico returned to their booth. They packed up quickly, to keep themself from watching her get dragged away. They went home quickly, to keep everyone else from watching them fall apart.

This was their fault. Their idea in the first place and their mark and their intentional attempt to provoke someone. This was on them. And they were going to fix it.

Chapter 38

It only took them a couple of hours to track down the residence of the group from the market—under the guise of getting them some more of their money back, of course—but when they knocked on the door to the hotel room that they'd been directed to, it was empty.

So, Nico sat down in the hall and waited. And then waited some more. And then, finally, hours later, the volunteer from the show appeared at the end of the hall.

Nico clicked out their cane, quickly rising to their feet.

The orc looked confused for half a second, but quickly shifted into false warmth. "Magician person!" He held out his arms in greeting. "What brings you to my humble abode?"

"I have more of your money," they said. "If you'd be kind enough to invite me in so we can figure it out."

He frowned. "I don't recall losing any more, actually. It must all be accounted for."

"I have more of your money," they repeated. "So I think you'd better let me in."

The orc's eyebrow quirked up, but he complied. "Take a seat," he gestured to his coffee table. "I'll go put on tea."

Nico was mentally trying to figure out how to bribe him, but when he returned, the orc took control of the conversation.

"What does Tobias want this time?" He demanded.

Nico blinked. "I... what?"

"He's hiring kids now? That's truly beneath him. Tell him that for me, will you? Absolutely positively beneath him. Disabled ones at that! There are easier ways to—"

Nico saw red. They had no clue who this Tobias was, but they did know that they were in the process of being insulted. "I'm not a kid," they said.

The man frowned. "How old are you?"

"Nineteen."

"Ah," he nodded. "A child."

"I'm not—" It wasn't the point. They should have just moved on. Nico was incredibly bad at knowing when to just move on. "And I don't know who this Tobias is, but he would have been lucky to hire me. Just because I'm disabled doesn't mean I'm—"

The corner of the orc's lips curved up. "Arm," he said. Nico frowned. "What?"

"Arm, small little magician child." He waved his left sleeve. His incredibly hollow left sleeve. Then, he pulled it up to reveal the stump at the end of his elbow.

"Okay" Nico said. "Well.... still a dick thing to say."

They were supposed to bribe this man. They were supposed to give this man whatever he wanted, get him to drop the charges against Tillie, and then leave. And here they were cussing him out.

The man, though, laughed. Then, he sighed. "You're not with Tobias then?" He squinted at them. "Truly?"

They shook their head.

"Ah," the man sighed. "Well that really is too bad then. You are with that little thief from the market though, correct?"

Nico nodded, though a little embarrassed that he'd already known. At least this way, they wouldn't have to spell it out for him.

"Well then, my sincerest apologies for getting your friend arrested," he said. "I really did think Tobias had sent her."

"Who is Tobias!" Their patience was wearing thin. Tillie would have been better at this. Probably. Maybe. Maybe they would have actually both made terrible bribers.

The man waved them off. "Unimportant. I, though, am Radclyffe. You may call me Captain Radclyffe, if it helps you feel fancier. I've found feeling fancier is almost always a good thing."

They absolutely would not be doing that. "Nicole," they mumbled. Then processed the 'Captain' and cape and (if they were being honest with themself) abnormal intact limb count, and realized. "You're a pirate."

He laughed. "Gods, you really don't work for Tobias."

"And neither did my friend," they reminded him. "So you should just drop the charges. Pirate's code and all that."

Radclyffe leaned back in his chair. "And how do I know you wouldn't instantly go rob more people?"

"You don't. And you don't care. You're a pirate."

He put a hand to his chest. "I'll have you know I care very deeply about the citizens of..." he frowned. "where are we again?"

"Harper."

"Harper!" He finished.

"I'll pay you," Nico deadpanned.

"Not good enough. I'm a pirate captain. I'm already rich."

"What do you want then?"

He considered. "What's your sob story?"

"Excuse me?"

"Your sob story. Every thief's got one, or at least a fake one. Tell me yours."

So, they did. Without any reference to selkies or duels, obviously. Telling a pirate they were on a quest for a magical object would have just been asking for disaster. Nico and Tillie were two people heading on a trip home to Kovienne who had gotten stranded on a deserted island and then re-stranded on a less deserted one after surviving a siren attack. And had been forced to rob their way back home even though it was absolutely against both of their moral codes, of course.

"So?" They prompted. "Charges? Dropping? Quickly, preferably?" They'd asked around and it seemed like Harper didn't have a huge jailhouse. They just used it to hold people temporarily before shipping them off to somewhere where a full-scale prison would have been less of an eye-sore and Nico knew that it would probably be exceptionally more difficult to try and retrieve Tillie once they started moving her around.

Radclyffe tapped his chin, considering. "Your partner's good at it," he finally said. "Pick-pocketing. That could be helpful on a pirate crew."

They flinched. "Tillie's not a pirate. Or my partner," they realized. "We're just—"

Radclyffe's eyes gleamed. "I meant business partners, of course. I would never assume someone offering to hand over their entire livelihoods for someone else could possibly be in a relationship with them. That'd be absurd."

Nico clenched their fists, feeling their face go red. "We really are just business partners."

"That's what I said," Radclyffe patronized them. "Anywho, how about I drop the charges, she joins my crew for ten days and helps with a few minor robberies—from a safe distance, of course. She is a child, after all—and then we drop you two off in Kovienne and call it even."

They hesitated. "You're going to Kovienne."

"In ten days, yes."

It was longer than they'd been counting on. Much longer. But it wasn't like they had many other options.

And Tillie would hate it, so there was also that.

"What about... I'd be coming too, right? You'd just what, let me catch a ride for free?"

"Of course not!" Radclyffe looked insulted. "I'd put you to work. I am a pirate, after all. Any pirating and or boating related skills?"

"I worked as a cook for an entire ship once," they said, which was technically true.

"Excellent," he held out his hand. "So that's a deal, then."

Nico sighed. They accepted the handshake. Maybe if Tillie really wasn't on board, they'd be able to scrounge up the last few coppers and leave Harper before the pirates came to collect.

"I'll get in touch with the jailhouse, then," Radclyffe said. "We leave the day after tomorrow. Have your *partner* be ready for then," he winked.

They got up and marched towards the door.

"Oh, and Nicole?" Radclyffe called. "I'll have a couple of my crew keep an eye on you too. You understand, of course. Can't have you fleeing on me."

"Right," they clenched their teeth. "Of course."

They were fucked.

Chapter 39

Tillie was going to be pissed.

And then she was going to be all quiet and apologetic about being pissed and Nico was going to have to feel like shit.

It had taken ages to even get her on board with robbing the occasional asshole, so Nico already knew that there was no way she'd be overjoyed about taking up piracy.

So maybe, they wanted to hold back on telling her for a bit.

Radclyffe had gone to drop the charges against her immediately after their conversation (Nico had followed him to double check. He was a pirate, after all), but Tillie still couldn't be officially released until the next morning.

They spent the night tossing and turning and worrying themself sick. Tillie was still so unused to existing in a human body that being out in public for more than an hour at a time freaked her out. They had no idea how she could have possibly been coping in a cell somewhere.

Nico was outside the jailhouse before the sun even finished rising the next morning. It was a tiny thing: cracking stone walls covered in moss and a brown, water damaged roof. They hoped it was a little bit better on the inside. The only thing left to do was wait, so they found a big enough stone to sit down on and did exactly that.

Nico hadn't bit their nails since they were a child, but they gnawed relentlessly as the minutes slowly pushed by.

And then, there she was. Blinking against the sunlight.

Nico sprung to their feet. "Tillie." They rushed to her.

The blinking didn't stop. She stumbled forward.

"Here, I..." they dug around in their pocket, pulling out a new glasses-cover. "I got you a new one."

They handed it to her. She balanced it over the ridge of her nose. She didn't say anything.

Nico's heart pounded. "Here, let's—"

They reached out to touch her and she pulled away. Even though she didn't even know about the deal yet. Nico frowned, confused. And then kept frowning because they no longer were. They'd been the one to first suggest pickpocketing. They'd been the one who'd kept pushing their luck just a little too far.

And she was the one who'd spent almost a full day in a cell because of that.

They squeezed their medallion. Tightened their grip on their cane until their fingers cramped. "Sorry," they said. "What can... are you okay? What can—"

Finally, she spoke. Just one word. Quiet and dry and croaking: "Home."

"Okay." Nico nodded. That, at least, was a thing that they could do for her here. "Alright. Let's get you home."

Tillie was clearly exhausted. They doubted she'd slept at all. She kept yawning and stumbling the entire way back to the hostel then lied down on her pile of floor-blankets before the door even finished closing.

"Take the bed, Tillie," they gently prompted. There was dust in her hair. She'd obviously already spent far too much time on floors. "It's like eight in the morning. Promise I won't be needing it any time soon."

She stumbled again on her way there, even though it was only a few steps. Nico panicked, but didn't let themself touch her. They were too scared she'd pull away again.

"They gave you food, didn't they?" They asked. "They must have—shit, sorry. Stupid question. I can go—" They started to get up, then froze. She was holding their hand.

"Stay?" Tillie yawned.

Nico stared. "I... okay. Yeah. Of course."

They sat down on the edge of the bed. They unfurled their cane just so they could pull the floor blankets into arms'

179

reach without letting go of her. One-armed and awkwardly, they covered her up.

Tillie smiled, eyes already closed. Lightly, obviously. "Night," she whispered.

Nico quickly threw their free hand over their mouth. Like they'd just told her, it was eight am. "Good night, Tillie."

Chapter 40

Nico didn't know what time it was when Tillie woke up again, but they did know that by the time she did, their fingers had fully finished going numb. Or at least, they'd thought that they had.

When Tillie let go to push herself up, their fingers still inexplicably managed to feel just a little bit colder.

She smiled lazily, leaning against the headboard. "I didn't mean you actually had to stay the whole time," she said. "Just... until I fell asleep."

Nico blushed, jumping to their feet. They winced, only in part due to their leg. "Oh. Right. I can—"

"Well *now* I want you to stay," she rolled her eyes. "I missed you." She frowned. "Is that... that's ridiculous, right? It was only a day, I shouldn't have—"

"I missed you too," Nico promised, voice suddenly thick. "But," they forced themself to take a step away. "You actually do have to eat. I'll go grab something."

"Something fast?" She requested. "We should plan next steps, right? Don't want to waste the whole morning."

They swallowed. "Okay. Be back in a few."

They wasted money on brunch. They wouldn't really need it anymore, after all. They got toast, eggs, donuts, and orange wedges. They got theirs in a to-go bag and balanced Tillie's carefully on a tray. She still wasn't used to land foods yet and them mixing was normally too much.

"Hey," they made themself smile when they returned because Tillie was sitting up on the bed, smiling back at them. They'd have to tell her and ruin that, though. Soon. They handed her the tray.

Tillie frowned. "This is... I'm seriously fine, Nico," she insisted. "We almost have enough to get to Kovienne. We shouldn't be—" she froze. Their face must have changed a little bit too much. "Oh," she said. "We don't... I suppose you would have had to pay to get me out. That's..." she squared her shoulders. "That's okay, though. Fuck rules, we'll take as much as we can from whoever we can and then get out of here today before anyone notices."

Their breath caught. "Tillie," they whispered.

She shook her head. "I know it's not... exactly an upstanding move, morally, but every time we get close, something ruins it and I need... the longer we wait the bigger the chance I never get to go home. So we'll—"

"We can't, Tillie." There was suddenly a film in front of Nico's eyes. Everything looked blurry. Their cheeks felt wet. They couldn't have possibly been crying, though. That wouldn't have made sense. "I'm sorry," they whispered. "I'm... I had to make a deal," they explained. "With the people who caught you. I'm..."

"That's okay," she pressed their knee. "That's not your fault. I'm the one who messed up. I'm not... what was the deal?"

They told her. But Tillie didn't get angry about the piracy. She seemed fairly nonplussed about the whole thing, actually. It wasn't the activity that upset her, it was how long it would take.

"Ten days," She echoed.

"It'll be fine, though. We'll have more money to actually buy the cloak, that way. If—"

"It's not going to be there!" Tillie started swaying so rapidly that she had to put her tray down on the bed to keep herself from knocking it over.

"It could be," Nico pretended to believe. "It was honestly like, super ugly, so I bet—"

"Stop doing that!" Tillie screamed. She froze for half a second, staring at them. Then, the tapping and swaying started up again. "It's not your fault," she said. Because they had been crying. There was no denying it, anymore. "It's... fuck!" She screamed. "This isn't fair! This isn't—"

"I know," they tried to be her. Tried to make the fingers that pressed against her shoulder feather-light. They weren't her though, so she whirled around, smacking their arm away.

"Go away!" She screamed. "I need... get the fuck away from me!"

They frowned. "Tillie, it's okay. We'll—" They reached for her again, but she shoved at their arm. Then, she kept shoving at the air.

"Go away go away go away go away!" She chanted. "Leave me the fuck alone!"

Nico chewed at their lip, studying her. Her hands were moving so quickly that they blurred when Nico tried to track them. Her hair looked more wild this way, somehow. In constant motion while she swayed. Oscillating between stretching out behind her and flying past the sides of her face. And her face was red. So red. And her eyes were red. So red. "I don't want to leave you alone right now," they said carefully. "I think we should—"

"Go!" All at once, the tray of food was flying through the air. Tillie watched it crash into the wall. Nico watched her. They both froze in the silent aftermath of her destruction.

And then, Tillie started to sway again. "You can't be here," she insisted. "You can't... I can't... you can't..."

"Okay," Nico picked up their to-go bag. "But... I'm going to be right outside, okay? If you need me. When you're ready to put up with me again."

They weren't quite sure she heard them though. She was swaying and hitting and her eyes weren't focused on anything in particular. If she had heard them, she was pretending not to.

Quietly, lightly, Nico left. Quietly, lightly, they pulled the door shut behind them.

Chapter 41

It took almost an hour for the door to open again and when it did, Tillie was still ignoring them.

Nico jumped to their feet the moment they heard it start to squeak, but Tillie had been faster. She was already silently walking back to the bed. Or, what remained of the bed.

The blankets and sheets had been strewn in so many directions that it seemed impossible that they'd all started out in the same place. One pillow was entirely out of its case, the other half-escaped and presumably the source of all the feathers that now coated the room. There were props in various stages of brokenness in every single nook and cranny and the floor was littered with coins. And torn cards. The cheapest of their now destroyed act, but also the only thing to make Nico's stomach churn.

It looked like a tornado had swept through the room but instead, there was a single swaying girl in faded white on the bed, arms wrapped around her shivering knees and eyes staring at the floor.

Nico wanted to do something. To say something. But they had no idea what that something could have possibly been, and the silence felt too thick to break all on their own. So, they got to work. The garbage, first. They piled bits of paper and plastic into a stained tablecloth. They paused to study Tillie before moving to the glass dishes, but she appeared to be completely unharmed. Physically. Even though she was still refusing to look at Nico, she must have felt their attention on her. She shrunk under their gaze.

They got back to work.

The garbage was disposed of outside.

They found cleaning supplies under one of the sinks in the communal kitchen and carried back a bucket of water to scrub at the wall.

The dirty water was poured down a drain.

They packed their remaining props and supplies back up. They carefully collected each and every coin. They piled the sheets in the corner then begged the landlord for a broom and swept the floor, just because it felt like it needed to be cleaned.

The dirt was dumped outside.

They sped-walked to the market; the closest to running they'd done in years. They stopped at all the same stands: eggs then toast then donut then orange wedges. They had one more thing to find and after asked enough people about it frantically enough, they were pointed in the right direction.

When they returned, Tillie was still swaying on the bed.

Nico rotated their tongue around the inside of their mouth, as if that would somehow alleviate their dried throat. "I need to make the bed, Tillie," they stayed behind her as they spoke. They couldn't deal with forcing her to look away again. They'd already reconstructed the pile of blankets on the floor to the best of their abilities—one of the sheets was stained with egg or icing and would need to be washed, but they didn't want to be gone for too long right now so that would have to be a future problem—but they still had to put back their sheets.

Tillie didn't respond. She didn't turn towards them. But, eventually, she slid onto the floor and scooted far enough forward that they'd be able to put the fitted sheet back in place. They put the tray down beside her. They didn't see her acknowledge it, but by the time Nico was done with the bed, an orange slice was gone.

Once everything was back in order, they eased themself down across from her.

Tillie kept her eyes on the tray.

For once in their life, Nico kept their lips shut.

They both waited, neither knowing what for. Slowly, Tillie reached to grab another slice. "Did I hurt you?" she asked. It was quiet. Not a whisper, just quiet. The volume didn't seem to fit.

Nico shook their head. "Of course not."

Tillie nodded to herself. They went back to quiet. For a very long time.

"You're not the one the pirates want," Tillie told the ground. Not a whisper, just quiet. "They'd probably be fine, if you left. If you wanted to—"

"Of course not."

Tillie nodded again. They were quiet, again. For even longer.

"I got you umm...." Nico felt around in their pocket. "Here." They slid the new box of cards towards her. "I figured you'd need..." they reached into their other pocket. "Most of the old cards were too far gone, but the box was fine? If you wanted to swap the new ones into it? I don't know how, honestly," they laughed, just to be making noise. "It was busted as fuck even the first time I saw it, but I should have known that if it managed to survive being submerged in water and who knows what else, of course it would—"

Tillie threw her arms around their neck. They paused in surprise before wrapping theirs around her back. And then, she came undone all over again.

Nico had seen Tillie cry before. They hadn't exactly been keeping track, but they were pretty sure it must have happened at least once a day. Crying was just an intrinsic part of Tillie being Tillie. But this time, it felt different. Heavier. So, they held on tight as she shook and sobbed against their shoulder and tried their best to take on a bit of that weight themself.

"I'm sorry," Tillie gasped. And then all at once, it was like she couldn't stop saying it. "I'm sorry, I'm sorry, I'm sorry, I'm—"

They rubbed circles against her back. "Gross. Stop it. Not allowed. You didn't do anything wrong."

She chuckled a little, pulling back. "I destroyed the entire room," she reminded them, face caked in snot. "And like, half of the things we own."

"Oh." Nico remembered. "Right. That. Well then," they got up to get her a tissue. "You still should have only said it once, so that was still rule breaking." They handed her the entire box and waited for her to clean herself up.

"You can really go," Tillie reminded them. "Seriously. We have more than enough to get you back home and it probably won't even be there anymore so..."

"I'm staying. Too invested in this, now. I need to know how it ends."

Tillie swallowed. "You might not get your wish," she whispered. "You'll go through all of this and then still not—"

They rolled their eyes. "I never even bothered picking one out," they admitted. "Didn't want to get my hopes up. I'll be fine either way."

She wrung her fingers together. "I'll never show up in Bayside, I swear. You can tell everyone... I don't want to waste even more of your time," she whispers. "It's almost definitely not there. And if it is, I can handle it on my own. I—"

They sighed. "I haven't cared about some ugly cloak for ages now," they admitted. "I mean... no offense. I care about you getting it so you can go home, obviously, but I never... I didn't care about it in the first place, okay? Like, at all. Like I made it extremely obvious that I had absolutely no investment in some maybe wish ages ago, actually. That's why I didn't want to come, at first. I've never... let me come, okay?" They said. "This has already taken a ridiculous amount of time. If people back home are worried about me or whatever, it's not like a bit longer'll make a massive difference. I mean fuck, if my friends hear I had the chance to be a temporary pirate and gave that up? They'd probably honestly be even more pissed." They wrapped their hand over hers. Squeezed. "But mostly... I've never insisted on seeing this through because of the wish, Tillie. It's..." Their throat tried to silence them. They pushed forward. Something about Tillie always seemed to make them strong enough to do that. "In ten days you might be going back home, right? And then you won't be able to come back for seven years, if you even decide to.

I need... if you're only spending a few more days in this form, I don't want to miss them."

Tillie studied their clasped hands. "I yelled at you," she whispered. "I'm... I didn't mean to, but I..."

They rolled their eyes. "I've actually lost count of the amount of times I've accidentally yelled at you."

"I *hit* you."

Nico swallowed. "You seriously didn't hurt me," they reasserted. "I barely—"

"But I could have. Next time, I might..." Her voice cracked. Her eyes started watering again. "I have before, okay? I'm... I know I'm practically a fucking adult and I'm... I was the oldest sibling, back home. I should've been the best at controlling myself, but I swear I didn't... it's like when I get overwhelmed I can't..." her chest shuttered. "I don't want to hurt you. I didn't want to... it's not as easy as deciding not to, though! I keep telling myself I won't let myself but then I get worked up again and—"

"Tillie." They squeezed her hand. "I'm an almost-adult too, okay? I am perfectly capable of defending myself or walking away or whatever. If I had to, I would have. And I'll go right when you tell me to next time, okay? Now that I know. If there is a next time. So you won't even have to worry about it, alright?"

She pulled her hands away from theirs and into her chest. "I don't know what's wrong with me," she whispered. "That's not... I need you to know... it's not a selkie thing. My... whatever's wrong with the way I feel things. It's not just..." she started tapping her fists together. "There's something wrong with me and I don't know what it is, but you deserve to at least know that... I can't let you keep putting yourself around me without knowing!" Her eyes widened at the sound of her own raised voice. She moved further away from them. Nico forced themself to stay put.

"I know," they promised. "Not... oh gods, not that there's something wrong with you," they corrected. "I didn't mean it like that. I meant... I know you. I don't think there's anything wrong with you, but I know all of the things that you think are and you've warned me about them a million times and I'm still here, okay? You gave me to option to leave weeks ago. You're not trapping me in anything. I said I'd stay and I meant it."

She shook her head. "You didn't know then, though. You don't have to follow through with that just because—"

They closed the gap between them. Pushed their forehead to hers because that was what Tillie did, when one of them was coming up done. It made shivers run up their spine and their skin go a bit too hot, but they knew that that was how Tillie held things together. "I know now," they swore. "I know you now. And I'm still here, promising all over again. Let me come, okay?" They searched her eyes. "Please? I'm umm..." they squirmed in place. "Not super great at asking people for things. Say yes before I have to do it again and it ends up killing me?"

She smiled. And in that moment—with her lips so close and beaming—they wanted to kiss her. Her eyes were still red though, so Nico knew that they couldn't. "Okay," she agreed. "I'm... okay. I'd like that. A lot."

"Yes!" They celebrated, pulling back to fist-pump the air. Tillie giggled.

"Now," Nico declared, pushing the tray of food towards her. "Eat some fucking food before I lose my mind."

She smiled. "You're a really good friend."

"Yeah, no shit," they rolled their eyes. But their stomach felt warm. Bright, somehow. "You are too," they relented. "I'm... sorry I spent so long calling you a bitch."

Tillie frowned. "I don't recall you ever doing that, actually."

They shrugged, scooting to finally sit down beside her. "Must've just been in my head."

Chapter 42

True to his word, Radclyffe showed up first thing the next morning to collect them.

"My newest crewmates!" He threw out his arms in celebration. He was entirely too chipper, both for a pirate and a person awake before the sun.

"More like hostages," Nico grumbled, throwing one of their bags over their shoulder. They'd packed everything up over night and then had added one of the sheets in the morning. Hopefully, the landlord wouldn't miss it. They'd found themself randomly stranded enough times to find the action justified.

Radclyffe ignored them though, moving towards Tillie. "Our newest little thief!" He declared. "Masterful work at the market, truly. So sorry about that little 'thought you were from a rival crew, got you arrested' mix-up. But if anything, you should really try and take it as a compliment."

Tillie frowned. "Oh, umm... right. Thank you?"

Radclyffe chucked, spinning towards the door. His cape billowed around him as he did. Nico felt newly stupid for taking so long to realize that he was a pirate. "We good to go then?" He asked. "Most of your jobs will be on land, of course—I do hope you're not planning on robbing any of my crew, that would be quite inconvenient—but I've got to show this one around the kitchens." He nodded towards Nico.

"I can't cook," Tillie quickly blurted. "Or clean or... pretty much anything. I'm sorry. I didn't realize... even if you train me, I wouldn't be able to—"

He rolled his eyes. "Good. I wanted to hire—"

"Blackmail," Nico contributed. They knew that they logically should have stopped arguing with the incredibly tall, fully adult pirate captain, but they were also ridiculously bad at biting their tongue.

"Hire," Radclyffe repeated pointedly. His tone was light though. Almost teasing. "a pirate," he finished. "Not an extra crewmen. He cupped a hand around the side of the mouth, pretending to block Nico out of the conversation. "Don't tell Nicole," he faux-whispered. "But you're the one I was after. They're just a bit of necessary deadweight."

"Oh," Tillie said, failing to stop herself from smiling. "Umm... right. I mean, that's not—"

Radclyffe didn't listen. He was already whirling around towards the exit, pausing only to flash Nico a quick wink as he went. And beside them, Tillie was a little less panicked and a little more relaxed so Nico decided that maybe they didn't quite hate the captain after all.

In another life, Nico would have loved to be a pirate. Maybe in this life too, eventually. Once they were old and crabby and bored. The *Rad-Ship* (an awful, terrible name that Radclyffe had first told them with a twinkle in his eye that had prompted Nico to do their very best not to vomit immediately) really had already had more than enough crewman, so Nico had just had to wash a few vegetables in the kitchen before being dismissed so that the actual seasoned cooks could take over.

"Go find your girlfriend," Gladdys, the gold-toothed wild-haired old woman who appeared to be in charge finally silenced their protests against leaving. Only because it resulted in several prologued seconds of nonsensical sputtering and shock on Nico's end, but still.

The rest of the kitchen stopped what they were doing to laugh.

"Not my girlfriend!" Nico was finally cognisant enough to protest, somehow managing to go even redder.

"Sure," Gladdys rolled her eyes. "Go find your not-girlfriend then."

And so, before they could be teased further, Nico gave in, took off their apron, and went to her.

True to his word, Radclyffe had provided them with their own cabin.

Also true to his word, it was remarkably small. It had bunkbeds though, so at least there was that.

They walked in on Tillie practicing card tricks on the bottom bunk. She'd insisted on taking the top since it was technically harder for Nico to reach, but Tillie was also incredibly clumsy for an able-bodied person when she was in her human form, so they'd both agreed that it would be best if she only ever made the climb at night.

"Oh!" She turned. "Hello! I thought you were..." she trialed off, confused.

"They really don't need my help, apparently," Nico sighed. "No one seems super keen about letting a random teenager interfere with their cooking. They take it incredibly seriously, for a bunch of pirates."

"Oh." Tillie repeated. She frowned for half a second, but then she was scooting back on the bed, beaming. "That's perfect, then. I needed your help." She patted across from her. "I can't figure out if someone would be able to see through this one? Could you—"

Nico bit their lip. Tillie absolutely did not need someone to practice on. And they weren't genuinely upset about being frozen out in the kitchen—or at least, they didn't think that they were—but if humouring her humouring them meant that they'd get to watch her do magic, then they were more than alright with playing along.

They were invited up for meals that Nico had slightly contributed to but Tillie clearly didn't want to go, so Nico brought their plates back for them. Until dinner.

"Nico," Tillie gently touched their knee. "If we both stay cooped up alone in here until we dock, we might go crazy. Go. Socialize."

They hesitated. "We could... you could come to? We can—"

"I'm a lot less land-people-y than you. Especially when there's a ton of different foods and smells and sounds involved. I'll be fine. I actually can survive a couple of hours on my own, you know."

"Of course you can," they said instantly.

Tillie smiled, rolling her eyes. "Go. Begone. Bug someone else for a bit." She froze. "You umm... you don't actually—"

"Grossss," they stopped her. "Don't 'nice' me. I'm not actually that insecure and mushy."

"Then go! And don't let me see you back here for at least a couple of hours!"

"But—"

She leaned towards them. "I'll make us talk about our feelings, again," she threatened. "I'll be so, so mushy that—"

Nico bolted up. "Going!" They raced for the door.

Her laughter carried all the way down the hall.

And so, up above deck, Nico learned that they really, really liked pirates. Or maybe just these pirates: with their wooden legs and arms and failing teeth. Some from work injuries, many apparently from before they'd joined the crew. These pirates who never blinked when they heard their pronouns and just casually moved on with the conversation or responded with "cool mine are..." or "is it just they/them then?" or even a knowing nod and a "love the haircut, by the way."

Radclyffe found them later that evening, sitting on the dock, staring out at the water. "So," he sat down beside them, taking care to not sit on his own cape. "How're we liking life on the sea?"

Nico glared, but a lot less intently than they would have that morning. "You could've mentioned that your crew was..." They trailed off, unable to find the word.

"Magnificent?" He guessed. "Fantastic? Ridiculously cool?"

They rolled their eyes.

Radclyffe laughed. "We're pirates, Nico. Why would you have assumed that we weren't pretty much all either ridiculously queer or disabled?" He rolled up his sleeve again to highlight the stump. "Or, you know. Both."

They groaned. "Could people tell?" They asked. "That I was..."

"Ogling them in awe? Absolutely. But they found it endearing. Cute."

This time, their glare was full force. "I'm nineteen."

"Yes." He patted their head. "Exactly."

Radclyffe stretched out his legs, leaning back against his hand. "Where's your girlfriend?"

"Friend!" They corrected. Nico never thought that they would be the kind of person adamantly declaring themself friends with someone.

Radclyffe laughed. "Fine. Where's the little pirate-to-be?"

They looked away, worried that they'd reveal too much. Radclyffe and his crew might have seemed relatively cool, but they weren't about to announce that Tillie was a magical creature in search of an incredibly rare, wish-granting object. "Mathilda's... not a people person. She likes her space."

He wiggled his eyebrows. He was really too old to be doing that. "Seems to me like she's at least a one-person person."

"Shut up!" They hit his arm. Then remembered that he was a pirate captain and that they probably shouldn't be randomly assaulting him.

Radclyffe laughed, getting back up. "Send my love!" He said. "Let her know we're excited for our first job together when we dock in two days!"

They didn't go back right away, though. Someone brought out a fiddle and started to play so Nico moved closer and watched the crew dance until they got yelled at for sitting on the sidelines and were forcibly adopted into the dance circle. Nico couldn't dance—hadn't been able to for years—but that felt like an awful excuse when over half of the dance floor had even more mobility issues than they did, so they did an appropriate amount of one-footed hopping and swaying and head nodding before returning below deck, stomach full and heart giddy. It was almost a perfect night. Until, of course, they got stuck talking about their feels again.

Chapter 43

"Hey," they whispered.

By the time Nico returned to the cabin, Tillie was already on her bunk and they didn't want to risk waking her. She leaned over the edge though, smiling at them. "How was dinner? You stayed out a while."

They tried to find the underlying annoyance there, but there wasn't any. "Good," they admitted. "People seem... nice. You know. For a bunch of old pirates. You should come with next time, if you want."

She chewed on her lip. "I umm... no. Thanks."

"Okay," they nodded, flopping into their own bunk. "Were you okay?" They asked. "Today?"

"I'm extremely good at sitting alone in a room for hours, actually."

"Right." They nodded again. "Will you be in two days?" They asked. "When you have to help..."

"Oh. Yes. Could be fun," she lied.

"I'm sorry I made the deal without you," they finally managed to say. "It just seemed like... if I'd saved up to bail you out, we would have had to start at zero and I figured that would have been worse, you know? Thank you. For not getting mad about that. I know you're probably not exactly thrilled about it, but thanks for not getting pissed at me specifically for it, I guess. Even right after getting out of somewhere that must have been crazy stressful. I thought you would be."

"Why would I..." Tillie sounded genuinely confused. "Obviously I wasn't mad. I'd assumed you'd already taken everything and gone home, by that point."

Nico froze.

Tillie couldn't see them though, so she just kept going. "Obviously I would have taken robbing people for petty cash a handful of times over going to prison."

They stumbled to their feet. She'd thought that they would have just left. They'd spent hours worrying themself sick about her, weeks trying to reassure her that they weren't actually a shitty person, and she'd still just assumed that they would have stolen all of their stuff and disappeared. And they cared, about what she thought about them. They cared so much it ached.

"What the fuck, Tillie?" They whispered. They knew that if they let themself get any louder, they'd start yelling and she'd start crying and then they'd somehow end up feeling like the asshole. Then they'd somehow accidentally prove her right.

She leaned over the bunk again. "What?" She asked. "Did I..."

"You thought I'd left?" They asked.

"Well, yes," she said. "Of course. Why would—"

"You thought I'd just *leave*?" They demanded.

Tillie frowned. "I don't know what... I'm sorry? Did I say something wrong?"

Nico laughed. It sounded angry. It sounded mean. It sounded like the creature in their stomach. They forced their lips shut, before it could escape. They tried to take a deep breath, but that just seemed to fuel it. "I... Gods, Tillie! It's been weeks and you still fucking—" their stomach churned. They felt it again. They staggered towards the door. "I need to not be here right now," they realized.

"Wait." Tillie scrambled down the ladder. "Wait, wait, I'm sorry, okay?" She grabbed at their sleeve. "I'm sorry. Please don't... I'm sorry."

They pulled themself free. They couldn't trust themself to talk.

"Nico!" She screamed, desperate now. Tillie raced around them to block the door. "You can't... don't go," she sniffled. "Please, don't... you can't... don't leave."

And all at once, they were filled with rage.

Chapter 44

Don't leave.

Nico hadn't been left. Not technically. They'd decided to run away, even if they hadn't known that that was what they were doing at the time. They'd decided to not go back.

Don't leave.

But still, the fear of being left was somehow woven into every overgrown purple strand of their hair.

Nico was a leaver, technically. Nico had never been the left. But that couldn't have been entirely true, right? If it was, then why were they always so fucking scared of it happening again?

Don't leave.

Nico had never been the left, technically, but they were still the left behind. The left out. Nico had never been the left, but they'd grown up in a household that laughed and celebrated without them while they sat alone in their room. Nico had never been the left, but they'd been the name—one originally always listed first—left off of ever parent or teacher or classmate's tongue. Nico had never been the left, but maybe only because they'd known that they were still there.

Don't leave.

Because back in that house—the first one. The worst one—everyone else had started mourning them long before they actually decided to leave. The person that they'd been before becoming disabled. The future that they were supposed to have. Nico was a leaver, technically, but they'd also spend half a decade standing in the shadow of a ghost that never was, desperate trying to convince the people who'd once claimed to love them that they were still real.

Nico was the leaver, but they would spend the rest of their life trying to shake off being the left. Ignoring everyone they wanted to cling to, just in case they stopped seeing them too.

Flinching at each and every reminder of the person that they'd been.

Nico was not the left—not technically—but they hadn't meant to be the leaver either. Sometimes, that was just the only way to escape your own ghost.

Chapter 45

"Nico," Tillie tried again, tears streaming down her face.

They'd gone quiet, too busy warring with their own throat to respond.

"Nico," she grabbed their arm. "Don't... please, okay? Don't go. We can—"

It made their blood boil, this reminder of their own terror. Even if they weren't the one feeling it. It made them feel pathetic. It made them feel worthless. And they knew that that was exactly what they would hurl at her if the thing in their stomach manages to escape.

They parted their lips, but just slightly. To exhale. To let a bit of the pressure escape. They squeezed their eyes shut. "I need some space," they managed to keep their voice even. "Move. We'll talk when I get back." They risked opening their eyes. She was still there. Still busy reflecting all of the parts of themself that they desperately wanted to pretend didn't exist. Because Tillie was a little bit broken too, maybe, in ways that terrify them. In ways that petrify them. "I'll be back, Tillie," they promised softly. "I'm coming back."

Slowly, she moved. Slowly, they left. And then slowly—after triple checking that they'd found an isolated enough part of the deck—Nico began to cry.

For the person that they'd been, since they were ten. For the person that they'd thought they'd get to be before that. For the two homes that they'd now accidentally left. For the serpent in their stomach that they could never seem to keep satiated, no matter how desperately they tried. For Tillie who probably wasn't going to get to go back home who they were pretty sure they'd fallen in love with. For Tillie, who would never see them as anything but a self-centered monster. For the serpent in their stomach that knew that they were. For being left and leaving and always being ready to flee. For Tillie, who obviously knew a bit too much about that who knew that they were a monster, but who they also couldn't help but cry for anyway.

    For everything and nothing and everything in between. They cried for the sake of crying and then got up, took a deep breath, and didn't let themself run away.

Chapter 46

"Hey," they whispered, slipping back into the cabin. Not voluntarily though, this time. There voice was just too raw to handle much of anything else.

Tillie rushed down the ladder. "You were crying," she whispered.

Nico rolled their eyes. Tried to laugh. "So were you."

"Yes, well... it's boring, when I do it." She chewed on her lip, tapping at her sides. "I'm so sorry."

They scoffed. "You didn't even know why I was upset."

"I made you *cry*," she said, as if that was that. As if that was explanation enough. And maybe it was. "Tell me what you need," she insisted. "Tell me how to fix it. Tell me how to make sure I never do that again."

Because she hadn't been being malicious. There wasn't a malicious bone in Tillie's body.

Nico sighed, sitting down on the bed. They gestured for her to join them. "I guess we're doing this again, then," they said. "The..." they shuddered. "*feelings*."

Tillie nodded solemnly. "It's a bit unavoidable at times, I'm afraid."

And they wanted to laugh but that would mean that it was over and they wanted to sit in this, for a little bit. This cool, quiet anger. Or sadness. They had trouble telling, sometimes. It was a hard thing to recognize, after they'd spent so long shoving it away. "You don't trust me," they accused.

Tillie frowned. "Of course I trust you. You're... more than anyone. Ever."

They shook their head. "You thought I'd let you fucking rot in prison for something we did together. Something that was my idea! We've been traveling together for weeks and you still think so little of me that you didn't even consider that I might have been trying to help!"

Her eyes narrowed. "That wasn't... it would have made sense, if you'd left. I'm... I wasn't useful anymore. People would have been paying more attention so it's not like we could've kept the scheme going, right? That wasn't because... you had all the money and supplied and people waiting for you and pickpocketing was the one thing I was good at so if I couldn't do that, I'd be useless again."

"Gods," Nico threw back their head. "I wish you were actually useless." Tillie flinched. They sighed. "That didn't come out right, it... I was a dick, Tillie," they admitted. "But then I stopped being a dick and I've been trying really hard to prove that I've stopped being a dick and—"

"You have," she said. "You're not. I- I know that, I—"

"Let me finish? Please?"

She went quiet.

Nico sighed again. "I wish me realizing I sucked and trying to do better didn't coincide with you feeling useful, okay? You don't have to serve a function to people for them to treat you with basic fucking decency. I hate..." they trailed off. "You're not useless, obviously. Never are, never have been. But if you were, I would still be here because I fucking care about you and I'd thought you cared back enough to know that I wouldn't just—"

"I think the world of you," Tillie interrupted. "You're... I've known you for like a month and you're already my single favourite person ever, actually. I suppose I just don't... you said that when you're upset you... You said you say things that are more about you than the other person, right? I suppose I also... I think the world of you, I supposed I just have trouble convincing myself that other people could think the world of me or... anything of... I don't know." She took a deep breath. "I'm sorry I said that, I'm sorry I thought that, I'm sorry I hurt you but it wasn't because... it's not because I don't know you're incredible, Nico. I do. It was because I don't know a single other person who wouldn't have just given up on me."

They rolled their eyes. "I'm sure that's not—"

Nonymous

"You were right, about my colony," she interrupted. "I know... I know you didn't mean it, when you said that they were probably glad that I was gone, but you did a little, right? You'd figured me out a little. I don't think..." she looked down. "I was really bad at being a selkie too, I suppose," she admitted. "And it wasn't my parents' fault. They taught me all of the things that they were supposed to and they clearly did a good enough job at it too since my siblings all turned out normal, I just wasn't... you were right. I came on land because everybody knew I was always going to be a burden and I wanted to give them a break and they still haven't... they're not looking. I know they're not. Because if they put all that effort into finding me, they're just going to have to waste even more of their energy taking care of me again once I'm found. I'm... I didn't belong there. They knew it and I knew it but I'm bad up here too so maybe—" She pressed a fist against her leaking eyes. "I'm sorry," she said. "Gods, even now I can't... I'm sorry, this was about you. I was trying to explain, not... I'm sorry."

So, finally, they told her. The story in full, spoken aloud for the first time ever. Some of their friends had gotten some pieces over the years and Leif had probably had the whole thing mapped out long before asking them to move in, but they'd never told the whole thing themself before. By the time they finished, they were hiccupping and sobbing and it made them feel like a pathetic child, but then they felt stupid for feeling pathetic for crying because there was Tillie, wrapping her arms around them. There was Tillie, who always wore her emotions defiantly, for all of the world to see. Who they'd never think lesser of just because she let herself feel things. Nico had always been their own worst critic, but for once, they decided to let themself not be.

They laughed a little. "Ta-da!" They shook their wrists. "There. Now we've both hijacked the other person's thing."

Tillie didn't laugh back though. She turned their chin. Pressed their foreheads together. Because she was Tillie, so of course she did. "Your parents were idiots," she said, less than an inch from them.

204

Nico tried their best not to spit on her when they laughed in surprise. For real this time.

Blindly, eyes still locked on theirs, Tillie found Nico's hands. "I would have found you, okay?" She promised. "If you'd randomly disappeared on me, I would have found a million excuses to rope people into quests and went on a million journeys and stayed on land for a million years until I found you and made sure you were alright. If you disappeared right now, I would immediately start looking for you, okay? Even if it meant I'd never get my cloak back."

They smiled past the lump in their throat. Tucked a clump of tangled curls behind her ear. "I know," they promised. "You jumped into monster infested waters for me, stupid. Even when I was still busy being an idiot. I already know." They hesitated. "I can't umm... I know I'm supposed to say that you're wrong, about your colony. That they're looking for you as we speak and always secretly appreciated you exactly as much as they should have, even if they never really showed it. But I don't want to.... I can't know that," they admitted. "And I don't think you'd want me to lie about it and pretend that I do, right? I've never met them and sometimes families just suck. But what if..." They were terrified. Of telling her, of course. Nico's throat was well trained in never letting anything seriously slip through. But mostly, of never being able to tell her. They squeezed her hands. "Maybe I can belong to you and you can belong to me, okay? And that doesn't mean I'm saying you definitely don't also belong with your colony and that doesn't mean I'm saying I don't belong anywhere else either, but we can belong to each other too, alright? That way, if one of us ever goes missing for a while, there'll always be someone there to start the search party. That way, neither of us can go missing ever again."

Tillie's lips parted. She leaned forward, not for a kiss, but just to hug them more effectively. "Okay," she whispered. "Deal."

Nico rested their head against her shoulder and they stayed like that—so incredibly found that it ached—until they must have somehow fallen asleep. They woke up hours later tucked into their bunk, listened to the soft sound of Tillie's breathing above them, and rolled back over to make the morning wait just a little while longer.

Chapter 47

It had not occurred to Nico that signing Tillie on to become a pirate would involve Tillie actually becoming a pirate.

The first job that she was a part of sounded—as promised—fairly safe and uneventful. She was just supposed to loiter outside some fancy expensive social club's yearly get together to rake in as much extra coin as she could while all of the actually pirating happened inside. But pickpocketing during magic shows had felt low risk too.

Nico paced their tiny room from the moment she left to the moment that their leg completely refused to let them keep going. The only thing entertaining left in the cabin was Tillie's deck of cards so they sorted and mixed and resorted just to keep themself busy. And then, finally, the door opened.

"Were you... practicing card tricks?"

They jumped to their feet. Tillie looked perfect, though. Tillie still looked like Tillie. "You're okay," Nico finally remembered to breathe.

She blushed. "I wasn't exactly doing anything dangerous."

They wrapped their arms around her, but she flinched. Nico frowned, letting go. They watched her a little more closely. "Are you.... not? Okay? Did something happen?"

"What? No. It was fine. Boring."

They couldn't see the problem, but there must have been one. "Are you sure? You could tell me. If—"

"Nothing happened!" She giggled. "I was incredibly competent and did an incredibly good job, actually."

"You flinched," they explained.

Her eyes widened. Her cheeks went pink. "That umm..." Tillie buried her fists in her pockets. "I'm fine. I'm just umm... not a fan of hugs."

They gaped. "Tillie! That's the kind of thing you have to tell me! I can't believe—"

"That wasn't right," she shook her head. "That wasn't... I mean I even start them, sometimes. I just... I'm still not used to it, I guess. Things touching this skin. Especially other land-people. But I like it, most of the time. If the placement's right."

Nico sighed. "I'll stop, okay?" They thought back to all of the times that they'd tried to touch her. All of the times that she'd flinched and they'd just brushed it off. "I'm sorry, I should have—"

"No!" She exclaimed. "I don't want..." she squeezed her eyes shut. "I like it, when you do. Because it's mostly because you like me and I like knowing that you like me, I just... don't stop. It's just some specific placements that I don't like."

"Okay," they nodded. "Where?"

She blushed. "I'm umm... I'm not actually sure. Or... okay, with hands," she held hers out. "You feel things more, on the palm. I really, really like holding hands but sometimes I don't want to feel things too much so if you grabbed the top instead, that would be..."

"Done. Where else."

She sighed. "I don't know. Pretend I didn't say anything. Or... that you didn't notice anything, I guess."

Nico rolled their eyes. "Tillie, we're absolutely not doing that." They considered. "You could tell me?" They offered. "When I get it wrong and I can like, I don't know, keep a list? Or... it might be easier to just remember how to do it right, actually." They held out their arms. "Show me where?"

"I seriously don't know where."

They nodded. "Okay. Them move me around until we figure it out? If you want. If that wouldn't be too much."

Tillie bit her lip. "That'd be ridiculous," she whispered.

They just glared.

"Okay," she smiled, lightly wrapping her fingers around their wrists. "Okay, sure. Thank you."

So, awkwardly, clumsily, and clinically, she moved their arms around her back. And it was awkward and clumsy and clinical and yet somehow still felt a little bit too intimate, so Nico tried their best to be distracting. "So," they said. "Tell me about this heist."

Tillie grinned and relayed every single detail to them, no matter how exciting or mundane. True to Radclyffe's word, he'd kept her outside, invisible, and far from any actual danger.

Nico already knew they'd be equally as worried when she went out again next time, though. Tillie interrupted her own storytelling with "you could try tighter?" or "looser?" or "there." Or "definitely not there." and they did their best to memorize all of it, but they knew that they'd probably have to double check with her for a bit. She'd been against having them literally write every single thing down. Apparently, that would have been a little bit too far.

"Oh!" Tillie remembered. "I got earplugs too? For both of us because they're seriously not that expensive and it would have looked suspicious if—tighter?—if I didn't get any. Just in case. Radclyffe says siren attacks are super uncommon out here, though. But keep them on you anyway, okay? All the time? Just in case?"

They nodded. "Sure."

She bent her neck to look right at them. "Seriously, Nico. Promise me."

They rolled their eyes. "I promise. I genuinely thought I wouldn't be affected last time, now I know I will be. I—"

"Looser there?"

They complied. "If they did just like, sexily seduce people, it really wouldn't have worked on me, for the record. I was wrong about sirens, not myself. I asked some of the crew about it and apparently they're sexy *and* romantic evil mer-monsters so... good for them, I guess. Bad for pretty much every other species, though."

Tillie froze.

"Bad spot?" They checked.

"Yeah," she nodded. "Yeah umm... not there, I guess."

Chapter 48

Secretly, Nico was dreading reaching Kovienne.

They knew that that wasn't fair. Tillie hated being on land. Tillie deserved the entire world so of course she also deserved her own fucking skin.

But they loved her, a little. Maybe even more than a little. And once they got to Kovienne, they'd have to let her go.

They tried to ignore it. If they ignored it, then maybe it wouldn't have to hurt as much when she inevitably left. But then, on the fifth day of their journey—when their remaining time was half-way up—they couldn't.

It wasn't because of anything particularly remarkable. Nico was relaxing in their room. Now that she'd been on official jobs with them, Tillie was getting more comfortable being around the rest of the crew.

"Guess what?" She burst in, cards in hand. "I learned a new trick! Lonnie apparently knows a few and..." she finally slowed down. "Are you busy? Are you doing anything?"

"Nope," they sat up. "Just waiting for you to come back."

"Oh," she smiled. "Good. Then you can watch." She hopped up onto the bed and crossed her legs. "Okay, shuffle the deck, alright?" She held it out to them. "As much as you want."

They smiled, taking the cards. Nico felt warm. Nico felt light. Tillie made every single thing she touched light. "Okay," they handed them back. "Done."

"Excellent!" Tillie clapped. "Okay. Ready?" she said. "I'm not going to look at the cards. I'm going to look right at you. You look right back." She moved the cards behind her back. And then, she looked right at them. And they had to look right back. And they couldn't just not tell her.

"Tillie," they licked their lips. "I—"

"Shh!" She giggled. "This one's new! I have to focus!"

They tried. They really did. "Tillie," they whispered.

"Shush!" They heard the cards fall to the floor. She finally broke eye contact. "Shoot!" Tillie got to work collecting them. She wasn't mad at them though, she was giddy. "Okay." She held out the cards again. "Okay, we'll go again. Just—"

"Tillie!" They cupped her chin. Right against the bone. Right where they supposed to.

She stared at them. Still smiling. Still giddy. And they only had to last five more days, but they couldn't not let her know. But they also weren't brave enough to say it. Not yet. So, they leaned in. Their lips grazed against hers.

And then Tillie jumped off of the bed.

They froze. They were an idiot. Just two days ago she'd told them that she wasn't okay with a lot of land-person forms of physical touch and then they'd tried to kiss her without checking if that was alright first. They'd tried to kiss her without checking while fucking applauding themself for remembering where to touch her chin.

Nico got to their feet. Tillie stumbled back, eyes wide and chest heaving and absolutely terrified. Of them. They opened their mouth to apologize or to explain or to promise that it would never, ever happen again, but Tillie beat them to whatever they'd been about to say.

"I'm not a selkie."

Chapter 49

"I... what?"

"I'm not a selkie. I'm.... I'm just human. I'm—"

And then, canon fire sounded up above.

Chapter 50

Nico clicked out their cane and rushed towards the door, but Tillie was faster.

"You can't go," she said. "That sounded... you can't—"

"What because I have a fucking cane?" They scoffed. "Half the crew's disabled. You don't get to—"

"Because I don't want you to get hurt!"

They flinched. "You don't get to pretend to care about that right now. You don't—"

"Okay," she nodded. "I'll come too. We'll—"

"No." They couldn't let her. Because she was a fucking liar and a life destroyer and they knew absolutely nothing about her, but they still loved her. They wouldn't be able to do this if they had to spend the whole time worrying about her. "You're staying."

"If you're going, I want to—"

"What the fuck would you do, Tillie! You can't handle the sound of people breathing without shutting down, you think you'll be useful surrounded by fucking cannon fire?" It was mean. It was intentional. They needed her to stay and she didn't deserve to know that it was because they cared about her.

"I'm... okay," she moved, already crying. And it crushed them. Even now, it still crushed them. She'd eaten up all of their anger. She'd transformed them into this thing incapable of hiding in it anymore. "Okay. Be careful though, alright? Be—" they slammed the door shut behind them.

And almost made it all the way to the main deck before they were scooped up into the air.

"Put me down!" They kicked and punched at nothing.

Radclyffe held tight, raising them to his eye level. "Back in your cabin. Now. Block the door."

"I'm not just going to fucking sit out a fight!" They protested. They needed this, actually. To lash out at something. Anything. To destroy. "Just because I'm disabled doesn't mean—"

Radclyffe sighed. It made their bangs shift. "I still have one and a half arms, Nicole."

"Oh," they remembered. "Right. Well... that's just more of a reason you should let me—"

He walked them back over to the door and pulled it open, putting them back inside the room. They kept their focus on him so that they wouldn't have to look at Tillie.

"I'd love to chat, but we're kind of preoccupied right now," Radclyffe said. "You," he pointed at the two of them. "Children—"

"Nineteen!" Nico protested.

"Nineteen-year-old children," he amended. "Are staying here until someone comes to get you or the actual ship sinks, got it? Don't make me barricade the door, because I will."

And then he left them. With her.

"Nico," Tillie rasped. "Nico, I'm—"

"You don't get to call me that," they spit.

"Okay," she nodded. "Alright. That's fair. I didn't... I need you to know that—"

They spun around to face her. "Was that the truth? Are you not actually a selkie?"

Her lip trembled. She nodded. "I'm so sorry."

"Then I don't need to know anything else." They lied down on their bunk and crossed their arms over their chest, spinning to face the wall. "I'm not talking to you. You're not talking to me. You're going to be fucking invisible until I can get out of here and then I never want to see you again, got it?"

"I can't... you said—"

"Gods, Mathilda! You at least owe me that!"

She took a deep breath. "I'm... okay," she sniffled. "I'm sorry. I just... I'm glad I got to know you, I guess. Even if I probably shouldn't have."

Nonymous

They squeezed their eyes shut against the sound of canon fire and did their best to not cry.

It didn't work.

Chapter 51

They'd run into one of Radclyffe's exes. Apparently, that had required a bit of canon fire and sword fighting.

Nothing lethal or ship destroying, of course, but enough to force them to dock and to put the *Rad-Ship* out of commission for a few days. Radclyffe put the entire crew up in a hotel. And Nico in a room with Tillie.

Nico didn't even bother starting to unpack. They went straight to Radclyffe's room and slammed their fist against the door.

"Nicole!" He beamed. "Sorry again, about all that swashbuckling. What can—"

"I need me own room."

He frowned. "Yeah. Not doing that. Already paid for one."

"I need a different one."

He sighed. "Gods, can't you wait to fight until after we've gotten the ship back?"

"Nope."

Radclyffe pushed the door the rest of the way open. "Come in then, I guess. You're taking the couch, though."

They smiled a little. "Did everyone else get a room big enough for a couch?"

"I am an esteemed pirate captain!" Radclyffe pulled his hand to his chest. "It would make my crew look bad if I didn't live in style."

They rolled their eyes.

"Are you taking the couch or not, Nicole?"

"Taking." They threw their bag down onto it. Radclyffe followed them.

"Should I be expecting you to be here until the ship's fixed or are you planning on making up with Mathilda before that?"

"Your ex just threw a bunch of cannonballs at us."

Radclyffe's eyes gleamed. "So, she's an ex, huh?"

Nico groaned, pulling a pillow over their face. "I'm staying here. I'm not talking to her."

He snorted. "Alright. Good luck with that."

But Nico was serious. They didn't leave his room at all for the rest of the day, too worried that she'd be right there waiting to ambush them. Or maybe that she wouldn't be.

They would hide away forever. Because if they didn't, they knew that they might accidentally forgive her.

Chapter 52

"Mathilda's at the beach," Radclyffe informed them when he returned the night. "You know. If you were curious."

Which, of course Mathilda was.

"Not talking to her."

"Okay. Good luck with that."

Chapter 53

"Mathilda's been asking about you," Radclyffe said the next day. "And I'm supposed to tell her..."
"Nothing."

Chapter 54

"Mathilda's at the beach, again." On the third.

Chapter 55

"She's still on the beach, if you wanted to go find her," on the fourth.

Chapter 56

"Alright then," Radclyffe abruptly pushed their legs off the couch.

Nico jumped, only half awake. He'd ruined their mid-day self-pity nap. It was their second favourite self-pity nap of the day.

"We are figuring out what's going on with you and Mathilda right now because we're boarding again tomorrow and I don't have the extra cabin space to keep putting up with this."

"I'll stay with you," they muttered, trying to kick at him with their left leg to get back to their nap. "Bet you have a ridiculously big room there."

"Yes, well, I'm supposed to be entertaining a visitor, so that probably isn't a good idea."

They sat the rest of the way up, suddenly curious. "A visitor," Nico reiterated. "On a pirate ship."

"*You're* a visitor on a pirate ship," Radclyffe reminded them. "I happen to just be an abnormally hospitable pirate. Tobias is used to it, anyhow. He—"

"Tobias as in your ex who just shot at us?" They exclaimed.

Radclyffe grinned. "We have quite the dramatic relationship actually. It's all horribly exciting. Now." He leaned towards them. "What do I have to do to get you and Mathilda tolerable again?"

"I can just go home," they rolled their eyes. "I'm not actually from Kovienne. Neither's Mathilda. There's just... I don't know what, actually. Waiting for her there. She's the one you want anyway and I don't actually have a debt. I'll just—"

Radclyffe sighed. "Nicole, Mathilda's not actually pirating, you know that, right? You must have realized you both only ever have busy jobs by now."

They frowned. "That doesn't... why the fuck are we here then?"

"I'm a *pirate*," he reminded them. "You were a teenage runaway telling me you'd managed to get yourself stranded and your partner arrested and I was just supposed to what? Let you keep trying to tough it out all on your own? That would have been dangerous."

"You got us shot at," they reminded him. He kept seeming to conveniently forget that part.

"Oh, barely," Radclyffe waved the thought off. "That was just Toby. He's a massive softy, really. Once you get to know him. People rarely ever attack us, anyhow. We're pretty bad at the actual pillaging part of pirating, I'm afraid. Not much of a foe to anyone. I'm a pirate though, Nicole. We're all queer runaways or disabled runaways or both. It's not like I was going to stumble upon a pair of teens like that and let them repeat all of the mistakes I've made. I just knew that there was no way I'd get you on board without acting like it was benefiting me because you know," he gestured to his outfit. "Pirate. We weren't even supposed to go to Kovienne, originally. I'm not letting you wander off on your own now just because you're in the middle of some little spat."

"I'm nineteen."

"Yes. Exactly."

Nico sighed. "Tillie's not," they realized. "Disabled. Or even queer, maybe. I don't know. She'd go, if you told her that she could. And then I could stay with you until you're near Bayside. That's where I'm from. Easy. No disabled queer runaway teenagers to project onto abandoned, and I also never need to see her again."

Radclyffe frowned. "Do you want me to do that?" He asked. "Send her off all on her own?"

"Well... no," they admitted. "Maybe. I don't know, but... can we get back to you being wrong about something, actually? That was a lot more fun, for me." And it was easier to deal with the fact that Tillie didn't like them back if it was something that they could gloat over.

He rolled his eyes. "You're gonna look me in the eye and tell me that girl experiences life just as easily as everyone else? I've talked to her maybe half a dozen times and even I could already—"

"There is nothing wrong with Tillie," they said, perhaps a bit too quickly.

Radclyffe smiled. "No," he patted their head. "No, of course there isn't. I'm sure she's wonderful and incredible and very, very pretty."

They blushed profusely.

"But she also definitely doesn't navigate the world the same way that non-disabled people do, Nicole. Which means she's welcome on my ship, whenever she wants to be. And also that I'm not kicking her off to placate your ego just because she..." he frowned. "What is it that we're all angry at her about, again?"

"She lied," they muttered.

His eyes widened. "It that all?"

"It was a very big lie! Huge. It—"

"Why'd she do it?"

Nico blinked. "I'm... what?"

"Why'd she lie? She doesn't quite seem like the type, does she? She must have had a pretty good reason. Especially for a very big, huge one."

"I don't know," Nico grumbled. "I didn't exactly feel like asking questions after finding out."

"Maybe you should have," Radclyffe shrugged. "I've lied about plenty of things, mostly with at least slightly good intentions."

They snorted. "I don't see how this could've possibly been with good intentions."

"Well, find out," he urged them. "Or don't and only see her once every couple of months when she gets lonely and decides to try and shoot at you to get your attention." With those parting words of wisdom, Radclyffe patted their knee and made his exit.

224

Nonymous

"I'm pretty sure those aren't the only two options there!" They yelled after him. But maybe he'd been at least a little bit right, because a few minutes later they got up, clicked out their cane, and started off towards where they knew she'd be waiting.

Chapter 57

The sun was setting over the water by the time they found Tillie sitting on the sand, watching it descend.

They sat down beside her. She instantly jumped and opened her mouth to say something, but Nico needed to have the first word here.

"I've been told that it'd be helpful," they said slowly. "To ask you to explain why the fuck you did all of this. Would it be? For me?"

Tillie took a long, shaking breath. "I don't know," she admitted. "I hope so."

"I want to hate you," they said.

She flinched. "That makes sense."

"But now," Nico continued. "Some slightly unhinged, overbearing pirate's gotten into my head and I don't think I'll fully be able to... tell me?" They asked. "Explain why the fuck anyone would do this so I don't have to keep wondering and can go back to hating you properly?"

Tillie's eyes welled. "I don't want you to," she whispered. "Hate me."

"Well, tough. I deserve to."

She didn't start to explain.

"I promise not to yell, Mathilda," they conceded. "Okay? Or say something mean or awful or... not until you're done, anyway. I'm just going to listen and you're going to talk and I'm going to keep listening until you're done talking and then I'm going to get to decide how to react because I deserve to react to this. But I won't," they promised. "Until you're done. Until we can both leave and never see each other again."

"Okay," she whispered, blinking back tears. "Okay."

And then, Tillie began.

Chapter 58

Tillie had been born near the coast. That was where it started. That was where it felt important to start. With the parts of her that hadn't been quite fake.

Tillie had been born near the water. And for a while, she had been sweet and small and wonderful.

But then she'd gotten old enough for people to notice.

Screaming at nothing at one, less consolable than any other baby that her entire extended family had ever seen. Missing milestones at two, getting out-lapped in some of them by her eldest little brother only a couple of years later.

"She'll grow out of it," her parents had been told. "They're always difficult, when they're small," but then it had just kept getting more difficult. Tillie had just kept messing up. So, she'd go to the water and cry or scream under the waves where no one else could hear and hate her for it and she'd promise herself that she would do better, but she never would.

And now, she was at the water again. Crying, again.

"I wasn't lying," she whispered. "When we talked about things being too much above water? I wasn't lying I just... I didn't have a better explanation. I thought I was one, actually, when I was small. A selkie. I was so obviously horrible at being human that I figured I was one that had just washed up one day and my parents were just waiting to tell me. But they don't look like me, you know? Their eyes are always black. That's how you could tell. I was so, so worried that you'd..." she took another breath. "I used to wait under the water, sometimes. That was true too. For as long as I could. Not because... I didn't want to drown myself or anything, I just knew I also didn't want to be here? I used to... I would wait under the water where everything was quiet and constant and *good* and tell myself that if I just waited another second, if I let my brain go just a little bit fuzzier, I'd transform. I'd become a selkie or... or a mermaid or a fish or *something* because I clearly wasn't supposed to be human. I—" her voice caught. "I'm awful at being a human, Nicole. I couldn't clean up after myself or cook for myself or even remember to brush my own hair most days so my parents had to and then my siblings had to and we all clearly hated it but they couldn't trust me to do anything and I could stand them doing everything and then getting mad at me because they had to do everything so... I left, last year. And I didn't know what to do or where to go and I had no tradeable skills so I remembered that—waiting under the water, praying to change—and I hunted down an actual selkie cloak and I was finally about to fix everything when I fucked it all up again and decided to sell all my land possessions so I could hide the money somewhere and come back for it, if I ever decided to come back on land and I somehow accidentally..." she looked at Nico.

They didn't look back.

"I wasn't planning on lying to you," she whispered. "It just... I was frustrated and ruining everything and it just... it happened. I thought you would've just somehow forced them to give it back right away, though. I didn't realize..." she tapped her side. "I'm sorry. I'm so, so sorry. You didn't deserve any of this. But I was... it didn't feel like lying, fully. Because that's what I would've used the wish for, you know. Becoming one for real. It didn't... no, that's wrong. Because I knew the whole time that you wouldn't get your wish and I didn't... I'm sorry," she repeated. "I'm sorry. It was selfish and awful and I'm so, so sorry but I couldn't... I couldn't keep doing this," she choked out. "I was so sick of trying to do this! I couldn't keep spending every day of my life feeling like I was somehow managing to fail at pretending to be the species that I actually am. I couldn't... I'd always known that I was human, actually. I think. At least a little. But once I was too old to keep lying to myself about it, it was too hard to... I couldn't keep having only myself to blame, for being like this. It was too much. I'm sorry, I shouldn't have lied, I shouldn't have pulled someone else into this, but I knew that I couldn't go back to living like that and I'm... I panicked. I'm sorry," she laughed a little, low and mocking. "That's pathetic, isn't it? That I was so fucking desperate to have someone else to blame for how bad at humaning I was that I had to go and invent something wrong with myself? If... if you decide to keep going, you get the wish. You always should have. I shouldn't... I'm sorry. I'm so, so sorry."

Nico still didn't speak. They'd said that they wouldn't, after all. But as Tillie shook and cried and watched the sunset, they slid their hand over the back of hers and squeezed. In silence, with red eyes and heaving chests, they watched the sky until the only light remaining was the stars.

Chapter 59

"Tell me what you need right now," Nico finally broke their silence after they'd been lying together on the sand for hours. They'd never let go of her hand.

"What?"

"What do you need right now, Tillie?"

"I'm..." she frowned, shaking her head. "No. I didn't mean to... I didn't mean to do that to you. I'll be fine. I'm actually not that... I don't need to guilt another person into taking care of me."

They sat up, pressing their palms against the sand. "We take care of each other, remember? We've been doing that this whole time. You haven't guilted me into anything."

Tillie was finally sitting too, so Nico moved closer and pressed their foreheads together.

"I'm sorry," they whispered. "That it took me days to come find you. I promise I'll be better at it, next time." They squeezed the backs of her hands. "Tell me what you need right now."

Tillie's lip quivered. Her shoulders shook. "I want to go home," she whispered. "I just... I don't know where that is. I'm..." she moved away to start to sway. "How do you know where—"

And then, for the third time in their life, Nico booped a nose.

Tillie frowned. "I'm umm... what..."

"There," they explained. "For me. That's one of mine. I have another too, but... I know that one of my homes is right there."

She frowned. "My... nose?"

"No!" Nico giggled. "You! Just you. That was an adorable callback, actually. To the first time we met?"

That just made her look even more confused.

230

"I booped your nose?" They reminded her. "Because you were like 'hello where's my skin' and I was all confused and flustered and..." they frowned. "Oh gods, you didn't even remember that."

Tillie blushed. "No. Sorry."

"Fuuuuck," they threw their head back towards the stars. "Can't believe I just reminded you. And awkwardly poked your nose. Again. I..." they sighed, returning their attention to her. "Just pretend that that was incredibly sweet then, alright? I can't define yours for you and I don't have to be a part of it, but home doesn't have to be a place, Tillie. That's why... I stopped rushing to get back to mine a while ago because they'll be fine without me for a bit, I think. They have each other. And I've been home for ages now."

Tillie sniffled. "You're mine too," she whispered. "You're... you are. Thank you, for being such a good one." She yawned. "But can we umm.... Can we go be home somewhere with a roof?" She asked. "And a bed, preferably?"

They laughed, clicking out their cane. "Of course. Excellent idea."

Hand in hand, they walked back to the hostel together. And Nico found that they didn't even care that Radclyffe was probably privately gloating about being right.

Chapter 60

For the first time in days, Nico woke up in an actual bed. They were cozy and warm and light and unwilling to leave any of that just yet, so they nuzzled further into the blankets.

Something tugged at their arm.

They frowned and forced their eyes open, only to find a dark green pair staring right back at them.

"Gods!" They practically jumped right out of their skin, pulling the sheets tighter with their free hand. Their only free hand. Because the other was locked around Tillie's. "Gods, Tillie, were you watching me sleep?"

She rolled her eyes. "I don't think it counts as watching, actually. If you can barely see anything. I was just waiting for you to get up so I could get out of bed without waking you."

She pulled her hand away and started rooting through her bedside table. Because there were two bedside tables, at least. And beds. They were just close enough—for some reason—for a bit of awkward hand-holding. Then Nico finished processing that the other bedside table was all the way by the door and realized with a sinking dread that they likely hadn't started that way.

Tillie frowned, watching their panicked confusion. "I seriously couldn't actually see anything, Nico," she whispered. "Promise."

"No," they corrected her. "That's not... it's fine. I'm over that. Not in general just... you know. You've seen me without it enough that it's not a big deal I just... bed," they remembered. "bed close why."

She laughed. "You moved it," she informed them. "Last night. You decided it was too far away. You were all, 'oh no, they're so far!' and when I pointed out that they weren't, you got all sweet and flowery about how you 'needed to be close enough to hold on to me so I wouldn't have to worry about you being stupid enough to let go again'." She blushed. "You know. Or something."

"I absolutely didn't say that!"

"You did," she nodded solemnly. "You're actually terribly sweet and dramatic when you're tired enough to be."

They groaned, flopping back onto their (still separate) bed. "I was last night too," Nico remembered. "Before that, I mean. On the beach. You asked a serious question and I was too busy being all dramatic and flowery to give you an actual answer."

"Oh," Tillie's tone shifted. "I... yes. Of course. Obviously it was late and I was just dumping... so much onto you. And... you're allowed to change your mind. About forgiving me. Obviously. I wouldn't—"

"Tillie," they swung themself back up. "Stop it. I do. We're fine." They tried to search her eyes, but she looked away. They leaned into the incredibly tiny chasm between them. "Tillie," they repeated. "We're fine. I'm sorry someone convinced you that you were a hard person to forgive. You're not. We're fine." They waited for her to nod before continuing. "You asked though. About homes. And I didn't... I mean yes, I meant what I said," it was harder to repeat, though. In the light of day. "But I get that pretty platitudes probably weren't exactly what you were looking for. If we don't find the cloak—which we will, obviously, but just in case—you can come back to Bayside with me, okay? We'll like... say we found the cloak and satisfied the duel but that you just decided to stay a human a while longer. If we can't get you home, you can share mine."

She shook her heads. "I'm... I wasn't fishing for that. That wasn't me asking—"

"I know," they pressed her knee. "Because you never ask for things. You should try it though, sometime. Because otherwise I'll have to overtly ask you to come stay with me myself and that'd be a lot more embarrassing."

She worried her lip. "You live with people, Nico. They might not—"

"They'll be fine with it," they nodded. "We collect people. That's what we do. I mean fuck, at this point we've been gone so long that if we show up together, they'll probably just assume that you're—" they froze. They realized. "That son of a bitch!"

Tillie frowned. "I... excuse me?"

"They..." Nico trailed off. "So the whole um, lying about being a magical creature thing. How often would you say you thought about that? Like... how many times daily. Before telling me."

"Constantly?" She guessed. "That's the kind of—"

She was interrupted, though, by another "That son of a bitch!"

Tillie frowned. "I'm... confused."

They sighed. "Leif? The big one? Three eyes? One of them incredibly freaky? He may have been umm..." they paused, remembering that most people considered random mind-readings an invasion of their privacy. "reading your mind," they quickly mumbled, just to get it over with.

"What?"

"Reading your mind," they admitted. "She tends to do that. A lot."

"And you didn't warn me!"

"I thought you were an annoying bitch, remember? We were trying to find out if you were a murderer! Anyway, I'm pretty sure Leif decided they wanted to adopt you ages ago. Everyone would be fine with you moving in no matter what, but they might actually already be expecting you." Nico rolled their eyes. "That sneaky little asshole."

"But..." Tillie still looked confused. "They... umm... Leif, I mean, umm..."

"He's fine with anything," they filled her in. "When they're not around to let people know what to use. As long as you don't just stick to one."

"Right," Tillie nodded. "She didn't tell you? You're friends, why would he not..."

"Leif likes to think that they're all sage and wise," they explained. "I think he knew that I needed you, a little bit. Or a lot bit I..." the blushed. "Whatever. Which doesn't make her any less of an asshole for conveniently forgetting to tell me that I didn't even have your species right, but... you know. Anyway, you can stay with us, if we don't find the cloak. You can definitely stay."

"You're still... coming then?" She checked. "To Kovienne? And... not taking the wish for yourself?"

They shrugged. "Might as well see it through at this point, right? I've come this far." They saw her get ready to protest and sighed, opting for something a little bit more true. A lot more terrifying. But something about her stopped it from being that. Tillie always did. "I need to come because I need to make sure you're alright, okay? You deserve to be in whatever skin you think would be the most comfortable on you and I don't.... I can't say that I get it. Not exactly. I can't say I fully agree with your reasoning either, because I think you're a fucking phenomenal human. If there is a right or wrong way to do it, I'd much rather the world be full of people doing it your way because I think you human beautifully, actually. But I know that it makes sense to you, so if you're saying that this is a thing that you need to do, then I'm going to help you do it, okay? And if it doesn't work out, I'll be there to help you figure out what comes next."

They were selfish. They were awful. Because they were absolutely hoping that the skin had already sold.

"Why?" Tillie asked.

Nico groaned. "Please don't force me to keep complimenting you. It's physically painful, Tillie."

She didn't laugh though. Because Tillie was light and perfect and everything and nobody had bothered to let her know any of that yet.

"Wait, no, it's..." Nico closed their eyes. Took a deep breath. "It's because I think you're wonderful, okay? It's because I

235

think you're phenomenal. So if you're potentially only spending a few more days on land, I can't let myself miss any of that." They reached for her hands, but she pulled away.

"I can't, Nico," she whispered.

And for a stupid, hopeful moment, they thought that she might have meant making the wish. Transforming. Leaving them. But she was moving away from them, not towards, so they quickly smothered the thought. They would not let their mind trick them into being more hurt by her leaving than absolutely necessary. "What?"

"I can't..." she tapped her blankets. "You tried to kiss me," she reminded them.

They winced. "Right. Listen, Tillie. I—"

"You tried to kiss me," she repeated, louder this time. Silencing, this time. "because you like me, right? Because I've tricked you into... I can't let you... I'm not a selkie, Nico."

"I know," they nodded slowly. "You've mentioned that. Quite a bit these last few days, actually."

She shook her head. The tapping transitioned into hitting. "I'm not a selkie," she told them. "I'm completely, entirely human."

"I know," they tried again. "And that's—"

"I didn't have earplugs in either!"

They blinked. Watched her avoid their eye.

"I didn't have earplugs in either," she repeated, less loud this time. A little more her. She pulled her hands into her lap and wrung them together. "and the sirens didn't affect me. I was *fine*."

"But—" Their breath caught, silencing the end of the thought. Because, oh.

Oh.

"I can't let you throw away your wish over something I can't give," Tillie was still rambling. "I'm... I can't... I'm so sorry. I want to. I wish I did. You'd be the perfect person to—"

"Tillie." Who didn't like them back, in that buzzing, nervous way that they liked her. Who never would.

236

"I can't!" She sobbed. "I don't know why! I just... it's just another..."

"Tillie." Who'd just broken some newly forming corner of their heart, a little. Who'd never like them back in that buzzing, nervous way that they'd thought she might.

"I'm so sorry. I'm... see? I told you. I can't do any of it! I can't get any of it—"

"Tillie." Who was breaking every bit of their heart that remained, right now. Who was reminding them a little bit too much of themself, all over again. The lost, confused version of themself who'd desperately longed to stay in those battered, mutilated boxes that they maybe still carried around with them, just a little. The reminder didn't make them mad anymore, though. Watching her feel that—feel anything even remotely like that—just made them want to shatter. They would be sad. They would nurse that tiny corner of their heart. But later. In private. It was the least important part of it anyway.

So, they crossed that tiny chasm. They sat down beside her, carefully turned her shoulders, and pressed their forehead to hers. "I love you," they whispered.

Tillie made a choking noise. It had been a terrible word choice. "No," she shook her head. "No, that's what I'm trying to—"

"I know," they squeezed her shoulders. "I know, okay? That's... I hadn't pieced it together yet, but I know now, alright? And I'm not mad. So you really have to stop apologizing."

"You're upset, though."

"A bit," they acknowledged. "But that'll go away, okay? I'm just... processing. But that's not your fault. I shouldn't have assumed anything."

"It made sense to. Most people..." she started. "*Humans...*"

"I am not most people," they reminded her. "Never have been, never intend to be. And I really hope you're not going to try to become them either. I can't stand most people, actually. I'd like to keep standing you."

She laughed, but it was obviously forced. "They screamed, Nico," she whispered. "After I followed you overboard. They demanded to know what I was and why I was immune, but..." her voice bubbled. "I'm just human! What does it mean if I can't get the one universal human thing right? What does that make me?"

"You," they said. "Perfect."

Tillie shook her head. "That's not... I want to," she said. "Like people. Gods, do I want to... I can't do anything by myself! Do you know how scary that is? Knowing that I won't be able to live on my own but that I'll also never fall in love or... or get married or... do you know how awful that is?" She pulled their hand to her lips. Kissed it once. Lightly. "You're perfect," she insisted. "You're everything. This has nothing to do with you. I love... I hate being around people, normally. That wasn't a lie either. But you... I love being around you even more than I love being alone. And I still can't... I can't. I'll never be able to."

"I don't need you to," they promised.

"You will," she shook her head. "Eventually. If my cloak's not there and I move in with you, you'll eventually... I'm not going to get better."

Nico pulled away slightly, keeping their focus on her eyes. "I don't want you to get better," they said slowly. "You can't anyway, okay? Because this is not worse. This is just you and I'm obsessed with everything about you." They hesitated. "I can't promise to stop liking you," they admitted. "Like that. Especially not all at once. I'm... that could take time. But I can promise not to act on it, okay? Or even bring it up, if that'd make you uncomfortable."

Tillie swallowed. "it's really not going to change," she fiddled with her fingers. "No matter how long you wait."

"I know," Nico promised. "I'm not exactly oblivious to the fact that some people feeling different kinds of attraction than others. I was like... stupid insecure about not feeling sexual attraction, a couple of years ago. Which was bullshit and I eventually was able to realize was bullshit, okay? If you do end up stuck with me, we'll figure out how to get you there too."

"It's not like that, though. Like you. It's... none of it. Not even the most important parts of it."

"Okay," they nodded. "I know." Nico held out their hands. Waited for her to meet them halfway. "I'd still want to come and be there and... for whatever comes next too, alright? Because I'm pretty sure I still love you," they admitted. "If that's alright. If that's okay to say. Not umm... in that way. No offense, I was definitely falling for you, but it was way too early for me to be *in* love with you. In that way. But as friends. Platonically. Separately. I think I love you a lot, actually. And I would... I'd like the chance to keep loving you. In whatever way you'd like to be loved for as long as we have left. And if you do end up underwater, I'm sure you'll find someone there smart enough to realize that too." They hesitated. "Is stuff like that alright?" they checked. "To say?"

She lunged at them, throwing her arms around their neck. "I love you," she cried into their hair. "So much."

"Praise the gods," they breathed. "Getting shot down twice would have been beyond embarrassing." They pulled away, holding her at arms length. "You know you could do that though, right? If that's also not a thing you feel, I'd still—"

Tillie rolled her eyes. "You're my favourite person," she said, as if that was that. And maybe it was. "Obviously I love you."

They beamed. "I have a pirate to go talk to," they announced, pushing themself to their feet. They did love Tillie. Quite a bit, actually. But they also knew themself and spending any longer physically talking about how much they loved Tillie might cause them to explode. "We have a cloak to go get and there's no fucking way we're waiting any longer to get it."

Chapter 61

After Nico had a very vague, very confusing conversation with Radclyffe, the *Rad-Ship* added in an immediate pitstop in Kovienne.

And so, a day later, they were there.

And Tillie was almost gone.

"Okay," Nico forced themself to smile as they left the docks together. The *Rad-Ship* had offered to wait for them if they were planning on being in Kovienne for less than a day, but Radclyffe had also given them each a substantial sum of money before letting them go—'wages', he'd called it. Like a pirate—so they'd sent them away. They didn't know how long it would be, after all. If the cloak wasn't there, then Tillie likely wouldn't want to be around other people right away. If it was, then Nico wouldn't be able to. "Homestretch."

Kovienne was a goliath. One of the biggest towns in the realm, in fact. It was why their *Interthrifter* tended to outsource. Tillie's tapping picked up beside them almost instantly.

"Tillie," they held out their hand, waiting for her to press against it. "You good?"

She leaned against them, adjusting her sunshade. "I'm good," she lied. Then, thinking better of it, "Don't let go."

They nodded. "Never."

The *Interthrifter* wasn't hard to find. Before they'd docked Nico had been worried that they'd spend the day looking for ways to stall, but now, they weren't even considering it. If Tillie was anxious, then they were anxious. They just wanted to get her okay again.

They had to let go of her hand for half a second to activate the welcome mat, but once they were inside, Nico grabbed for her right away. Tillie, though, stepped away.

"Sorry," Nico shoved their fists into their pockets. "Was that not..."

"Perfect," Tillie smiled. "Still perfect. I just..." her eyes flicked around the very full store. "We should split up here, right? In case it's still here? In case..."

They hesitated. "You sure?"

Tillie nodded. "Just... don't leave without me, okay? In case I get stuck?"

They rolled their eyes. "Still not leaving you until I have to, Tillie."

They walked together to the Middle section. Tillie started at the left. Nico started at the right.

They shouldn't have done that.

It only took five minutes. Five minutes of 'maybe it's not here' and 'maybe she'll stay' and maybe most importantly, 'maybe she won't leave' until Nico found it. Firm. Soft. A black-speckled light brown that they knew instantly must have been it.

Because they did remember it, somehow. In some corner of their mind lost to them until this specific moment. They didn't even have plausible deniability.

They'd thought of this moment. They'd been having dreams—or maybe nightmares—about it. Them being the one to find it. Them being to one to have to decide whether or not to give it to her. Them having to be the one to choose to let someone they loved leave them behind, again. But now, it wasn't even a choice. Now, the cloak was here and it was soft and firm and warm and Tillie's. So obviously Tillie's.

Nico had left people before, because they thought that their lives would be better without them in it. Tillie had too. And maybe Nico regretted it sometimes and maybe they both would regret it a little forever, but this was different.

Nico knew that Tillie wouldn't be happier without them. Because Tillie loved Nico and Nico loved Tillie and that was real and true and solid and good and maybe the only thing that they'd ever been sure of. That wasn't the point, though. How happy she made them or how happy they made her had never truly been a factor here. Because Nico knew that Tillie wouldn't be happier without them, but they also knew that she could never be her happiest with them. And that was all that had ever mattered.

"Tillie," they found her between the racks. Their voice was already hoarse by the time they reached her, but Nico was not going to break down. Not in an *Interthrifter*, of all places.

Tillie turned. Her eyes widened. And Nico already knew, but they still had to check. "Is this—"

"Thank you," Tillie's arms were already around their neck. She hopped up and down against them. "Thank you thank you thank you thank you."

And Nico, despite everything, smiled. Because this was it. All that had ever mattered.

Chapter 62

They spent the rest of the day together.

This was a decision that neither of them had to voice. Perhaps one that neither of them could. They walked aimlessly through less populated stretches of beaches. Picnicked on park benches.

They didn't talk much. Sometimes, they went hours without exchanging a word. One of the greatest gifts that Tillie had given Nico was the ability to do the exact opposite. To talk openly and endlessly even when it terrified them. But now, when Nico should have been the most scared, they were just calm. Because they were with her. Because they weren't about to waste their final day with her on terror.

As the sun set, the moved back towards the dock. Tillie helped them down a path of giant rocks until the shore was far behind them. And they didn't feel helpless, they just felt light. They sat together at its furthest point. Waiting, for something. For the end.

"I'm umm..." Tillie started. "Sorry again. For—"

"Don't you dare."

She laughed, leaning against them. Wrapping her arm around their back, just to get that little bit closer. Waves slammed against the rocks and showered them in mist, but neither shivered. Tillie, in her cloak. Them, in a flannel. "I'm going to miss you," she whispered. "So much."

Nico rolled their eyes. "I'm sure seals don't even miss people. I'm sure you'll be fine."

She shook her head. "I'll miss you," she insisted. "It'd be impossible not to. I'm going to miss you forever."

Nico swallowed. Their eyes welled. "Yeah, I... yeah. You too."

"It'll be easier, though." Tillie stretched her legs towards the waiting sea. "Right? Once I... it'll be worth it. Everything will finally stop being so complicated, all the time. Everything'll be... it'll be better."

They squeezed her fist. "And you'll be happy."

She nodded. "And I'll be happy. And..." she turned to look at them. "You don't think they'd still be able to tell, right? That... I mean I'm sure they will at first, but it has to be easier, right? Being a seal? Even if I'm bad at that too, they won't be able to tell that I'm... that something's wrong with me?"

Nico frowned. "There's nothing wrong with you."

She laughed a little. "I can't even—"

"No, Tillie. There's something... different, with you. Maybe multiple things different with you. And I get that that can make this form hard and I get why you'd want to change it, but none of that's wrong, okay? I'm not letting you go until you actually get that. None of that makes you any less incredible."

"I love you," she whispered. "I'll miss you."

They laughed. It made snot shoot out of their nose. They hadn't even realized that they'd been crying. "You already said that."

Tillie reached into her pocket. "Here," she held out her battered, worn box of cards. "Keep it."

Nico frowned. "No, I... that's yours. I can't—"

"Seals don't have opposable thumbs, silly," she whispered. A ridiculous thing to say while crying, really. It made Nico want to unravel. Tillie pressed the box into their palm. "I'm fairly certain they barely have fingers, actually. So... you keep it, okay? You never know. You might decide to start doing magic full time."

Nico barked out a laugh. "Yeah. Definitely not happening. No offense," they quickly added. Because they were nicer, now. A little. She'd made them nicer. Or maybe she'd just made them comfortable enough to let people know that they were nice. "I'm pretty sure I only ever actually liked it because you were the one teaching me," they admitted. They slipped the deck into their pocket. Triple checked that it was secure. "Thank you, though. I'll keep it forever." They hesitated. "I umm... here," they leaned away from her, slipping the medallion over their neck. "Take it. I don't know if... I guess seals can't like, wear jewelry, or whatever, but bury it somewhere, I guess. Keep it with you. In case you ever come back on land."

"I can't take that," Tillie argued. "I'm... that's different. You need that."

"I don't think I have, actually," Nico admitted. "Not for a while."

She just kept shaking her head. "Nico, when you lost it, you—"

"I need you to take it," they stopped her. "It... it was a family heirloom." From their first one. Their worst one. "But I don't want.... I don't think they're mine, anymore," they admitted. "Family, I mean. And carrying it around forever would be..." they sighed. "I wore it everywhere because I wanted to remember that we belonged to each other, but I don't think... we don't. They never even knew I was trans. I never even got the chance to choose whether or not they'd get to actually know me." They watched her. "I belong to you though, remember? We promised. So I need... It's a family heirloom, right? So I need you to take it with you."

Tillie's lips parted. Her shoulders shuttered. "I... okay." She pulled it over her head. "Okay, I... I love you," her voice broke. "I'll miss you."

They laughed, pushing her hair off of her tear-streaked face. "Third time you've said that, Tillie," they whispered.

They stared at the moon. They bided their time.

"You should go," Nico admitted, once they realized that maybe, that thing that she'd been waiting for was their permission. "You should..." they swallowed. "Help me back first, though?" They held out their arm. "I don't think... I love you, I'll wait by the shore so still come and like, wave at me when you're all cool and awesome and seal-y, but I don't think I can watch you go."

"Okay," she got up. "Of course."

Nonymous

They stood on the shore. They hugged her, one final time. She grabbed their hands. Pressed their foreheads together, one final time. "Thank you," Tillie whispered. "For... you changed my life."

They laughed. Smiled. Memorized every spot of colour in her eyes. "Ditto."

And then, she left. She went—for the first time—to where she was always supposed to be.

Chapter 63

Nico waited.

And waited.

They watched every single wave for a sign of her, but there was nothing. And they were getting cold now, with her gone.

They didn't start to cry again, when they realized that she probably wasn't coming. Maybe she'd had to transform somewhere deeper. Maybe selkies couldn't remember much of their human lives, once they'd changed forms. She was gone. The more time ticked by, the more certain of it Nico became. And they didn't cry. Not because they weren't able to—they could, now. She'd given them that—but because they weren't upset. Devastated, maybe, but not upset. Because somewhere, deep beneath the waves, she was happy. They turned to leave. To go home. To the other one. The only other one that had ever actually been theirs.

"Nico!"

They didn't turn. They couldn't. They'd accepted it, once. They wouldn't be able to do it again. They took another step.

"Nico!"

She was calling for them, though. She was needing them, maybe. They stopped. They turned. And then she collapsed into their arms, the cloak now clutched in her fists, pressed between them. "I can't," she sobbed. "I couldn't... I can't. I couldn't do it."

Nico frowned, easing them both down onto the sand.

"I can't," she repeated. "I couldn't... I can't do it."

Palms on her shoulders, forehead against hers. "Tell me what you need right now." they said, failing to meet her water-logged eyes. "What can I do?"

She shook her head. "I- I can't do it. I couldn't..." she pressed the sealskin into their lap. "Take it. Please."

They swallowed. They would do anything for her, but not this. Not wish her away themself. "Tillie," they said slowly. "I..."

"I can't do it. I can't change. I can't go, I—" It was everything Nico had wanted to hear, but now, it terrified them.

"Okay," they squeezed her shoulders. "I... you wouldn't have to right away, right? You get to decide when the seven years starts. Make the wish now and then..."

"No," Tillie kept shaking. "I can't... don't let me. I can't do it. You need to... make a wish. Get rid of it."

Their pulse spiked. "Tillie," they tried to look at her. They desperately needed to look at her. "You said you needed this, remember? You said..." their throat went dry. "You said you can't keep living like this. You can't just throw away—"

"I said I couldn't keep living like *that*," she whispered, finally smiling a little. "Trying and pretend and getting it wrong over and over again and I'm... I can't. I couldn't. But I... I don't have to, right? I can just... I could wear ridiculously massive earmuffs and... and I can let myself jump at loud noises and when I'm exciting and..." she frowned a little. "I think I do a lot of jumping actually. For pretty much every single emotion."

Nico laughed. Nico cried.

"But I could..." she pulled away, wringing her fingers together. "Maybe then it'd be okay? If I stopped pretending? This last little bit's been... more than okay, actually, so maybe if I just let myself be okay with other people being able to tell that I'm awful at passing for human, than I could... I don't want to—"

"Hey," they found her hands. Squeezed. "You are not 'passing', alright? You're still a human, Tillie," they reminded her. "For now. Which means that everything you do is automatically so, so incredibly human."

She sniffled. "How can you know that?" She whispered. "For sure?"

"You're my favourite human, right?" Nico said instantly. "So you must be one, then. It's the only option." They hesitated. "You don't have to be, though," they whispered. "You don't have

248

to... if you'd be happier being something else, then you go become that something else, okay?"

Tillie shook her head. "No. You take the wish."

"You could still be a selkie, though. All of the human things while still having the option to—"

"I don't want the option," she insisted. "I don't..." she took a shuttering breath. "I have a bad track record," she admitted. "With running away. I can't... I have to commit to it. I don't... I'm pretty sure living in any skin would be hard, sometimes. For me. But this one's mine. I need to commit... I want to figure out how much I can actually do, in this one. How happy I can actually get." She licked her lips. "So you need to make a wish, okay? Because this? Having to choose to not to take the easy way out over and over ago every other second? I'm... it's going to destroy me."

They couldn't, though. If she ended up regretting this, they'd never be able to forgive themself.

"In the morning," they compromised. "I need to come up with something first anyway, right? We'll wait until you're well rested, in case you change your mind." They spread the sealskin out over the sand. They both curled up on top of it.

Tillie fell asleep almost instantly, "thank you," she whispered as she nodded off.

Almost exactly what her last words to them were originally supposed to be. Because maybe she'd change her mind in the middle of the night. Maybe Nico would wake up and she'd be gone. But for now, she was here for a few more hours and so were they, so they let themself enjoy them.

And then, they both woke up with the dawn and she sent Nico off to meet the sea.

Chapter 64

Unlike Tillie—unlike even some of their housemate—Nico had spent no time researching selkie skins or wishes. They'd always figured, somehow, that they wouldn't end up making one. And yet, here they were. They threw the cloak into the sea like Tillie had instructed them to. They waited for it to sink. And then, in the back of their mind, they heard it: the sea.

Its voice was a lot higher than Nico had thought it would be. It's accent distinctly foreign, but from where they couldn't quite tell.

Thank you, the sea whispered. *How can I repay you?*

"A million gold," Nico decided. It was an incredibly lame request, but they hadn't had enough time to think up a better one.

Hmmm, the sea hummed. *Inflation. Too disruptive.*

Nico cursed under their breath. The sea was, apparently, incredibly picky. They tried dozens of work arounds, but infinite money was apparently not something that the sea was eager to give away. Nor was world peace, the end of all hunger, or a 'sickass dragon I can ride around everywhere who can talk and is also my best friend' (there was a clause against creating new life, apparently). They weighed their options. And thought of it, of course. *Fix me,* they could have asked. Surely that would have been a small enough request. *Make me what I could have been, before I was ten.* But a little extra mobility felt like a horrible waste of a wish. And if they made it, they'd have to spend the rest of their life knowing that when it had mattered, they'd decided that that was the most important thing about themself.

And then, Nico remembered what actually was. They spoke with the sea. Finally—after several tweaks and follow up questions—the sea agreed.

Nico couldn't believe they hadn't thought of it right away. After all, what trans person didn't secretly dream of shapeshifting?

Chapter 65

They found Tillie back on the beach, sand in her hair and eyes red-rimmed. "It's done?" She asked. "It's gone?"

They nodded. "It's gone."

She didn't ask what their wish was. They didn't tell her. It'd feel like gloating, to do it now. They were worried that she'd freak out now that the truth of what she'd given up had finished settling in, but instead her shoulders relaxed. For a moment, Tillie was entirely still. "Thank you," she whispered.

They rolled their eyes. "You gave me a magical wish granting cloak, Tillie. I should be thanking you." They sighed when she glared in response. "You're welcome." They leaned against their cane. Tillie didn't seem surprised in the slightest to see that they were still using it and something about that made them feel a little bit lighter. "Let's go get breakfast," they said. "I'm starving. We'll look into rides home after that."

But Tillie stayed on the beach.

"Tillie?" They turned around. Their heartbeat picked up. She couldn't be leaving them now. Not when they'd finally let themself start to daydream about her staying. "You coming?"

"I'm..." she kicked at the sand. "I didn't stay for you, just so you're aware."

"Okay," they put a hand over their heart. Smiled against the thing currently squeezing it. "Ouch."

"No!" She quickly corrected. "No, I didn't... I love you," she said. She was always saying that, now that they'd established that she didn't mean it romantically. "I just... I didn't stay *because* of you, I meant. Because you helped me realize that I might be... less than awful," she admitted. "At the human thing, yeah, but not... I don't have to come back with you. That's all I was trying to say."

They swallowed. Nodded. "Of course you don't."

"And it's different, right? You said I could if we couldn't find it, but we did. And I have money now, to get started on my own here. Or... somewhere quieter than here preferably, but..."

Nico frowned. "Tillie, do you not want to come with me?"

"Of course I do," her voice broke, even as she rolled her eyes. "I can't hold you to that though. Just because you got the wish doesn't mean you're obligated to—"

"I want you to come with me," they promised. "I feel like I've made that... incredibly clear, actually."

"I don't want to burden you," she whispered. "I don't want you to feel stuck with me forever just because—"

"Bold of you to assume I wasn't planning on burdening you forever," Nico interrupted.

She sighed. "Nico. I still can't... you pay rent. And make your own food and do your own chores and I... I don't how much of that I'd be able to do. If I'd be able to do any of it."

They nodded. "All the more reason to come with me, then," they said. "That way I can help."

"*Nico,*" she said.

"*Tillie,*" they responded. She didn't smile though, so they walked back over to her. "I think..." they said slowly, trying to pick their words carefully. She'd done that. She gave them enough space to be careful. "Expectations are on the floor, okay? Lower than that. The bottom of the fucking ocean, alright? I'm not expecting anything from you so nothing you can or can't do could possibly upset me. But... I don't want to that say I'm sure you'll be able to do everything because that's a bullshit expectation to put on you, yeah? But I also think it's important... I think you can actually do a lot more than you think you can. You *have* been doing a lot more than you thought you could, right? This last little bit? I think... we'll figure it out," they decided. "Which things you can do and how to make doing them easier for you. And if that turns out to be nothing more than you know how to do right now, then that's fine. We'll figure it out. There are tons of things I can't do either, so we'll just keep doing what we've already been doing. I help you, you help me. Easy. And... my friends are awesome. Seriously, I swear. I'm extremely picking about the people I decide to love. So we'd actually have even more people to help us figure it out."

She wouldn't look at them. "I don't... I just need to know that you know this doesn't have to be forever. I didn't give the wish up because I was counting on it being forever. If you get sick of me or... or fall in love, *real* love—"

"I am," they stopped her. "This is."

Tillie smiled. "I didn't say it wasn't," she said. "I love you as much as I can love a person but that's not... it isn't what you want. It's—"

"Tillie," they stopped her. "I need you to stop deciding what I do or don't want, okay?" They watched her. "Deal?"

She nodded.

"Okay. Good. Then I seriously want you to come home with me. I seriously want to love you exactly like this for as long as you'll have me. And I seriously want to go get some fucking breakfast."

She took a deep breath. Smiled lightly. "I'm sorry I keep freaking out," she said. "I'm... I'll get better at that. Eventually. Hopefully."

Nico laughed. They crossed the distance between them. Pressed their forehead to hers. "I'd take you exactly as you are," they promised. "But it would definitely be helpful if you could remember that for more than ten minutes at a time."

"Deal," Tillie giggled. "I'll work on that."

"Tell me what you—" Nico started.

Tillie shook her head against theirs. "Tell me what *you* need right now," she said. "Your turn."

Nico let themself smile. "I need to go home," they admitted. "I need you to come with me." Because it wouldn't be home anymore, without her there. Not now that they knew that she existed. But they'd already been missing it for far too long to keep stalling.

"Okay," Tillie took their hand, leading them back off the beach. "Let's go, then."

Chapter 66

Tillie refused to come with them, that first time Nico that was finally able to return to The House.

"Go ease them into it," she insisted. "Catch up for a bit, before you tell them."

They didn't ease anyone into anything. But to be fair, none of them eased Nico either. They didn't even get the chance to put their key in the door before it was thrown open and they were tugged inside by six eager, hugging arms. Eight, once Milo had performed a sufficient level of eye-rolling from the corner, of course.

"How did—" they started. Then realized. "Fucking roses."

There was chatter. There were questions. A lot of them. "Alright," they ducked their way out of the hug after letting themself revel in it for a suitable amount of time. They swatted away their friends' arms, cackling. "I missed you guys too, okay? But I need to—"

The room fell silent. Milo whistled.

"You missed us," Leif sang, following them to the couch. There was an undercurrent there, though. Because Leif hadn't read them yet. None of them knew what had kept Nico away for so long.

They rolled their eyes. "Shut up." But it felt good to say it. It felt good to be able to say it.

They filled them in, slowly. About the parts that mattered. About the parts that they had permission to tell. Like they'd thought, Tillie coming back with them had not been unexpected. Late, definitely, but far from unexpected. Kya had gotten half-way through growing an extension on the roof for her before announcing that she and Pat were going to start sharing a room instead.

Nonymous

And Nico found that they weren't even a little bit disgusted at that, just happy for them. Maybe being away really had changed them.

"So?" Kya asked. "When do we get to officially meet her?"

"Soon," they promised, suddenly anxious about it. "She's waiting for me to go get her. But you need... everyone has to be nice, okay?" They stressed. "Not like, disgusting fake nice, but tolerable, at least. Until she gets comfortable. She... hasn't had enough people be nice to her to deal with us being assholes right off the bat."

"Perfect," Kya smiled.

"Got it," Leif nodded.

"Done," Pat agreed.

They all turned to where Milo sat slouched against the armchair. He sighed dramatically. Sat up a little straighter. "I get to be mean after, though?" He checked. "Once she's all..." he gestured lazily. "Acclimated?"

Nico rolled their eyes. "Yes, Milo."

"Okay," he finally nodded. "I can play nice. For now."

Nico grinned. They were happy. They were home.

But there were still a few more things that they had to attend to.

"You," they pointed at Milo. "We're having a meeting actually. In my room. Right now."

He rolled his eyes. "I wasn't actually—"

"Meeting!" They stopped him. This kind of conversation had to be private. They knew that no one would be upset about it—if anything, they'd be elated—but they weren't about to let anyone pressure him into saying yes. But Leif ruined it.

"I'd like one first, actually," Leif said. "Let him stew."

Nico nodded and followed Leif to their room. They could wait a little longer.

256

Chapter 67

"You figured out I knew," Leif announced, sitting down on their bed. "And you didn't tell anyone."

Nico sat down beside Leif. And instantly regretted it. They'd missed this bed. They would have to spend a long time getting reacquainted with this bed again soon. Later, though. Once everything was settled. "Were you reading up the path again? You can't keep—"

"No reading," Leif put Leif's hands up in surrender. "I could just... tell."

They nodded. "Figured it out a little bit ago."

"Are you pissed?" Leif checked. "I didn't think she'd keep you away for months, obviously. I didn't—"

"No," they interrupted. "Are you?" They asked. "Because I'm pretty sure... I said I wouldn't change. I think I might have."

Leif barked out a laugh. "Oh, praise the gods."

"Hey!" They reached up to hit Leif's arms. "You're supposed to tell me I was perfect!"

"You are," Leif nodded. "But I've been..." Leif blushed. "Maybe the blindfold doesn't block things out, right now," Leif admitted. "Entirely. I'm looking for work arounds but my power's been getting... you're perfect. You always were. It just seems like you're finally starting to become okay with other people knowing that and honestly, it's about fucking time."

They laughed. "Do the other know?" They asked. "About your powers?"

Leif nodded. "We're figuring it out." Leif got up. "But you want me to get out of your hair as quickly as humanly possible so you can go collect our newest tenant." Leif paused in the doorway. "I know what you're about to do, by the way. I didn't read it on purpose or anything, but... that's really fucking cool, Neek. You're really fucking cool."

They rolled their eyes. "Yeah, well, duh."

Leif grinned. "I'll send him in."

Chapter 68

Milo was already muttering before he'd even finished crossing the threshold. "I wasn't actually going to be a dick to your friend."

Nico nodded. "I know. You're a sweetheart. You'd never."

He groaned. "Almost drowning's clearly rotted your brain even further, Nico. You're—"

"I got a wish," they interrupted. They couldn't wait to tell him. They were terrified to tell him. "For returning the selkie skin."

Milo's spine straightened as his attention clearly piqued, but then he quickly shifted back to being him. "Yes, that would be what that typically entails, I've heard. What'd you get, infinite riches?"

They shoot their head. "Not allowed, unfortunately."

"Pity." He said it like it was nothing, but they knew that it would have been. That's why it had been the first thing he'd checked for. If Nico was rich, then he wouldn't have to be anymore. If he decided not to be.

They'd made the right decision. They knew that they'd made the right decision.

"Yeah, the sea's incredibly stingy with wishes, apparently," they said. "I tried for all the cool powers, but none of them worked."

Milo frowned. "I don't see why I'm the one who has to—"

"I went with shapeshifting," they informed him. "Minor, though. Changing to other species at will would apparently also be too big an ask. But as long as the species stays the same, then any change should work."

He smiled slightly. His small one. His genuine one. "That's great, Neek," he said quietly, touching their shoulder. "Good for you." Milo cleared his throat. "Charmed a not-selkie and got a wish. Seems like you really—"

"Do you want it?" They asked.

He froze. "I... what?"

"The wish. Do you..." Nico pulled the vial out of their pocket. "You have to drink it, unfortunately. Willingly too. The sea made it incredibly clear that pouring it down your throat wouldn't work. But it's yours, if you want it."

He stared at them. "You're fucking with me."

They stared back. "I'm not."

Milo laughed. A little higher than he normally let himself. A little bit delirious. "You thought I'd what? Take a shot of nasty ocean water just because—"

"Milo," they stopped him. "I would never fuck with you about something like this."

He nodded a little. Swallowed. "I know," he admitted. "I know, I..." he laughed again. "Shit, Nico. What the fuck am I supposed to say to that?"

"Yes or no?" They suggested. "Preferably quickly so I can go collect Tillie and finish moving in?"

He stared at the vial. "I can't just... gods, Nico! You're fucking trans too! And I'm the one who can afford a reassignment spell! Why the fuck would you—"

If he was Tillie, they would have been able to explain it. That it felt more important that he take it, somehow. That they hated their parents and knew that they had every right to hate their parents but that they missed them a lot, sometimes. That if they'd had the option to go back—not to erase the parts of themself that were disabled or queer or anything else that their birth family might have deemed unsuitable, but just to pause it for a little—that they might have taken it. Milo still had a chance to have it all. The ability to present the way that he was supposed to without having to cut his birth family off. And maybe it really was just the threat of them withdrawing their money and stability that kept him from transitioning, but if it was something more too, then they needed him to have that choice. If he was Tillie, Nico would have been able to tell him that they'd been stranded penniless on a deserted island a few of weeks ago and had somehow gotten back from that with money to spare so if they did decide to change things someday, they knew that they'd be able to figure out how to afford it. That they knew that they would never need this, not as much as he might have. But he wasn't Tillie. And Nico wasn't quite ready to start baring their entire soul to the other people that they loved (not yet anyway), so they said, "maybe I just really don't want to have to drink sea water."

He wasn't Tillie at all. He was a lot more like them, actually. So, they also knew that if they told him the truth, he'd never accept the wish.

Milo took a deep breath. His hands shook, just slightly. "So if I don't take it, you're the one who gets to—"

"If you don't take it, I'll pour it out the window right now," they stopped him.

He gaped. "See! You are fucking with me!"

They smiled. Their throat went tight. "You wanna bet?"

Slowly, he took the vial. He uncorked it. He winced as he chugged it down.

And nothing happened.

"I really wasn't fucking with you," Nico said, pulse picking up speed. "I'm... not intentionally, anyway. Maybe I pissed off the sea enough that it—"

But then, in the blink of an eye, he was him. Different than he had been a few second ago, but so incredibly clearly him that Nico could barely remember what he'd looked like before.

Milo got up to stare at himself in the mirror. "It can go back and forth," he said, studying his hands. "Right? Just in case—"

"It can," Nico whispered, feeling their eyes well. They wiped it away though, before he turned around. Milo would never put up with any of that. "I made sure."

He went to them. In only two strides because, Nico realized, he'd made himself a bit taller. They snorted. Of course he had. Trust them to give someone else the ability to make them feel short. "You're fucking insane," Milo whispered, voice thicker—and lower—than they'd ever heard it. "You're such a fucking idiot."

    Nico smiled, letting themself be pulled into a hug. "I love you too."

Chapter 69

Tillie was waiting at a picnic bench down the road for them, just where they'd left her.

Nico couldn't help but smile as they approached. Tillie never failed to make them feel giddy.

A less nervous giddiness, now though. Still that undercurrent of nervousness—they still had a little bit of a crush on her, maybe they always would—but deep, deep beneath the surface. Mostly, already, she just made them happy.

"Hey," they slid in across from her. "Everyone's wildly excited to meet you. In an incredibly non-intimidating way."

She smiled back at them. And everything was good. "Oh!" Tillie's eyebrows shot up. "Here!" She started to pull off the medallion, but Nico held out a hand to stop her.

"It's an heirloom, Till. It was always supposed to be. Keep it."

She giggled. "Aren't those supposed to be passed down through different generations?" She reminded them. "Kids, and all that."

Nico scrunched up their face in horror. "Eww! Gross! I'm not making any future generations, I'm wildly too self-centred for that. You'll just have to do instead, then. Keep it. I don't need it anymore anyway." They found her cards in their pocket. "You actually can still use these though, so—"

She pressed down on their hand, trapping the box on the table. "Keep it," Tillie smiled. "Heirloom."

Nico raised an eyebrow. "Your parents did card tricks?"

"Oh. Well... no," Tillie blushed. "But... you already redefined it!" She protested, stomping her foot beneath the table to accentuate the point. "I get to do that too!"

Nico laughed. "Okay," they slipped it back into their pocket. They'd have to find a place for it, back home. They'd have to keep it forever. "Heirloom. Deal."

Nonymous

They stood up, clicked out their cane, and held out their free hand. "Let's get you home then, okay?" they said. "Finally."
And so, hand-over-hand, together, they chose not to leave.

Nonymous

About the Author

Alex (any pronouns, feel free to talk about me behind my back at will I'm impossible to mispronoun) published their first book a month after turning 20, promptly decided to publish a book a month those next ten months because that was reasonable, and is now trying to hit 22 before turning 22 because he has no concept of time. To join her reading list and get an email a month (when she's organized enough to send it with info on new and upcoming releases, early reader opportunities, genre polls, and other polls (Alex really likes polls), message them at alexnonymouswrites@gmail.com

Also, does this book contain a lot of incredibly short (sometimes one line) chapters that have no business being their own chapters specifically because Alex thought having 69 chapters in a book with an ace main character and love interest would be a fun bit? Who's to say.

Content Warnings: ableism, negative self-talk about queerness, negative internal and external talk about disability, (non-malicious) mispronouning, brief mention of suicidal ideation (not a plot line), alluded to transphobia, characters lashing out at each other, autistic meltdown, gender dysphoria, alluded to unsafe binding, swearing **this is not an aro book. The love interest is aroace, the main character is just ace. If you picked this up looking for n aro-book and you're romance repulsed, the main character does clearly experience romantic attraction.**

Printed in Great Britain
by Amazon